"I guess this is where we say good-night,"
Mandy managed lightly, throwing Jake
a smile as she turned and pushed the
door closed.

How had that kiss happened? she asked herself, collapsing into the nearest chair. One minute they were almost friends, the next, close to taking a step toward intimacy they had no right thinking about.

Mandy groaned, trying to think straight, but it felt impossible when she thought that Jake might be just on the other side of the door. She touched her fingers to her lips and closed her eyes as a shivery sensation rocked across her midsection. Why had Jake kissed her? More disturbingly, why had she let him? Did either one of them want to retrace old history?

She felt kind of tingly, almost like a limb regaining circulation after being in a cramped position. The inside of her that had felt dead since the accident felt vibrantly alive. All because of a kiss. One little kiss.

Not so little, whispered a small voice....

Dear Reader,

"It was a high like no other," says Elaine Nichols. She's speaking, of course, about getting "the call." After numerous submissions, Elaine sold her first manuscript to Silhouette Special Edition and we're pleased to publish *Cowgirl Be Mine* this month—a reunion romance between a heroine whose body needs healing and a hero whose wounds are hidden inside. Elaine has many more Special Edition books planned, so keep an eye out for this fresh new voice.

And be sure to pick up all the novels Special Edition has to offer. Marrying the Bravo fortune heir granted the heroine custody of her son, but once the two are under the same roof, they're *unable* to sleep in separate beds, in Christine Rimmer's *The Marriage Conspiracy.* Then a hungry reporter wishes his tempting waitress would offer him a tasty dish of *her* each morning, in *Dateline Matrimony* by reader favorite Gina Wilkins.

What's *The Truth About Tate?* Marilyn Pappano tells you when her journalist heroine threatens to expose the illegitimate brother of the hero, a man who would do anything to protect his family. She hadn't giggled since her mother died, so *His Little Girl's Laughter* by Karen Rose Smith is music to Rafe Pierson's ears. And in Tori Carrington's *The Woman for Dusty Conrad,* a firefighter hero has returned to divorce his wife, but discovers a still-burning flame.

We hope you enjoy this month's exciting selections, and if you have a dream of being published, like Elaine Nichols, please send a self-addressed stamped query letter to my attention at: Silhouette Books, 300 East 42nd St, 6th floor, New York, NY 10017.

Best,

Karen Taylor Richman
Senior Editor

Please address questions and book requests to:
Silhouette Reader Service
U.S.: 3010 Walden Ave., P.O. Box 1325, Buffalo, NY 14269
Canadian: P.O. Box 609, Fort Erie, Ont. L2A 5X3

Cowgirl Be Mine

ELAINE NICHOLS

SPECIAL EDITION™

Published by Silhouette Books

America's Publisher of Contemporary Romance

To amputees everywhere,
who somehow find the courage to adjust and go on.
To Trenda, a real cowgirl; and Dick for finding her.
My family, critique group and Great Titles Inc.;
thanks is too simple a word.

 SILHOUETTE BOOKS

ISBN 0-373-24428-2

COWGIRL BE MINE

ELAINE NICHOLS

lives in the scenic Catskill Mountains with her family in a renovated 150-year-old farmhouse. Reading and writing romances have been her favorite pastimes for as long as she can recall. A romantic at heart, Elaine could never resist a happy ending. This year, a long-held dream has come to pass with the publication of her first story with Silhouette Books. She firmly believes the old adage "Keep writing, hone your craft and continue to submit" is the true road to publishing success. Elaine enjoys writing contemporary romance, time-travel romance, children's fiction and nonfiction. Elaine has also dabbled in illustrating children's book covers. Elaine is an avid horseperson and has always been fascinated by cowboys and cowgirls, so it's only natural she would write about them.

You can visit Elaine's Web site at www.elainenichols.com. If you would like to contact Elaine to hear about upcoming news or send your comments, you can send her an e-mail at elaine@elainenichols.com or write to her: Elaine Nichols, P.O. Box 100, East Jewett, NY, 12424.

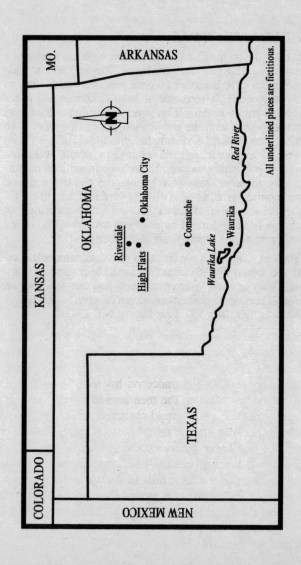

All underlined places are fictitious.

Prologue

Someday, that bull would kill someone. Mandy Thomson just knew it. She straddled the top rail of the bull chute as old Hit Man moved restlessly from side to side.

Mandy let her gaze roam the rodeo yard. Her heart jumped like a young colt on a brisk morning as she stared, transfixed, at a dark-haired man. Jake Miller. He stood close by, a cocky look of assurance on his lean face. He was a head taller than most of the men around him, a stranger in business clothes among mud-spattered cowboys. His suit looked expensive, not the most common attire down by the pens. She had never before seen him dressed like that, yet he carried it off with nonchalance and elegance. His dark head was bare to the faint mist in the air and his long legs were spread, feet planted on ground churned up by countless boots and three days of rain. Mandy didn't try to stop the smile spreading across her face. Only Jake could pull off a suit at a rodeo in the drizzling rain.

She hadn't seen or heard from Jake in ten years, not since that terrible night she'd left. He'd showed up now, the night she planned to remember for the rest of her life—the night she'd make the rodeo finals. With the bittersweet knowledge of the past firmly in her mind, Mandy sensed it was fitting Jake should be here to see her triumph.

Even knowing she was short on time before her ride, she continued to stare at Jake. Why was he here? What was that expression in his face—a mixture of pain and want? Mandy wiped the mist from her eyes, knowing she was wrong. She drew a deep breath.

He had changed, matured, yet something in his eyes remained the same. How long had she loved that strong face with its wide cheekbones, no-nonsense jaw touched by the faintest shadow of beard, and deep-set eyes of the lightest blue? Her seventeenth summer she had loved him with a young woman's vibrancy. They'd spent endless time together, planning, talking…dreaming. Back then, Mandy had thought Jake could do no wrong.

She drew a deep breath and looked around. Why was he here? It wasn't to see her! He was already drawing attention; she could see some of the girls nudging each other. Her throat dry, Mandy drew a deep breath and then pressed her lips together. There were a lot of handsome faces like Jake's, but he had a presence. He always had. Jake was special, that's why she had loved him so much, until she had walked away….

"Mandy Thomson!"

Hearing her call, Mandy stood up against the metal bars, gripping the top rail tightly. As she did so the bull in the chute hopped sideways, rattling the metal gates.

Adrenaline pumping, Mandy jerked her gloves on, her gaze sweeping the yard, oblivious to everything until her glance lit once more on Jake. He was still there. Seeing him broke her concentration, brought in a flood of memories.

Live, intense heat struck Mandy and she closed her eyes tightly for a brief moment in exasperation. She had gotten over him. Anyone with a lick of sense knew ten years was a long time to pine over any man.

Deliberately, she looked away. Rubbing rosin on her gloves and rope, Mandy centered her attention one hundred percent on what she knew of the bull, Hit Man. True to form, he was bouncing in the chute like a young kid throwing a temper tantrum. Hit Man shot her a glance now and then, probably to see if his head games were rattling her. He was one of the oldest bulls on the circuit, but anyone in rodeo knew he'd give you the ride of your life.

Mandy's heart pounded wildly in her chest and up into her throat as she threw her leg over the chute and climbed down on the bulky-muscled bull. Quickly, she gripped the flat, braided rope as the bull lunged from side to side. Dry-mouthed, Mandy wrapped her hand while the bull bellowed. He turned his head and seemed to glare at her with one eye, then with a quick twist tried to horn her.

"Watch your legs there, Mandy!" someone shouted, but she had already pulled them up. Mandy focused on keeping her feet from being pinned between the animal's sides and the metal bars. Steadying hands of the cowboys at her back helped her stay upright as the bull continued to ram the sides of the chute.

Her fingers tightened on the rope and she gave the signal to open the gate. With vivid clarity Mandy saw the gate swing open, felt the rush of air from her lungs. Like a race car in its first heat, a ton of Brahma bull exploded into the rodeo arena, twisting and spinning. His cloven hooves sank into the mix of mud and manure.

The ornery bull did his best to defy the laws of gravity. He lunged forward, coiled to the right, came down, whipped to the left and dove again. Mandy had watched this bull and knew what to expect, but every bone in her body was being jolted to hell and back. She was determined to ride it out and do it in style. As the bull spun, she spurred him, her concentration intense.

The clock in her head ticked off. Mandy held fast like a winter's burr on a blanket. Two...three... This was the longest six-second ride of her life. Five... Triumph began to burgeon in her chest. She had him. Hit Man wasn't getting away.

As the bull reared his head up, they hung suspended in the air for a moment. Then, with surely no more than a quarter of a second left, Mandy felt him twisting, going over, taking her with him.

All time stopped, silence reigned, the cheering crowd disappeared. There was only she and Hit Man. It seemed to Mandy, in that split second of realization, that the bull had won. She tried to throw herself clear, but she couldn't get her hand free.

They slammed into bone-chilling mud. Mandy felt her head snap sideways, saw the dull gray sky overhead. Clods of dirt and mud slapped her. She smelled manure, then sweat and heat rolling off the animal, which lay atop her. When she tried, she couldn't move, so she lay still, her legs pinned under the deadweight. If looks could be believed, the bull had dropped dead.

A kaleidoscope of images flashed before Mandy. Her first pony, the mare Daddy brought home from the rodeo. Ribbons on her wall, the first bull she had ridden. The gate opened and Mandy knew again exhilaration mixed with fear. What a ride. A high like no other.

Daddy, a hard-drinking, fun-loving man. A family man, when he was home. He had been gone a lot when she was growing up. One rodeo after the other. Daddy said he lived to rodeo.

Mandy experienced again the guilt inside her, but she

hadn't spoken up, not even when her brother, Ben, smashed the plaque listing Daddy's rodeo honors. If only she had told her family it was her fault Daddy had left. If she had tried harder to win more ribbons and trophies, maybe Daddy would have stayed.

A dark-haired man flitted in front of her, with piercing blue eyes, so light they looked ghostly. Jake. She had always loved him, never stopped. But he hated her for what she'd done. His mouth moved, his beautiful mouth. She didn't understand the words, but they had a calming effect.

The crazy swirl of remembrances slowed and dimmed as Mandy floated gently.

Chapter One

Mandy moved her wheelchair into place on the van's elevated ramp. The motor whirred as the lift lowered her to ground level, then came the gentle bump: sounds and sensations that had become all too familiar over the last months. Gripping the chair's wheels nervously, Mandy assessed her surroundings. After four weeks in the hospital and another eight weeks at the rehab center, she found this place was a sight for sore eyes.

Some of the tenseness eased from her shoulders. She had left her new living arrangements up to Ben, and he hadn't disappointed her. The ranch was set right in the heart of Oklahoma, and yet appeared to be in the middle of nowhere. For a brief moment, as she stared at the modern, one-story ranch house and dark brown stained barns off in the distance, she was reminded of home. An ache began to churn below her ribs. Home.

Some day she would have to deal with the mess she had made of her life.

Mandy thought back to that fearful night three months ago. When she woke up in the hospital recovery room, Mama had been there. And surprisingly, so had Daddy.

Mandy's memory flashed to her first glimpse of the empty space where her leg should have been. In a span of seconds, fear, desperation and finally disbelief had ripped through her. She would never be the same. Her life was over. Mandy recalled again, with shame, the hateful words she had flung at her mama....

When she had finally accepted the fact that her lower leg was gone, she had made a vow: nothing and no one was going to keep her from returning to rodeo. She wanted it back with a vengeance. She'd worked hard at her therapy and religiously performed the exercises.

Just because her leg had been amputated below the knee didn't mean she was quitting. Getting to the rodeo finals might take longer than she'd first anticipated. She had to believe she could make it, or she'd go crazy. Rodeo had consumed her life for so long, there was nothing to fill the void.

She had seen the look in her daddy's eyes that one time he had come to see her. The pity there had made her angry and determined to get back to one hundred percent. She wouldn't give up. She would see what look he wore when she made the finals. Finally leaving the rehab and coming to this place to regroup was the first step in achieving that goal.

She also needed to repair the strained relationship between her and Mama. Each day Mandy put it off, it became that much harder. Pride wouldn't allow her to go back home after the terrible things she'd said to Mama in the hospital. As for her apartment, it had been taken over after the accident by someone who could afford expensive rent. So she had no place else to go—except here.

Looking around, Mandy began to feel a surge of hope.

For the first time since her accident she could be comfortable and relax somewhere. Wherever she looked was pure Oklahoma. Vast and familiar.

Mandy wheeled her chair onto the smooth blacktop. The walkway continued toward the house, to a side door with a short ramp.

Ben had assured her the ranch house was fully equipped to handle special needs. It belonged to a friend of his, but Mandy hadn't been interested enough to inquire further. At the time she'd been in an apathetic frame of mind. She had never dealt with depression before. Now she struggled with it almost daily, and it depleted her.

At the best of times she doubted herself, wondered if she was crazy to try and be normal once more. At the worst, she wondered how she could resume normalcy if part of her, a leg she'd always took for granted, was gone. The doubts raged mostly at night, but sometimes they crept into her daylight hours.

"I'm going inside," Mandy told the driver. "I'll get my bag later."

"That's okay, Mandy," he said with a quick smile. "I'll bring it in."

Mandy shrugged, unable to summon the energy necessary for ordinary responses. She wheeled herself up the short ramp. A large knobbed handle had been screwed into the door above the doorknob. Mandy pushed it down and the door swung inward.

She wheeled herself through the doorway and into a large, bright room lined with floor-to-ceiling windows. The walls were painted a warm ecru with darker wood trim.

A kitchenette occupied the far right side of the room, and grab bars were placed at various points throughout the kitchen. The stove and sink were open beneath for wheelchair access. The cabinets were low and also had large handle pulls.

Mandy moved into the bedroom. Attached to the head-board of an attractive maple-wood bed was a trapeze for ease of movement. Closets with wide handles lined one wall.

Mandy inspected the small bathroom off the bedroom. This room had also been equipped with grab bars for the tub and toilet, with an optional bath seat for the tub.

She rolled her head back, the remainder of the tension draining from her body. The apartment had been well planned. Mandy heard someone in the other room. She wheeled her chair back to the living room, irritated that the driver hadn't left.

"I told you to leave them..." Her voice trailed off as surprise—shock—clutched her insides.

Jake stood in her doorway.

Mandy's heart fluttered in a panic, anxiety churning in her chest. "Jake...dammit, what's going on?" she whispered. He stepped inside, holding her suitcase and overnight bag, then leaned down and placed a case on either side of his booted feet.

He straightened and walked forward. He looked taller and bulkier than Mandy remembered, but then ten years was a long time. Light blue eyes in a dark, lean face caught her off guard, making her grip her fingers together. He'd always been so handsome, and so unaware of it. Needing time to collect herself, she drew a short, choppy breath. The sensation of panic escalated. She needed to ease it, but all she could do was stare. Jake. God! Why was she being punished? Hadn't the empty years been punishment enough?

Jake nodded at her, his gaze steady. She sensed the wariness in him. She'd always been able to pick up on Jake's emotions. They used to laugh about it. Mandy wasn't laughing now; she was doing her best to ease the pain in her throat.

She couldn't tear her gaze away from him, but she wanted

to. Lord, how she needed something else to concentrate on. She felt vaguely disoriented, then something clicked into place. She remembered him from the night of the accident— the dark, almost black hair; those eyes, so direct and piercing... Those recollections caused her breath to grow shallow. She rubbed her palms together, his voice swirling through her memory. She was in quicksand, flailing. She hated this lack of control.

Anxiety made her flinch back from the hand he held out now. She needed to catch her breath, but it was erratic, getting away from her. It all seemed too much. She prayed she wasn't in for another anxiety attack.

"Hello, Mandy. It's good to see you." Some part of her registered his deep voice, rich and smoky. He appeared so calm, as if seeing her didn't bother him at all. Her presence conjured no emotion in him, at least none that showed on his face. Mandy's panic subsided just a fraction. She ignored his outstretched hand. She couldn't touch him. How could she be expected to touch him as if they hadn't parted with harsh words and tears ten years ago? All those wasted years.

Her breath escaped noisily and she heard a sound come from her throat, a weird, short bark of surprise. She tried again. "What are you doing here in my apartment...?" She tried to see around him and knew instinctively they were alone. "Where's the driver?"

"I told him I'd bring in your cases. He left."

"What the hell is going on?" she asked. Mandy could feel herself losing control, but she didn't care. She needed answers while she could concentrate. Damn, she felt ready to drop. Those light eyes gazed at her, but she couldn't even begin to guess at his thoughts. Ten years!

"This is my place—part of my house, that is. Ben said you needed somewhere to stay." One large hand indicated the room. "It's been empty, so I told Ben you could use it."

Not liking the feeling of being cornered, Mandy wheeled away from him. "This is your place. Your house. Ben rented me a room at your house?" Mandy held her breath, waiting for him to deny it. She needed to stall for time. Her thinking process felt like mush.

"Yes. I assumed Ben had told you."

"Guess it slipped his mind," Mandy snapped. "He just told me I'd be renting a room from a *friend* of his. I don't recall him mentioning that *you* were that friend."

Mandy didn't want to feel the tightness in her chest. She was confused, not a feeling she welcomed. No way could this man be her blue-eyed protector from that terrible night. Her memory of that time seemed skewed, as if she'd seen it through someone else's eyes. She had thought often of that night, but it didn't seem real.

Her senses ultraheightened, Mandy knew he stood behind her. She could hear him breathing. She clenched her thigh, looking down at her legs, the one pant leg empty and flat. Why was she like this?

Jake cleared his throat. "I…was there that day."

"That day?" she repeated hoarsely, turning back to him. Desperately, she searched his face.

Jake nodded.

"I don't want to talk about it." Mandy knew the truth and it tore at her. She had known from the moment she saw his eyes. She would never forget the look there, the compassion, the fear. Why had he been afraid? He had been her protector the night of the accident. In a hidden recess of her mind, she had clung to the memory of his strength during her hospital stay, and then later during the stressful, intense rehabilitation process.

"It wasn't real," she muttered. She had thought of him as a guardian angel, not a real man. Not her Jake. Damn! Mandy clenched her hands. *Get over it,* a voice screamed inside, *he's not your Jake.*

She hadn't asked anyone about him. She had wanted to believe it was all a figment of her imagination, a spiritual presence sent during her desperate time of need. He had kept her calm while she had been extricated from under that bull. He had been her lifeline, then when medical help arrived, she hadn't seen him again. He had left her, but knowing he had been there during the worst of it had made her feel protected and special. It was strange, but she had never felt so protected in her life, and all because of a man who now looked at her as if she meant no more than a stranger.

Mandy pulled her thoughts back. They *were* strangers.

She clenched her jaw and set her shoulders. "This is too much. I cannot handle this." She had said the words out loud. Oddly, she felt as if all her dreams were being ripped away. Mandy tried to stay calm, but as her gaze darted around the room, regret sliced through her.

"This place would have been perfect," she muttered. "Now it's all ruined." It wasn't quite clear as to why, but she knew she couldn't stay here in such close proximity to Jake. The real Jake was no guardian angel, but a man who despised her. Maybe he had a right to after what she had done that night long ago.

"Mandy..."

Without thinking about it, Mandy wheeled quickly toward him, adroitly aiming the chair between the door and his legs.

Jake quickly pulled his toes in. "Hey," he said, "I've brought all the bags in. There's nothing else out there."

Mandy threw back her shoulder-length blond hair and looked straight up at him. "As soon as you move, there'll be something out there. Me."

He looked startled and lifted his brows. Deftly, Mandy wheeled past him. She heard his footsteps follow her down the ramp. She wheeled the chair faster, faster, her arms feeling as if they'd fall off. Damn! Why had the driver left so quickly?

Mandy stopped at the edge of the driveway just in time to see the van disappear. Her shoulders slumped. She cursed under her breath as Jake moved into her line of vision.

"What's the problem, Mandy? If something needs changing, I can have it done—"

"No." Hurriedly, she shook her head, refusing to look at him. It hurt so much, the thoughts in her head. He was too handsome, too much for her to look at. Memories slammed her once more. Jake bending down tenderly to kiss her, helping her over some rough spots when they went hiking… She recalled how he'd surprised her with flowers when they'd been dating for a month and how he'd cheered her up when she lost a rodeo event. Every minute detail she remembered about him was the same: the blueness of his eyes; the small crinkles alongside his straight, firm mouth; the square, clean line of his jaw…

Mandy again looked at her legs, intense, emotional pain tightening her mouth. Why did she have to be like this? Why wasn't she normal? The regret of wasted years, what now felt like a wasted life, was too much.

"This won't work," she said through gritted teeth. "I need complete privacy. N-nothing personal, but I need to be totally alone. How could you imagine this would ever work? We haven't seen each other in years, and then to be thrown together like this…"

"I live in another part of the house. If you don't want contact, I won't intrude. I work all day, anyhow. I thought I'd help you get settled in, is all." His voice sounded so calm and practical.

Mandy shook her head quickly. "No, it won't work. I need a phone. Can I use your phone?"

Jake said, "Sure. Come on over to my house. Your phone should be working later tonight."

Jake sensed any offer of help on his part would be swiftly rejected. He walked ahead of Mandy, leading the way. For the hundredth time he asked himself how he could have been so stupid as to agree to let her stay in the empty apartment at his ranch.

Because you're a sucker, he thought as they neared his house. That wasn't true and Jake knew it. He and Mandy went back a long way, and a part of him still cared about her. She had nowhere else to go and she needed help.

Having Mandy at the ranch would be a small price to pay if it meant closing doors on old wounds. Why had he left it so long? Finding a picture of Mandy from some old clippings had prompted him to go to the rodeo that night, three months ago. Curiosity had taken him there. Fascination had made him stay, and now an urgent compulsion drew him further into her sphere.

Jake hoped to God he could handle the reality of her injury. His father had lost both legs before he died, so Jake knew what was involved. He wasn't sure he wanted to deal with it—all over again. But his personal feelings had no importance in the scheme of things. After all, he'd gotten over Mandy years ago. The best thing to do would be to stay out of each other's way. He had promised her brother that she could recuperate here; there was no going back.

This reunion scene with Mandy was playing out like he had been afraid it would. She had taken one look at him and her hackles had risen full speed. Why? She had walked out on him, so why would she be afraid of him? She looked bone tired, frail, and her voice was bordering on panic. Jake had to keep her from leaving at all costs. He was afraid something would happen to her if she left in the state she was now. He needed to think fast. He had six sisters; he should know what to do, right?

He opened the atrium door into his living room and stood aside. "The phone is over by the windows."

He saw her look around his house—the place he had

bought after she'd left him. Jake was proud of his home, the hand-hewn beams, the natural, light-colored woods. He had spent a lot of time making it comfortable. He thought he saw interest in her gaze, but then tiredness seemed to shut down her face.

Thinking fast, he followed behind her. "It's too bad this won't work out," he said softly. "I, uh, I'm kind of strapped for cash right now. I thought it would be an ideal arrangement." Jake thought she hesitated, her hands on the wheels, then she moved on into the room. The late afternoon sun spilled through the casement windows and touched her. Jake was close enough to see that her knuckles were white from the way she was clenching the wheels. She turned the chair so her back was to him, and quickly picked up the phone.

As she began to punch in numbers, Jake knew he had nothing to lose. She was prepared to get out as fast as she could. He had scared her, maybe brought back the bad memories of that night, not that she would admit to it. Mandy had never been one to admit to anything that she felt was a weakness. She covered it up with bravado and brash nerve. Once she set her mind on a course, there was no persuading her otherwise. But now, Jake knew, he had to persuade her to stay, for her own sake.

He stepped forward, noting the soft curve of her cheek, the swing of her naturally blond hair spilling past her blue, blue eyes. She was the kind of woman a man could lose himself in and not care if he ever surfaced. Once, Jake had almost let himself get lost in her.

His gaze dropped to the empty space where her right leg should be. He swallowed hard. Pain lanced through him, and he didn't want to feel it. He didn't want to feel connected to a woman who had thrown his love in his face.

In his mind, Jake replayed the night of the rodeo accident. Once again he saw the bull falling on her. The bull had been old and just died. It was a scene he would never forget.

He'd gone to see her once in the hospital, though she didn't know that. He hadn't gone back. Somehow, he didn't think she'd want to see him and be reminded of that terrible night.

He felt the anger well in him. Her lifestyle had finally caught up with her—the wild living, the parties. Jake read the papers. He shook his head in disgust. The bottom line was he'd wanted forever with Mandy, but all she'd wanted was new excitement down the road. It seemed she had gotten what she wanted, in spades.

Returning to the present, Jake watched Mandy's eyes, saw the overwhelming pain, the sad defeat. His gut clenched. Despite his bitterness, he knew he could not let her leave. Something told him she needed this place. He had promised Ben he would help her, and dammit, he wouldn't go back on that promise. Before long it would be dark, and it was an hour's drive to the center, not counting how long it would take to get a driver back out here. No matter where she was going, it would take time.

Mandy held her shoulders straight, but she looked exhausted. Violet shadows emphasized her eyes and hollows lay in her cheeks. Jake figured she needed a good night's rest and then some. As his thoughts rambled on, he heard her mutter something about voice mail into the phone. Going for broke, Jake said, "I never thought I'd see the day you'd give up at the first obstacle. I guess you've changed over the years, Mandy. But then, ten years is a long time."

Chapter Two

As if he'd touched her with a live wire, Mandy's head jerked around, her eyes narrowing and shooting fire. "What...what did you say?" She demanded. She dropped the phone back on its cradle with a loud clatter. She hoped she'd broken it, she was so mad, but she glanced at it quickly and saw it was still in one piece.

Jake had the nerve to turn away and saunter toward the kitchen. She stared after him, for the moment speechless. Hurriedly, she jerked her eyes from his long back and legs. She wondered why he wore perfectly creased dress pants. He'd look great in tight, faded jeans. Years ago he'd worn jeans all the time. Mandy made an exasperated sound, irritated with her thoughts. With a jerky movement, she propelled her chair across a short-napped, gray carpet.

"What the hell are you implying? I've never given up on anything in my life. You don't know what you're talking about, Jake Miller. I suppose this is some kind of reverse psychology?'' Her entire body felt ready to snap from the tension riding her. She gripped the arms of her chair, feeling an ache shoot up into her neck. ''Well, it's not going to work. I'm not seventeen anymore. You don't know a damn thing about me.''

Jake reached into the refrigerator and calmly took out two cans of soda. He handed one to Mandy, then popped the top on his. Taking a deep gulp, he lowered the can and looked her straight in the eye. ''You're right, I don't know a thing about you. You seemed okay with everything, the arrangements and the place, until you saw me. What we might have had is long over, so it can't be that. So if you're not giving up, what is it that makes you want to run like a rabbit for a hole?''

Mandy had never in her life been likened to a rabbit running for a hole. The analogy caused the beginnings of a smile. She caught herself and looked away from him. She needed to stay angry so he wouldn't catch her off guard. God knows she'd crumble into the ground if she let him get past her defenses.

I don't want to deal with people, anyone, the way I am now, she wanted to scream at him. *I want to be selfish and alone. I don't want to remember how I loved you.*

''I'm uncomfortable with this whole situation. I thought I was out here by myself.'' The truth was extremely difficult for her to admit. Mandy felt as if she had no pride left. And yet, suddenly, she remembered Jake saying he needed the money.

He shrugged his big shoulders. ''Well, there's only me. Except for Sundays, there usually isn't a gang of people hanging around,'' he said dryly. ''If you're worried about the connecting door between your side and mine, I'll hand over the keys. My mom and dad used to live here, so I have an extra set.''

Mandy gripped the ice-cold can in her hand, feeling the

aluminum indent under the pressure. Jerkily, she placed the can on the table beside her and pushed it toward him.

"You shared the house with your parents?"

"Yes. My mom needed help with my dad. It was easier this way."

Mandy felt an unexpected ache deep down. Easier for whom? Everyone but Jake. She pushed that thought aside.

"What happens on Sundays?" A faint curiosity stirred inside her.

"A bunch of friends come and play football. It shouldn't bother you. We play in the pasture away from your side of the house."

"Football?" Something clicked in Mandy's mind. "Ben plays football on Sundays since he moved back from New York. He hardly ever misses it."

Jake shifted his feet. "Yeah, well, Ben's one of the guys."

Things began to sharpen into focus. If she hadn't felt so wrapped up in herself, she might have figured it out earlier. When had she gotten so self-absorbed? "I've been so stuck in my own thoughts, I haven't paid attention to what Ben's been telling me." Mandy put a weary hand to the back of her head, then flipped her hair away from her face. "God! Ben must have told me."

Jake's expression turned wary. "He told you about this place, that I owned it?"

"Maybe…" Something on the wall beyond Jake's shoulder caught Mandy's attention. She had been staring at it fixedly, but her brain finally assimilated that it was a large antler, the end of which was carved into the head of a bear. The work was so breathtakingly beautiful and delicate that Mandy lost her train of thought. She moved her chair toward it, then slowly reached out to run her fingertips delicately over the face of the animal.

"Jake, I've never seen anything so stunning." She lifted

her gaze to his in wonder. "This carving is a work of art. The detail is so exquisite and fine."

"Thank you," Jake said simply.

"Where did you get it?"

"It's an elk antler. It was given to me by a friend last year. He finds antlers in the woods when they're shed by elk or moose—"

"No, the carving—who did the carving?" Memories snapped into place. Mandy let her gaze touch his, her eyes wide with amazement. "Jake, did you do this? I remember…" She recalled so clearly the small wooden animals Jake used to carve. Mandy had about a dozen of them in her room at Mama's ranch.

"You did this, Jake. You carved this antler. I had no idea you were into it so seriously."

"There's probably a lot we don't know about each other," Jake said slowly. "It's been a long time."

Confused, exhausted, Mandy felt suddenly overwhelmed by the pressures of the day. She was tired beyond belief. She needed to lie down. Coming to a snap decision, she tore her eyes away from the carved antler and wheeled herself to the door. "Maybe I'll stay the night and call a taxi in the morning." She couldn't help the stiffness of her voice or the determined tilt of her chin.

Mandy paused in the doorway and waited for Jake to say something. When he didn't, she looked back at him.

"You can stay as long as you need to," he said.

She splayed her fingers and rubbed her forehead. "Why are you doing this, Jake?" she asked, looking up at him. "Why would you offer this place to me at the low rent Ben quoted me?" She knew her voice was too high, and made an attempt to lower it. "Why me, of all people?"

"The apartment's been empty. You needed a place to stay for a while and the solution seemed right."

I'm kind of strapped for cash…. Mandy looked at him.

He wouldn't beg her to stay, and she wouldn't want him to. Was this a small way for her to repay him for what she had done years ago? The small amount she paid him in rent might help him out now.

Mandy had another split-second flashback to the night of the accident. Once more she saw him at her side, his face filled with determination and concern, the drizzle of rain blurring his features. They should have been strangers after ten years apart, yet he had helped her that night, had stayed with her, and she felt an unwanted connection to him. Darn him! Why had he come back into her life now? How could she deal with this?

"Why, Jake? Why were you there that night?"

She eyed him across the room, noting a certain hardness in his expression. Mandy knew he wasn't going to answer. Why?

The thoughts ran too fast for her to catch them. At the moment, she couldn't think properly. She had to lie down. "I've got to get some sleep," she said. "What time do you leave for work? Will I see you in the morning?"

"I'll be around," he promised.

Jake moved up behind her, as if to help propel her chair out the door.

"I'm fine," she lied, gripping the rubber-edged wheels. "I can get myself the rest of the way."

"I can help," Jake said. Mandy twisted in the chair and narrowed her eyes challengingly. Finally, he seemed to get the message, because he stepped away from her and merely opened the door.

It took every ounce of strength Mandy possessed to move the chair out the door onto their shared front deck. At the door of her apartment, she turned her head and looked back. Jake stood in his doorway watching her. He lifted a hand slowly and saluted her. Mandy turned her head away and closed her eyes tightly. That gesture of farewell was familiar, one she hadn't seen in many years. Emotion overloaded her. Mandy felt the threatening burn behind her eyes.

Firming her lips to stop the trembling, she said loudly, "For the record, Jake, I never give up." *Except once, when I shouldn't have,* she amended silently. *I was only seventeen, and maybe I made a mistake.* A mistake she could never undo and would forever regret.

"Ben, find me another place. I can't stay here," Mandy typed on her notebook computer early the next morning.

Ben's reply came almost immediately via modem. "Why not? The place is perfect. What's the matter? Has something happened to upset you?"

Mandy looked at the ceiling, then typed, "No." She swallowed hard and typed quickly, "Jake's been great. I just can't stay here. It's not right for me. By the way, you might have told me, but I don't recall you mentioning the place was owned by Jake." Mandy hit the Send button.

After a while, another e-mail came. "I did tell you, Sis. I know you two were hot when you were kids, but it didn't seem to be a problem for Jake. You two have hardly mentioned each other in all these years."

Mandy felt a sharp lance of pain. She hadn't told anyone the truth about her leaving, and apparently Jake hadn't confided in her brother, either.

"It'll take me a while to find another place with such a perfect setup. I told Jake it was only temporary."

Mandy felt a curl of disappointment. The apartment was perfect, but how could she explain the twisting emotions she herself didn't understand? She couldn't stay around Jake Miller. He touched something raw in her, the part of her that had never fully recovered from loving him. She was attracted to him, plain and simple. It was the first real emotion she'd felt in months. Maybe before the accident she might have done something about it if Jake walked back into her life, but not now, not when she felt so inadequate as a woman, as a person.

Mandy had never felt inadequate in her life. Now the feeling seemed to seep into every segment of her existence. Even her writing career suffered. Since the accident, she hadn't touched a freelance article she'd once been incredibly enthusiastic about. She had to get her life back on track. Seeing Jake brought into vivid recall the day of the accident, the pain and her own vulnerability. All her absurd fantasies about him aside, how could she move on with her life if she were constantly reminded of the life they might have had together?

Mandy looked down at the computer screen.

"...so the only alternative I can see is to have you move in with me." Ben had put a smiley face at the end of the message.

Mandy zeroed in on the words. "What?" she practically screeched.

Furiously, she typed, "Whoa! Hold on, Ben. No way." Mandy managed a laugh, and typed again, "No way. I'll stay here until you find something else, but find me something fast."

Mandy sent the e-mail and disconnected, mixed emotions snaking through her. She looked out the window at the sun creeping across the pasture. This ranch looked so beautiful. She felt enfolded by it, protected. When had she ever wanted to be protected from anything in her life? But now she welcomed the feeling.

"It looks like I'm stuck here, at least for a while." She would make the most of it. Surely on a ranch as spacious as this one appeared to be, she could easily keep out of Jake's way. Jake, who had a new life, one that would never involve her. They had both moved beyond a teenage love.

Mandy glared at the artificial limb, which lay on the table across the room. She could wish it away, throw it in the corner, hope it would rot there forever, but she knew it was a lifeline, the one thing that could make her independent, her ticket to getting back into rodeo. An expensive ticket, but one she had to invest in.

Her crutches leaned against the wall by the refrigerator. First step: renew her acquaintance with the leg that had been specially fitted for her....

Jake rose early, took a swim in the pool and got ready for work. All the while he thought about the events of last night. Mandy had baffled him, telling him out of the blue that she was leaving, then deciding to stay. His ploy might have made her change her mind and stay the night, but he had seen the determined look in her eye that told him she would be gone by daybreak, if humanly possible. This was a new situation for Jake. None of his sisters had ever been so obstinate or determined to go their own way. They had always turned to him and welcomed his help.

Jake recalled a time when Mandy could be swayed by him. No more. She'd made that abundantly clear last night. She'd been furious when he'd tried to help her out the door. Jake couldn't help staring at her amputated limb. It had been covered by her jeans, but he had woken up in the middle of the night thinking about it, remembering the accident. Would he ever get that scene out of his mind? The bull half covering Mandy. Both her legs pinned under its weight. Mandy lying so still and white...

Jake looked at the pinkening sky, running a hand over the front of his silk shirt and finding a button he had missed. Daybreak had come and gone, and as far as he knew, she was still here.

With thoughts of Mandy on his mind, Jake glanced at his watch, then left the house and strode to the barn. He'd fed the horses earlier, but had neglected to close the gate leading from the barn to the pasture.

Now he smoothed a hand through his hair for the hundredth time and glowered at the ground. It didn't sit well that he had tossed and turned most of the night. He wouldn't have been surprised to hear a vehicle arrive to pick up Mandy.

He came to an abrupt halt at the barn door, surprised to see Mandy in the barn. There was no wheelchair, just her, standing there on her own. Another quick look at his watch assured him it was barely six, but there she was, staring out over his pasture, a relaxed, almost tranquil expression on her face. Jake swallowed hard and shoved his hands into his pants pockets. Long ago he had dreamed of sharing every morning with her. His mouth twisted. They both had been so young.

Jake figured the gentlemanly thing would be to let her have some privacy. He should turn and walk away. She probably wouldn't be happy to see him this morning.

"Good morning, Mandy," he said instead. As if he had startled her, she swiftly turned her head. At least she didn't look nearly as tired. Even tired, she looked damned good.

Mandy walked toward him, slim in worn jeans and a gray cotton T-shirt. Her gait was somewhat awkward, but she wore a determined smile on her face, and he couldn't help but stare at her blue, blue eyes. She had shown up yesterday looking bone tired and sitting in a wheelchair. Today, with her prosthesis in place, he got the message that she wanted to act as if everything was normal. As far as he was concerned, normal was good. The way she was watching him, Jake had a feeling this was a trial of sorts. Was she testing him, or anyone who came into contact with her? Jake squashed the voice that warned him he'd made a mistake in letting her come here.

"Good morning, Jake. I wanted to see your stock. Mind if I look around?"

"No, feel free. The horses are pretty friendly. They're always interested in carrots or treats."

"Are they yours, Jake?"

"Yes. A friend fell on some hard times and needed somewhere to park the horses. That was three years ago. I ended up buying the trio."

Jake watched Mandy lean a moment against a fence post. He wondered about her leg, if it bothered her, but something in her face warned him not to ask. He balled his fists deeper in his pockets and said with determination, "Are you...do you need any help?" Inwardly, he cursed his own awkwardness. She narrowed her eyes, but he ignored the warning. "If you find you need anything or I've forgotten something, I'll be around later this afternoon. Look around at whatever you like, Mandy. I'll be leaving for work in the next hour." He made himself walk away from her. Everything in him wanted to stick around and talk to her, make sure she was okay. But her wary expression told him she had to make the first move. Jake pushed the barn gate closed and latched it.

"Jake?"

He turned quickly, then cursed his eagerness. What was the matter with him?

"Do you usually work on Saturdays?"

"Not usually. In a little while I have to go in and check a few things and meet with some people."

"I guess I'm not used to seeing you in a suit," she remarked.

Jake smoothed his tie, feeling the cool breeze, seeing it lift several strands of Mandy's hair. "I run a manufacturing company. I have a lot of business meetings—that's the reason for the suit." He couldn't resist adding, "I'm not the same man you knew, Mandy."

His box manufacturing business had reached a level of success where he could hire a manager. His wildlife-carving business thrived; Jake never would have guessed his hobby would turn into such a success. Come hell or high water, he was heading down the road, and he wasn't looking back.

"I know what you do—I do remember your father's business." There was a slight curve to Mandy's mouth, as if something amused her. Jake wondered at the quick, almost assessing glance she ran over him. A ripple of awareness moved between them as their gazes met. He slid a finger under his suddenly tight collar. Did she think he was the same gullible kid he'd been, blindly in love with her? Holding back from taking their kisses too far...

It piqued Jake that Mandy seemed to ignore him as she turned her gaze back to his pasture. He wondered if she saw the same beauty in the flat, desolate expanse as he did. He loved this land. It was his, something he had worked hard for. A place of permanence he came back to at the end of a long day.

"I really appreciate you stocking the fridge and the cupboards for me," she told him softly, still not looking at him.

"No problem, Mandy. Ben helped me with suggestions about what you might like. I go shopping once a week. Make a list if you need anything."

She looked surprised, then disappointed. "Oh...I thought maybe you remembered what I like." Quickly, she put up a hand to brush the hair from her eyes, her laugh sounding forced. "Isn't that silly? We wouldn't remember anything from that long ago."

Jake's smile felt frozen. He remembered that she liked strawberries piled with whipped cream. He recalled the time he'd kissed the cream from her lips, then deliberately sprayed some whipped cream on her neck and licked that sweetness from her skin....

"Mama's bringing my vehicle out sometime this week." Mandy ran her fingertips over the rough-cut wallboards. "By the way, I talked to Ben this morning."

"Really? Is he back in the country?"

"He is. I contacted him via modem. I want to reassure you I won't impose any longer than necessary. Ben's looking around for somewhere else for me to rent." Mandy looked Jake in the eye and blurted, "If it's okay, I'd like to stay here until he comes up with something. I—I can't go home right now. I promise to stay out of your way."

"Yeah, sure, no problem." Jake tried to keep his voice offhand, while something inside him lifted. She wasn't leaving, at least not immediately. Then he felt irritated with his thoughts. He wanted her to get well and leave; he had to keep that firmly in mind. They weren't in love anymore. Maybe they could find a comfortable solution for her, or maybe she would realize on her own that this arrangement could work. She could rest and get her life together. Once things settled down for her, she could leave, and they could all go on as before. Jake felt satisfied with that conclusion. He was only helping someone in need. When she was on her feet once more, good riddance.

"I have things to do," he said abruptly, exasperated with his own meandering. He made himself walk away and left her standing by the barn. It was best for both of them if they stayed out of each other's way.

Chapter Three

Mandy watched Jake walk toward the house, still unable to shake the sense of unreality each time she saw him. She had had him pegged a certain way in her mind, and to see him now, it felt as if she'd never left. She must have been out of her mind that night, to think he was an angel sent especially for her.

Once Jake was out of sight, she determinedly walked away from the barn to the split rail fence enclosing the pasture. If it killed her, she would learn to walk normally with this fool artificial leg.

The barn itself was in good repair. Mandy found three horses out in the pasture. The first two were beautiful bays, their coats the color of copper, with legs dark and fine. The third horse, a deep, true black, was of a heavier build. Mandy immediately felt drawn to him. He reminded her of her favorite horse, Pongo, a black-and-white Paint.

The black horse trotted over to the fence and poked his

dark muzzle over the rail next to Mandy. Speaking softly, she leaned against the wood for support and rubbed her palm down his sleek neck.

"You're gorgeous," she told him, and an unexpected homesickness hit her. Because of her stubbornness, she hadn't seen her horses in over three months.

The horse dipped his head and, in the next moment, pushed against Mandy's chest. The unexpected movement made her take a step backward on her right leg. She lost her balance and landed awkwardly on the ground. Hearing running footsteps, she turned her head to see Jake coming toward her, alarm all over his face.

"Damn." Mandy tried to scramble up, but only managed to rise to one knee by the time Jake reached her side. She held herself off the ground with her hands in the dirt, looking up at him awkwardly, her face flushed, her shirt damp from her exertions.

"Mandy, are you okay? I just happened to see you fall." Jake knelt down. The concern on his face, combined with his dark hair tumbling over one eye, set off an uneasy feeling in Mandy. Attraction stirred dark and needy. Damn! She didn't want to feel attracted to him. They couldn't pick up where they'd left off. Life didn't work out that way, as much as she wanted to turn back the clock.

Mandy felt herself tense. Where had those thoughts come from?

He helped her to her feet and, still slightly off center, she took a nosedive into his shirt. Instantly, she panicked, trying to straighten as she slapped his helpful hands away. Jake stepped back and released her upper arms, but not before Mandy felt a pulsing awareness that made her nerve endings jump. The subtle scent of his freshly showered skin played around her nostrils. Soap and shaving lotion...

What was the matter with her? She couldn't go back;

there were too many years and too many words between them.

Angry with herself, she snapped, "I'm fine! Leave me alone. I don't need your help." Mandy turned her head away from him, blinking hard as moisture filmed her eyes. "I guess I'm a hazard around the barn," she muttered, angry with her own awkwardness. She felt as inadequate as hell.

Jake stepped back, and she heard him say, "I forgot to mention Tibald's got a knack for rubbing against you. He's gotten the best of me a time or two."

Mandy again blinked rapidly, not daring to look at Jake as she slapped the dust from her jeans with her palms. If he knew there were angry tears rimming her eyes, he was smart enough not to mention it.

After a moment, she ran her gaze up and down him, not bothering to hide her disbelieving frown.

"Tibald…that's his name? He's knocked you down?" she asked incredulously.

"Well, knocked me backward," Jake admitted with a grin. Mandy decided to ignore the smile in his eyes telling her it was no big deal. The connection she felt was too dangerous for her peace of mind. "Of course, you can't compare my two hundred pounds to your one hundred," he added quickly.

"One twenty-five," Mandy told him automatically. Without her lower leg she was minus five pounds, give or take.

Jake reached up and affectionately rubbed the heel of his palm between the horse's eyes. "There's not a bit of malice in him, but he forgets his size."

Mandy stepped back to get a better look at the horse. "He reminds me of my Paint horse," she said, giving voice to her earlier thoughts.

"Ben said your horses are out at your mother's ranch."

She looked away. "Yes, Mama's got lots of pasture." Mandy suddenly felt uncomfortable with that explanation.

"I—I let Mama assume responsibility for my animals the entire time I've been in the hospital and rehabilitation." She looked down, angry with herself. She had never asked about them, nor offered Mama anything for their upkeep. Mandy bit her lip at her apathy. It wasn't like her to let other people shoulder her obligations. "I have some things to sort out with her."

"I'm sure you will. If you should decide to start riding, Mandy, there's plenty of room here for an extra horse."

Mandy opened her mouth, then quickly closed it. Did he think she was ready to pick up the pieces and begin to ride? "I'll ride when I'm ready." She swallowed hard. "That's...very generous of you, but I won't be here that long. I wouldn't impose on you, anyway," she ended stiffly.

As Jake scrubbed a hand under the black's wide jaw, the animal stretched his nose out and closed his eyes. "Old Tibald here is as mellow as they come, but he can race like the wind if he's in the mood."

Mandy stared at the back of Jake's head, her eyes unwillingly moving down the thick column of his neck, where it went down into his white shirt. She wondered what changes had occurred physically with Jake. He looked to be in superb shape.

Frowning heavily, still feeling slightly out of sync, Mandy swung her hair off her shoulders. "I'm probably jumping to assumptions here, but you strike me as being too busy to have time for horses. Ben mentioned you've made a great success out of your father's business. He said you work all the time."

Jake turned slowly to face her, his brows lifted in surprise. "I've always owned horses, Mandy. I ride whenever I can. During the day they pretty much fend for themselves." Something in his eyes reminded her of the Jake she'd known long ago, the Jake she'd loved. There was almost a softness when he spoke of his horses. Mandy drew in a hard breath.

She wondered fleetingly if there was a woman in his life. How would his face look when he spoke about the woman he loved? She swallowed hard, an edge of desperation gripping her.

"So you still enjoy making boxes for a living?" she quipped, needing to shake the attraction nipping at her.

"Sure. Why not? Miller manufactures the best cardboard boxes this side of the Mississippi." Jake's mouth quirked up at the corners as if he were amused by her.

"I'm having a hard time putting the two together," Mandy said smartly. She put her hands on her hips. "You know, man who makes boxes, horse that races like the wind."

Jake looked at her thoughtfully. "After my dad's accident I had to take over the family business. That doesn't mean I've turned into a dead bore," he finished dryly. "I have managed to come up with a semblance of a life in the time you've been away." His words were smooth, but cutting all the same.

Embarrassed by her own deliberate lack of finesse, Mandy felt heat mount into her cheeks. "I—I didn't mean that," she said hurriedly.

Jake dusted his hands off and moved away. "I think you did. I have a few things to take care of before I leave, so if you'll excuse me…"

Mandy knew he didn't give a damn if she minded him walking away. She had offended him, unintentionally…or perhaps intentionally. She had wanted to distance him from herself, and maybe that was her warped way of doing it. Nothing like implying a guy was as boring as dirt or boxes. She didn't really believe that, but she needed a defense. The same intense feelings she'd always felt for Jake gripped her. She didn't want to feel them. What Jake stirred in her made her feel vulnerable. She'd never survive loving and leaving

Jake a second time. And she would leave. They both knew it was a given. There was no place for her here, with Jake.

Mandy could only guess at the pain Jake had experienced when he'd been forced to give up a promising football career. He had been on the verge of a scholarship. Then, abruptly, he'd had to shoulder responsibility for his family, the business, his father's care. Mandy knew at the time they were too young. She'd been too young. She had left, and it had broken her heart.

Being near him did something to her hormones, no doubt about it. The man was that good-looking, but then, she had known plenty of good-looking men on the rodeo circuit. Mandy felt a momentary remorse for the partying lifestyle she had led, then immediately put a rein on her thoughts. She had never worried about her lifestyle before the accident, so why was she giving it a second thought now? Darn Jake; it was his fault she was suffering all this introspection.

Confused, Mandy stared after Jake as he walked away. He wore creased gray pants and a pristine white shirt with a tie that looked like silk. Didn't he ever relax? He used to know how to kick back and have a good time. Mandy tried to recall that night he had stayed with her while she was pinned under the bull, but most of it still remained hazy. Except for his eyes. They haunted her still, but not in a bad way, and that worried her.

Since she had left Jake all those years ago, she had never been tempted to spend too much time with any one man. She had chosen her path and stuck to it. Rodeo, first and foremost. Her mama had taken that path for a time, then quit to raise Mandy and Ben. Daddy had never left rodeo for very long, and probably wouldn't until the day he died. The plan had always been for Mandy to follow in her daddy's footsteps. Although he had won dozens of buckles, trophies, saddles and the like, he had never made it to the finals. Making the finals had been Mandy's dream for as long as she could remember. Daddy used to call her his "wild child." He'd bragged to anyone who would listen that she had the guts and grit to win big. Daddy had made her believe it.

Mandy had witnessed firsthand what the rodeo life did to families. She knew of the loneliness Mama couldn't hide. Daddy had made a good living at rodeo, but it had come at a cost to everyone. Mandy wouldn't marry and raise kids the way she had been raised. It wouldn't be fair to anybody. She was her own person, and she had decided, selfish or not, that she was living her life the way she chose. Jake would never know how her decision to leave him had torn her apart. How do you recover from a once-in-a-lifetime love who you threw away?

No doubt there were plenty of women willing to take on the position of Mrs. Jake Miller. But not her. With a grimace, Mandy laughed at herself. Who was she kidding? She had never stopped yearning for him, but she'd never be asked again. Jake had his pride, just as she had hers. She would never beg him to take her back.

Mandy recalled how Jake had watched her in the rodeo yard before that fateful ride on old Hit Man. She had even thought of boldly seeking him out after her ride. They might have joined the gang and gone out for a good time.

It was too bad she had alienated him, because now she couldn't ask him all the questions inside her head. He had so much land, a big, spacious barn...why was it all going to waste? Mandy stopped in her tracks. Why in the world should she care? she asked herself. Jake might look like a cowgirl's idea of heaven, but he was as steady as any Mr. Right. Thank God finding a Mr. Right wasn't on her agenda.

There had been a time when she'd do anything for Jake. Her seventeenth summer had been happy, idyllic. Jake had followed the rodeos with her and fit right in. They'd had vague plans for the future. Jake would take his scholarship, play football, and some day they would buy a ranch. But Mandy hadn't really looked further ahead than that summer. When Jake's father had had a car accident and then suffered a stroke, it was the end of their world as Mandy knew it. Overnight the welfare of his family had rested on Jake's shoulders. He was running in ten directions, trying to keep everything from falling apart.

Mandy knew she was part of the problem. Jake needed to concentrate on his family, not follow her around. He had no time for her. Their plans to marry when she turned eighteen fell to dust. Mandy had told Jake she needed breathing space. The idea of marriage had suddenly been too real, and had begun to scare the hell out of her. She didn't know anything about being a wife or caring for babies. She wanted to play, not be bogged down with responsibility, the way Jake had suddenly been.

He hadn't seen it that way. Despite everything, he didn't want what was between them to change. It tore her apart, but her decision had totally alienated Jake. Afterward, she'd tried writing to him, calling him, but he'd cut her out of his life. His indifference had sliced her to the bone. He didn't understand that the rodeo wouldn't wait, that she had to make her mark.

In the intervening years Mandy had wondered if she had made the right decision. At the time, the situation had seemed so hopeless, Jake's burdens so heavy. Leaving had seemed the only solution.

Mandy put a brake on her own thoughts now. Here she was, worrying about a relationship between her and Jake, when no doubt it was the furthest thing from his mind. He had matured into a sensible, solid citizen, too smart to hook up with a loose cannon like herself, especially now that she had a bum leg. He would want a homemaker, a round-the-clock mother for his kids, someone dependable with a capital *D*. Mandy had long ago discarded any such notions.

Angrily, she swiped at the wetness on her cheek. She had made her life her own. All the faults were hers, and it wouldn't do any good to regret the decisions she'd made.

Stopping to rest a moment near the barn, Mandy leaned against the open wooden door, staring at the fields as the sun crept higher in the sky.

With a wry grin, she dropped onto an old rickety bench beside the doorway, stretching her legs out before her. Her right leg ached just the tiniest bit, but it was a good ache. She had to be careful not to overdo it, or she would be back on crutches, with blisters and sores. It was a constant battle, having to be careful about things she'd never had to think about before.

Gently, Mandy massaged the limb. Looking around, she had to admit Jake's ranch, with its seemingly endless stretch of pasture and low hills, was a rancher's dream.

Mandy decided she wanted to explore the layout of the land and become familiar with the place. Even if she didn't stay long, she liked to know her way around. Maybe Jake would let her work with the horses, even if she just brushed them or exercised them on a lunge line.

Right now a walk would strengthen her leg. The long driveway to the house would be the ideal place to start, for she could negotiate the slight inclines. Her therapist had told her walking would become easier the more she did it.

Resolutely, Mandy got to her feet.

Jake was getting ready to leave for town when Mandy passed his office window. Curious as to where she was going, he watched her walk down the driveway and disappear around a curve.

Mentally, he shrugged his shoulders, then pulled on his suit jacket. It wasn't any of his business, was it, if she wanted to go for a walk? Then a thought hit him. What if she fell and hurt herself? Who would be around to help her?

There were some uneven stretches along the driveway. He opened the glass door leading to his back deck and skirted the swimming pool. Quickly, he strode around the house.

Jake felt a need to keep an eye on Mandy, if only for her own safety. He remembered how rebellious she could be, how full of determination, but he also knew this could be a real touchy situation. He had a feeling she'd be furious if she knew he was worried about her. Still, Jake told himself, he didn't need a lawsuit on his hands if she got hurt.

Rounding the first curve in the driveway, he spotted her and quickly ducked into the woods on one side. At least the driveway had been paved last year and the going was fairly smooth. Jake wondered if Mandy realized that the way back to the house would be a steady incline. He reminded himself that he had good reasons for staying out of sight, but felt slightly foolish, sneaking around his own property.

Jake pushed his hair back, feeling sweat dampening his forehead and the shirt under his jacket. He should have left the jacket at the house. Mandy didn't seem to be having any problems. In fact, she seemed steadier on her feet than when he had seen her at the barn earlier. Jake began to feel he'd worried needlessly, until she suddenly left the paved driveway and wandered toward the woods. Why the devil was she going there? She could really get hurt on the uneven ground.

Jake pushed tree limbs back so he could see her better. She looked around a few times, but he ducked down quickly. He muttered a curse when he heard the sharp snap of a twig beneath his shoe.

''Who's there?'' Mandy called out.

Resignedly, Jake pushed aside a tangle of brush and stepped forward.

''Jake?''

''Hello, Mandy.'' Casually, he straightened his tie and ran his palms over his hair to smooth it down.

Her hands were on her hips and she had a suspicious look on her face. "What are you doing in the woods?"

Jake felt heat slide up his cheeks and he cleared his throat. "I forgot to mention the hot water was off because of a power shortage earlier this morning, so if you want to take a shower, it'll take a while for the water to heat up."

"Oh, okay, Jake. Thanks." She moved close to him and lifted a hand toward his head. Jake felt her fingers on his hair, and a tingling spread through his scalp. He gripped her wrist and jerked it away from his head. He stared at the small twigs in her fingers, then looked into her face. She seemed ready to burst into laughter. Some of the tension eased from Jake.

"Somehow, I don't think these will go well with your business meeting."

Jake released her wrist. "Thanks. Anyway, I wanted to tell you about the water." He looked at his watch. He was going to be late. "Do you want company walking back to the house?"

"Sure, if you have time. You can show me the path you took through the woods."

"The path?" Jake thought fast, then took her arm and guided her to the edge of the trees. There was no path. "Sure, follow me."

Jake managed to find a fairly clear area for them to walk through. Worried about her falling, he deliberately shortened his pace, holding her arm the entire time. Strangely, she didn't protest, and he began to feel some of the tension ease from his body.

Partway to the house he heard Mandy give a small laugh. He looked at her questioningly, seeing the light in her eyes, the relaxed curve of her lush lips. He smothered a groan, then looked fixedly ahead. How different she looked from last night, when everything had seemed to weigh her down.

"Well, Jake, it's understandable why Ben has kept in touch with you all these years."

Surprised, Jake came to a standstill. "Why is that?"

"Ben's a pretty smart guy. It's because you're such a good friend, and friends like you are hard to find. I'm glad you're his friend." To Jake's ears her voice sounded almost wistful. In the next moment, the thought was banished when she gave him a brilliant, almost carefree smile. "Do you think we could manage to be friends?"

"Friends?" Jake felt a rush of anger. What the hell was she asking? How could they be friends? He didn't want to be her friend. He wanted her to get well and leave, so he'd never have to think about her again. He wouldn't think of her as a friend. Friends didn't go away, they kept in touch. If she didn't leave, all the old emotion might surface and he'd make a fool of himself again. He knew the pain of trying to hold on to a woman who wanted to let go.

"I think we can do it, Jake. It's been a long time since we were anything to each other."

Mandy's gaze was turned away from him, and Jake wasn't sure if that was deliberate or not. He swallowed hard, stopping the protest about to jerk from his throat.

"You're right, ten years is a helluva long time," he said. He told himself he'd better remember that. She had her life and he was working on his.

"I think we should try for friendship the short time I'll be here. It might be easier all around." Tentatively, it seemed, Mandy held out a slim hand to him.

Jake looked down at her, then let his gaze drift over her palm, the skin pale and smooth, with hardly a trace of a callus. His thoughts flashed back to the night of the accident. He recalled taking her hand then, remembered, too, the slight calluses against his own larger palm. Drawing a deep, fortifying breath, he slowly grasped her hand in his.

Mandy shook his hand firmly. "I won't break, Jake. If

we're going to be friends, I want you to remember that. We're both adults now. I think we can work through the past and leave it where it belongs."

She looked too damned fragile to him, but Jake merely nodded and said, "Sure," with a smile. He knew he'd ruin this tentative overture if he did what he wanted to do—step forward and plant a kiss on her luscious mouth, lose himself in her scent and warmth, like old times. "Friends," he heard himself say.

Jake liked the feel of her hand in his. Was he such a glutton for punishment, that he thought any contact was better than none? Dangerous road there! Back up, he warned himself.

"I think I'd enjoy that, too," she murmured. They reached the house and stopped beside his truck. As Jake opened the door and began to climb inside, Mandy said almost musingly, "You didn't fool me, you know."

Warily, he swung back to look at her. "About what?"

"I knew you were keeping an eye on me." Before he could think up a plausible protest, she went on. "While it's kind of nice to know you were looking out for me, it's not necessary." Gently but firmly, Mandy continued, "I'm a big girl. I can take care of myself. Forget any notions about taking me under your wing. I know you're used to looking out for your family, but I don't need that." She added emphatically, "What I need now is a friend."

For the second time that morning Jake felt heat creep up his neck. Taking the bull by the horns, he said, "You keep using the word *friend*. Do you really think it's possible, us being friends at this late stage?"

Mandy avoided his gaze, as if she, too, was revisiting past memories and what they had meant to each other. "I've been thinking about this arrangement. You've got a beautiful place and it's close to town. I'd be crazy to think I could do better." She turned her head and finally met his eyes. "But it creates problems if you feel like you have to watch over me."

Jake nodded, trying to soothe the deep ache inside him. He wanted Mandy to get well, but he began to wonder if he could keep his emotions in check. Why had these feelings resurfaced after so long? He should be reassured that she wanted nothing more than friendship. In a few days or weeks or months she'd be gone, and he could pick up the threads of his life. He'd been getting along fine, hadn't he? He hadn't needed her in all these years.

"Sorry, Mandy, it's merely habit that made me follow you. I—I would have done the same for any of my sisters. You're right, we can be friends. Old history is old history and we've both moved on."

"Do you still look out for your family?"

"Of course, but my sisters are settled now, with families of their own."

"All except you. You're pretty special, Jake." Mandy looked away from him, but Jake thought he saw a flash of pain or perhaps regret. "I've never taken care of anyone in my life, except for myself, and sometimes I wasn't very good at that." She threw her head up almost defiantly and flashed him a smile. "Makes me seem pretty self-absorbed, doesn't it?"

Jake had a flashback to that night long ago when she'd walked away from him. He'd seen the same pain in her eyes then, but it hadn't stopped her from pursuing the rodeo, and he had let her go.

"How is your little sister, Amy, these days?" Mandy asked, when he didn't reply to her comment. "Last time I saw her she was about eight."

"Amy moved out a few weeks ago. She's sharing an apartment with some friends in the city."

Mandy jerked her head up and her eyes widened as if a thought suddenly occurred to her. "And here I am, intruding on your life, when you've finally got your house to yourself.''

''You've been through a bad time, Mandy. You need some space to pull your life back together.''

''Yeah, I guess.'' Jake heard the uncertainty in her voice. As she dipped her head, her hair fell forward. Jake stuffed his fists in his pockets, squashing the urge to push back the locks hiding her eyes.

He couldn't touch her. They were going to be friends. There was room for nothing more, even though his traitorous heart wanted more. He wouldn't allow this to happen again. Jake forced himself to step back and take a deep breath before he did something stupid, like start wanting Mandy again, and acting on it.

Chapter Four

Later that afternoon Mandy sat on the edge of a lounge chair beside the swimming pool. As she stared at the crystal clear depths she admitted to herself that she was a coward. She didn't dare hop into the pool with Jake somewhere close by.

If she wanted to swim she would have to take off the leg. She didn't want to do that with anyone around, especially Jake. He was a man, a good-looking man, and that seemed to matter in her mind. He had known her when she was young and whole. She'd be virtually trapped in the pool if he came out. Of course, she could hop on one leg and escape; she had become pretty proficient at that during therapy. But she wasn't comfortable doing that in front of an audience.

Mandy pushed her dark glasses up on her nose and leaned back in the lounge chair. She was a fraud. She had told Jake she wanted to be friends. It was a ploy to protect herself, to hide. She was drawn to him and kept thinking about him, as if the time apart had never been.

She had to snap out of the damnable lethargy that sapped her. She had to find another place to live. It felt like torture to be this close to Jake. God! She still loved him, and he felt nothing for her—nothing more than concern for a fellow human being. He had made that so clear with his friendly indifference.

If she allowed herself to get closer, to actually give in to the urge to kiss Jake, which was the way her thoughts were wandering, she'd lose her perspective. She was here to recover, to pick up the pieces of her life, not get involved. She couldn't afford any more mistakes. They just kept piling up.

Mandy remembered Jake from way back when they were kids. He had been Ben's childhood friend. He had never called her a tomboy, like her brother's other friends had, but he'd told her once she was spoiled. For a brief moment Mandy wondered what might have happened if she hadn't left. Would she and Jake have a family by now? For the first time in her life, Mandy began to question the reasons she had left Jake. It had been a highly emotional time, too much for a seventeen-year-old to handle. Mandy clenched her fists. She had run away all those years ago. She, who declared she never ran from anything.

With an exasperated sigh, she moved to stand beside the deck rail. Looking out over the flats, she watched the sun drop in the sky. Her first day at the ranch was almost over. Mandy liked it here. That was strange, because she had never taken to solitude and tranquility. If the rodeo crowd could see her they would think she had gone loco. Who would believe Mandy Thomson craved quiet surroundings?

Mandy shook back her hair. There was no way her friends were going to see her until she could walk perfectly, with no hitch, no hesitation....

"Hey, Mandy, are you thinking about going for a swim?"

Drawing a startled breath, Mandy swung her head around. Jake stood on the opposite side of the pool, clad only in a pair of tight, faded jeans, his wide, tanned shoulders sleekly muscled and brown. Mandy sucked in a deep breath, her gaze tracing over him. This was what he hid under those business suits! The man looked amazing. The jeans hugged long legs and fit perfectly over every bit of him. Mandy checked herself abruptly. To see him nearly naked like this just about did her in.

"I—I thought you might have gone out," she muttered, tearing her eyes from his pectorals. Her brain seemed locked on his body. His size had always made her feel small...and safe.

"I decided to stay in tonight. How about you, Mandy? Do you have any plans?"

"No, I plan to forgo the nightlife for a while." She threw him a daring smile. "I'm sure the urge will come back in time. I have a reputation to uphold, you know—number one party girl." The words tasted bitter. Mandy shrugged at her own irreverence.

Without her conscious permission her gaze moved again over Jake. His chest hair was as dark as his head; at nineteen, he'd had only a smattering of it. The flesh covering his chest was more muscled now, yet Mandy could see the hollow beneath each rib.

She dropped her eyes to his bare feet. Swallowing past a tight lump in her throat, she watched him throw his towel onto a bench and unbutton his pants. Damn, the man's body was to die for. Mandy wondered if he planned on skinny-dipping with her there. The thought made her mouth go dry, then she rejected the idea. Not Jake.

He began to pull his pants down.

"Whoa, Jake, what are you doing—that is, I don't think

I've ever seen you without your suit," she murmured weakly.

He looked up, his gaze level. "I intend to cool off. Do you want to join me?"

Cool off! Mandy felt as if the heat of the day had caught up with her and pooled in her stomach. Didn't he know his jeans were unsnapped and just kind of hanging open? She sure as heck did. She wished she wasn't quite so conscious of it.

In response to his invitation, she shook her head. One look at his perfectly proportioned body and there was no way she'd strip down and let him see the stub that was her leg.

Mandy's mood suddenly went sour. A dry sob nearly choked her. Damn the wasted years! She cleared her throat and reached down to pick up her book. "Thanks, but I think I'll go inside. I've got some things to take care of...."

Biting her lips hard, Mandy maneuvered her way around the pool, cursing her awkward steps. She had to escape into her apartment. The door was located right behind Jake. She moved too fast and the leather sole of one boot slipped off the pool edge. Mandy fell toward the water. A startled yelp left her lips, then she quickly shut her mouth as water closed over her head. Automatically, she flailed her arms and pulled herself upward.

As Mandy broke the surface she felt herself being hauled against a hard chest, with arms banding around her back. She sputtered and cursed, her hair over her eyes and in her mouth.

"Mandy, are you okay?" Jake asked with concern.

Pushing back the clinging strands of hair, she met him eye-to-eye. "What a stupid thing to do," she hissed in disgust. "My foot slipped."

He shook his head, a smile curving the lips so close to hers. "Glad you decided to join me, after all," he said softly, his eyes full of some cryptic emotion. Meeting his gaze, Mandy felt her insides twist. Slowly, so slowly that she could have pulled back, Jake's mouth moved to touch hers. His tongue flicked out and traced her upper lip, then her lower lip. He lifted his head, his gaze locking with hers. Frozen, Mandy stared at him. Confusion held her speechless. Desire made her wish he would do that again.

"You taste like chlorine," he murmured.

Mandy felt herself softening under the influence of that masculine smile, the genuine enjoyment she read there. Her insides were all aflutter and felt like mush. The years melted away. She moved her legs to tread water and then frowned. *Ten years.*

"This isn't a good idea. I have to get out." She pushed away from him.

Jake moved with her to the side of the pool. Before Mandy could protest, he put his hands on her hips and lifted her as if she weighed nothing. He climbed easily from the pool and pulled a chaise longue toward her. Mandy sat on it, her wet clothes weighing her down. She began to shiver, trying not to dwell on the kiss, but it consumed her thoughts. The heat, the fire inside should have warmed her, but she shivered again.

Mandy pulled a towel around her shoulders and huddled into its dry warmth. She looked down, alarm clutching at her. "My leg," she said quickly. "I don't know what effect water will have on it. For what it cost, I can't afford to have it ruined."

Jake seemed to hesitate. "Take it off," he finally said, as if it were the most natural thing in the world.

Outraged, Mandy jerked her head up to meet his eyes. "What?"

Jake's expression bordered on exasperation. "It's not like I asked you to strip naked and dance."

Mandy felt heat flood into her face. A smart retort leaped to her lips, but she bit it back.

"Wise girl," Jake said easily. "Don't argue. Take it off so we can dry it out. Maybe the water won't hurt it."

Calming herself, Mandy realized he was suggesting the smartest thing to do at that moment. Yet she knew she couldn't remove the prosthesis with him standing there. She couldn't bear for anyone to see the ugliness of her scarred stump. She felt paralyzed by her own indecision.

"I—I…"

"Relax," he said, moving closer. "Let me take a look."

Mandy drew a deep, shaky breath. Inconsequentially, she noticed the growing puddle his wet pants made on the stone. The jeans clung to him. She tried not to look at the zipper area of the fabric, but her eyes were drawn there nonetheless. She snapped her gaze back up.

"Do you want to take up where we left off in the pool?" Jake asked huskily. Mandy blinked hard, expecting to see him grinning. He looked dead serious.

"No," she said shortly. "I've got to get this leg dry."

Squatting in front of her, Jake pulled her left boot off, tipped it upside down and let the water run out.

Mandy stared at the boot. "My new boots," she wailed, abruptly overcome by impending tears. Why should a pair of wet boots cause such upset?

"They'll dry," Jake said reassuringly.

Mandy tried to stand, but Jake pushed her gently back on the chair and proceeded to roll up her wet right pant leg. "What do you think you're doing?" she demanded.

While she watched in horror, Jake eased the boot off the artificial leg and tipped it upside down. Mandy stared at the metal components of the prosthesis, then at the top of Jake's head as he knelt before her.

"I'm helping," Jake said shortly. "Don't be so defensive.

I'm only going to unhook the leg and see if we can dry it out."

"What? Unhook it?" Mandy did stand up then. "You darned well are not, Jake Miller! I can do that myself." Panic struck. Mandy knew he must not see her stump. No one had seen it except the nurses and doctors in the hospital and rehabilitation. Even her family hadn't seen it.

Jake, still kneeling, caught her by the arm. Dread escalated as Mandy looked down into light blue eyes framed by water-spiked black lashes. Fear rioted through her, then desire tried to curl around her insides. Fear won. Frantically, she licked her lips, but words didn't come. Inconsequentially, she noticed the black hair on his chest still dripped with water.

"If it bothers you, I won't look," he said calmly. "You can cover it with a towel. I used to help my mother with my dad."

Slowly, Mandy sat, her fingers gripping the armrests as Jake finished rolling up her pant leg. Why did his fingers feel so hot against her water-cooled flesh? She looked at the metal limb exposed so starkly between them. She felt like she was living through a scene out of a science fiction movie, and she was the monster.

True to his promise, Jake kept his eyes on her face, no doubt seeing the apprehension that raged, the coward inside that couldn't bear for him to see her leg. If he saw her residual limb, Mandy knew he would be repelled. How could he not be? She remembered her first reaction to seeing the stump. She didn't think she could bear to see disgust in his eyes. She didn't care that he had helped with his father. This was her body, her scars. Her body no longer felt whole. And Jake used to know her as a whole woman. Quickly, she dropped the towel over her thigh.

Mandy held her breath as a deep hurt echoed through her.

She didn't know why it would bother her to see a reaction of disgust from Jake, she just knew she couldn't chance it.

In the next moment he stood and walked across the pool area, her prosthesis in his hand. He picked up the towel he had earlier discarded and carefully dried the artificial limb.

Wide-eyed, Mandy watched him. Jake acted as if he were drying off a plate, or a pan, she thought hysterically. He had her leg in his hands, for God's sake!

"I can do that," she managed to protest, surreptitiously tugging down the rolled-up jean to cover the atrophied stump.

Jake moved closer, but not close enough for her to reach the leg. "Believe it or not, there's no ulterior motive in my helping you. It's help, plain and simple, so stop looking for something that isn't there. We're supposed to be friends, right? My dad had both his legs amputated."

"I—I know that, of course I know that. It's just that I could have done it myself," Mandy said quickly. Needing something to do with her hands, she pushed her wet hair behind her ears, then pulled it forward again.

"I know you can do it yourself," he said impatiently. "I also know you could've gotten out of the pool by yourself. Nobody's saying you can't do anything and everything on your own. It's just that there's nothing wrong with accepting a helping hand."

"Help isn't going to do me any good when I'm alone," she retorted bitterly. "If I start depending on people, pretty soon I won't be able to do anything."

Jake gave a short laugh.

Incredulous, Mandy jerked her head up. "Are you laughing at me?"

"Yes," he said, shaking his head with amusement. "I can't imagine you not being able to fend for yourself. You're the most independent woman I know. It's laughable."

"Now you're saying I'm a joke?" Mandy demanded, unable to keep the hurt from her voice.

"Mandy, come on, get over it. You know that's not what I'm implying. You have never been helpless in your life. Your grit and determination will never allow you to be helpless. You'll always be able to climb out of any pit—that's the way you are. It's what I admire about you. If you cool off a minute and think about it, you'll know I'm speaking the truth."

If Jake wanted to strike her speechless, he'd done so.

"Anyway," he demanded, "who says you have to be alone?"

Mandy narrowed her eyes, anger bursting inside as her temper took over. "I do, dammit! Who wants to look at this leg every day? I certainly don't. It makes me sick."

"Your anger is understandable, but you've got to accept the leg is gone and nothing's going to change that."

"You can talk till you're blue in the face, Jake Miller, but you haven't got a clue what it's like to go your own way and find one day it's all gone. To wake up and discover your mother gave them the okay to hack off a leg."

"Your mother would never okay that unless it was absolutely, medically necessary."

Jake's voice sounded cold. So cold Mandy shivered with self-disgust.

She put her head down, misery a tangible pain inside. "Oh God! I know you're right. I—I was unconscious for three days. Mama had to make the decision."

She darted Jake a glance. His face looked white, maybe with anger and disgust, but he didn't say anything.

"Everything went down the tubes. My life, my career. Everything." The damning tears ran down her cheeks. Mandy wiped ineffectively at them with her wet shirtsleeve. She felt embarrassed, ashamed by her outburst, hardly able to believe the resentment she had been harboring.

"I do know what it's like," Jake said into the silence that followed. His voice was stark and he sounded fed up with her.

Mandy looked at him. "I'm sorry, Jake. I'm insensitive. Of course you do. You gave up everything to take care of your family. Everything was pulled out from under you." She dropped her voice to a whisper. "Even I abandoned you."

"Drop it, it's in the past."

Mandy wanted to say more, but the dark look on Jake's face stopped her. She drew a shaky breath instead. "You're right, it's the past, old history." She tossed her hair back, feeling a shiver work its way across her shoulders. "Everything was fine until you started using amateur psychology on me."

Jake put the towel and limb under his arm and squatted beside Mandy. "You weren't doing fine. You were pretending and running scared. We all do it from time to time. You're so afraid of being vulnerable, you step away from anything even remotely related to help. But you can't be strong every minute." His palm reached out to cradle her jaw. For a moment Mandy let herself go weak and lean into that touch. Right now she did not want to be strong. She wanted to be enfolded in Jake's arms. She wanted him to kiss her again, but longer and deeper. Mandy pulled herself back from temptation with difficulty.

"You're damn fool crazy," she retorted. His words made sense, but Mandy didn't want to admit it. She was afraid it would give him some kind of power over her. She wasn't that same young girl who had adored him.

"Am I, Mandy? When you arrived yesterday the first thing on your mind was bolting. I know I remind you of the accident, and that's got to be damned hard, hard enough that it pulls at your gut, but maybe in a way it'll help the healing process."

Mandy bit the inside of her cheek and didn't answer. Jake had pretty much hit the nail on the head. She could never let him know about the acute, wrenching disappointment she had felt. It caused a strange mixture of emotions, learning that the man whose image she had clung to had in actual fact been a real, fallible human. A man who hadn't believed in her enough to continue loving a mixed-up teenager. *Why, Jake,* she cried inside, *why didn't you come after me all those years ago?* Mandy held her breath, afraid for a moment she had said the words aloud.

"Mandy, I'm sorry you got hurt…sorry if it bothers you that I was there that day. At some point you'll have to come to terms with your life, and all that it can be. Not what it used to be." Jake stood up, an almost stern expression on his face. "Despite what's happened, your life isn't over. You must realize that."

"I know that! I'm going to get better, then I'm going back to my old life," she said defiantly, crossing her arms.

Jake lifted a brow. "You don't have to convince me. You always had more determination than two people. I'm sure you'll do it if that's what you want."

"Of course it is." Mandy clenched her jaw, her eyes fixed on the water. "Rodeo is my life."

"What if what you're wishing for might not be what you want in the end?"

Mandy snapped her gaze up to meet Jake's. "Rodeo is what I've always wanted. There's never been any doubt." Except for the brief period she had thought she wanted kids, and Jake as a husband. Mandy dismissed that memory. It had been long ago. Instead, she focused on her daddy's words. *She could have the world at her feet…. She needed to win, and win big.* Somehow, the thought didn't soothe her.

"You're a survivor, Mandy, but there's no rule book that says survivors have to go it alone."

"What are you suggesting—that I shack up with you?" she asked sarcastically. "That would be convenient. We could share the electric bill, the newspaper and toothpaste, wedded life ad nauseam." Even as she spoke, Mandy felt a sick, twisting ache inside. She wanted to stop the terrible words, but they spilled from her lips, a wealth of bitterness she'd kept stored.

"Wow. You've got a real active imagination." Carefully, Jake placed the now-dry prosthesis beside her. "Believe me, I'm not about to go down that road with you again."

"Well, the whole institution of marriage is boring," Mandy said rudely, trying to pretend his words hadn't stung. She felt as if she was being torn up inside, but the words just kept coming. "I'm not cut out for sitting still or putting down roots."

"Maybe…maybe not. I guess if you say it enough times you'll take it as gospel."

"What makes you so smart? I don't see anyone around here sharing your life. You haven't done anything about getting married or having kids."

Jake went still, then he dipped his head in acknowledgment before he turned and began to walk away. "Point well taken."

Ashamed of herself, Mandy wondered for a moment if she had hurt him. With shaking fingers, she reached for the leg, then muttered an almost desperate, "Damn."

Jake looked at her over his shoulder. She couldn't read the expression on his face, but it seemed to be somewhere between indifference and mild curiosity.

"Need something?" he drawled.

Taking a deep breath, Mandy realized she could hop all the way to her door or she could ask for Jake's help. She wasn't sure which bothered her more. "Yes. It's my sock—the special socks for my leg. They're all wet. I need some dry ones."

"Where are they?"

"They're in the bathroom on a towel on the counter. They should be dry. I'll need two pairs."

"I'll be right back." Jake pushed his wet jeans down and stepped out of them. Mandy watched them fall to the deck, wondering if they would be ruined by the chlorinated water. Underneath he wore dark blue swimming shorts. Mandy stared at the muscular length of his legs, his perfect legs, then hurriedly turned her head away. She felt as if she was on fire.

Jake entered her apartment and came back quickly. "I brought you some dry clothes, too."

Surprised, Mandy looked up and saw the assortment of clothes in his big hands. "But..."

"Your suitcase was open, so I picked some stuff off the top." Jake dropped the pile in her lap and turned away. "I'll be in the pool." He dove into the water without saying anything more.

Mandy sat and watched him for several moments, but he ignored her. Setting her teeth, she lay back on the chaise longue and wriggled out of the cold, wet jeans, her eyes on Jake as he continued to swim.

Carefully, she pulled on the special sock for her leg, smoothed the wrinkles, then put on the second one. Sitting on the edge of the chaise, she bent her knee slightly and slowly pushed her leg into the socket of the artificial limb. She fastened the straps into place, all the while darting glances at the pool.

As quickly as possible, Mandy lay down on the chaise and pulled the dry jeans up over her damp underpants. She whipped off her T-shirt and quickly pulled the dry one over her head. Her breath came fast and her heart pounded hard with nerves. Jake hadn't brought her any regular socks for her other foot, so she left her boots off.

Gathering up her wet clothes, conscious of her underclothes soaking through, Mandy walked jerkily toward her apartment door, careful to stay well away from the edge of the pool this time.

The sound of her metal foot on the concrete sounded like an old peg-legged sailor she had seen on television as a kid. Mandy wanted to laugh, but a deep down sadness was strangling her. Emotion gripped her throat, and something akin to panic swirled inside, trying to take over. She had to get inside and sit down so she could close her eyes until the feeling passed.

Before the accident she hadn't known about anxiety attacks. They had started while she was in rehabilitation. Apart from relaxing, there wasn't much she could do about them.

Her doctor had suggested some type of antidepressant, but the very idea scared the hell out of Mandy, even worse than the attacks themselves. They usually lasted only a minute or so.

Entering the sanctuary of her apartment, Mandy was glad to feel the beating in her chest ease. Damn Jake. Damn him and his accuracy about her fears.

Chapter Five

Jake heard the door to Mandy's apartment slam. He swam another lap. Back and forth, he swam as hard as he could, another twenty strokes before he stopped to tread water, hearing the sound of his harsh breathing on the evening air.

He felt the anger pouring from him. If Mandy expected him to keep his mouth shut, she was in for a surprise. He wasn't a lovesick kid anymore. Jake closed his eyes, thinking about that kiss in the pool. It had been a damn fool thing to do. Why had he done it? It had just seemed so right at the time. Now, it kept coming into his thoughts, making him want more.

Maybe he should've kept his mouth shut, but Mandy had gotten her licks in, too, and they'd felt like salt in a wound. Jake gritted his teeth. She was getting under his skin and he didn't like it.

For all the women he had in his life, including his six sisters, Jake felt right now he didn't know squat about the gender. Mandy had acted as if he were a Peeping Tom who wanted to sneak a peek at her leg. Why couldn't she see he was helping her? He knew what an atrophied stump looked like.

Jake hadn't wanted to see her leg. He had told her so, but he had lied. He had looked. He had seen the leg briefly when she'd closed her eyes. He had felt an aching twist of pain and fear—her fear mixed with his own. His mind dwelled on the pain she had gone through. He didn't want to think of the emotional stress she still obviously suffered.

Jake had a feeling he could tell her till he was blue in the face that her leg didn't matter to him, but he'd be wasting his breath. Perhaps he'd be lying, too. He didn't want it to matter, but it did. It was gone; that was a fact. At least the doctors had done a better job on Mandy than they had with his father. Viewing it for the first time made it all very real. Knowledge was one thing, seeing was another.

Mandy had made up her mind that it made her deficient in some way. She was doing her best to pick up the pieces and resume her life. That took courage and persistence. No easy task for a woman hell-bent on relying only on herself.

Jake knew this was something Mandy had to resolve on her own. But the worst thing she could do was shut herself away from the very people who might help her—her family and friends. Maybe in helping Mandy, Jake could rid himself of the fascination still pulling at him. It was obvious she didn't think she needed anyone in her life. She had made it clear ten years ago she didn't need him. This time around Jake wasn't going to be a stop along the way.

He dove into the water and pushed himself harder, but the memories howled after him. At no time could he let himself forget he wanted her to get well and leave.

The next day, Ben showed up on her doorstep. Spotting her brother through her living-room window, Mandy opened the door with a squeal of delight and threw herself into his arms. Ben promptly dropped the bouquet of flowers he held and caught her in a tight bear hug.

"Ben, you're back!"

"Glad to see you, too," he said with a big smile. "You look like your old self," he added approvingly, stepping back.

"I'm settling in, Ben."

He squatted to retrieve the flowers he had dropped. "I'm glad you're getting along okay out here."

"I like it here," Mandy admitted. "I'll miss it when I find another place."

"Actually, I haven't had much luck in finding anything yet. I was planning on tackling that next week."

"I'm looking, too. I don't want to hold Jake up any longer than necessary." Mandy stepped back and invited Ben into the house. "Come on, let me show you the place."

Ben held the flowers out to her and this time Mandy took them. Lifting them to her nose, she drew in a deep breath.

"So Jake told you his plans for the apartment?" Ben asked.

Startled, Mandy looked askance at her brother. "What are you talking about?" A sinking feeling began in her stomach.

"Never mind," Ben said, too quickly.

"Ben. Tell me what you're talking about."

He grimaced. "I thought you knew. Jake's going to be renovating the house. He's making a combination showroom and workroom out of the area where you're living, since it's got the best lighting in the entire house. Don't worry, though, he said a few month's delay wouldn't matter, since nothing's been finalized with the contractor."

Mandy gripped the bouquet to her chest. "He never said anything. Is that why he's got boxes all over his house?"

"Well, he's been in the middle of some general clearing out, what with Amy moving."

"Is the workroom going to be for his carvings?"

"So you know about that? Yes. He's gotten a lot of interest in the last few years, and with the elk and moose antlers he's carving now, he needs more display room." Ben was looking at her with a worried frown.

Mandy pasted a smile on her face. "Maybe there're other plans I'm messing up that I don't know about." She felt pain jab at her heart. She might as well be a bulldozer wreaking havoc.

"I don't know of any other plans, Mandy. You'll have to ask Jake."

"I intend to." With determination, she grabbed Ben's arm. "Let me show you my place."

Ben pulled her back around. "We can do that later, Mandy. I have a surprise that has first priority."

Mandy looked at her brother, narrowing her gaze. Placing the bouquet on a small table, she asked, "What kind of surprise?"

"Don't look so suspicious. Come outside," was all he said.

Once outside, Mandy looked toward the driveway. She caught her breath and gave Ben a disbelieving look. She moved carefully down the ramp toward his truck and the familiar fire-engine red horse trailer hitched behind. Her horse trailer.

"Jake figured right about now you'd be missing your babies," Ben said, following her to the back gate of the trailer. "So I stopped at Mom's place first and brought you—" The horse inside the trailer whinnied loudly.

"Pongo!" Mandy finished excitedly, immediately recognizing her Paint's voice. As Mandy moved toward the back of the trailer, steel shoes moved restlessly on the wooden flooring. Mandy unlatched the back gate with trembling fingers. She wanted to cry and run away at the same time. It had been an eternity since she had ridden.

"Pongo!" she called. "Hello there, you black beauty." Indescribable joy filled her as she looked through the metal slats and saw Pongo's wide black hindquarters with their splash of white. She swallowed the tightness in her throat, emotion very close to the surface. She almost couldn't control the urge to cry. Ben had caught her totally off guard. Mandy blinked rapidly as she swung the back door open.

"Here, let me bring him out." Ben moved past her and pulled the quick-release knot on the lead line where he had tied the horse to the front trailer rail.

Mandy held the door open as Ben backed Pongo down the ramp. Once on the driveway, Pongo turned toward her and softly rumbled a greeting. Immediately, she slung an arm over her gelding's neck and buried her face in his smooth black coat. Mandy inhaled deeply the lingering smell of hay and the warm scent of horse. How had she stayed away from him so long?

"You remembered me, Pongo. I've all but ignored you and you forgive me, don't you?" Mandy whispered into his neck, stretching her arm to stroke lovingly under his jaw.

"I see you didn't come alone, Ben," Jake said from behind Mandy. Mandy didn't move her arm from her horse's neck, but turned her head to look at him. Some of her excitement dimmed.

"Why did you do it, Jake?" She felt her hackles rise, disrupting her previously excited mood.

"I think you need him."

"Since when do you know what I need?" she blurted, unable to still her tongue. All these years Jake had never questioned her decision to leave, yet now he suddenly knew what she needed! Mandy looked away from Jake as Pongo nickered softly, standing perfectly still as she leaned her weight against him.

For a moment a wild urge took hold of Mandy. She wanted to jump on his back and ride off. There was a small hedge at the end of the drive. Pongo loved to jump; he could clear the hedge with room to spare. Mandy grabbed a handful of black mane and her gaze met Jake's. She hesitated, her fingers gripping the long hair tightly. Fear sliced into her.

If circumstances had been different, that's what she would have done. It's what she had done countless times in the past—jumped on a horse's back when the urge struck her. She had been riding bareback since she was four years old.

Now, things were different. Uncertainty stabbed through her, attacking her confidence in her riding skills. With Ben and Jake as witnesses, she could do nothing but stand beside Pongo. Mandy loosened her grip on the gelding's mane and smoothed the hair with shaking fingers. Apprehension she didn't want to acknowledge twisted through her. She could no longer measure up to her own standards. What was happening to her?

When she rode her beauty, she'd have to be by herself. If she was going to humiliate herself, she wanted no witnesses. Still, the urge to run was not easily suppressed, and Mandy fought an inner battle for several more moments.

Jake, as if guessing her thoughts, gave voice to the desire riding her so hard. "You look like you want to jump on Pongo. Come on, I'll give you a leg up."

"No!" she said sharply. Mandy took a jerky step away from Jake. "No." She lowered her voice. "Pongo hates to be trailered, and I want to give him time to settle down. I'll take him over to the barn. He might as well get introduced to Tibald right away, since Tibald's top horse in the pecking order here." Mandy knew she was talking too fast, but she felt mortified of her cowardice. She put her shoulders back, trying not to let dejection override her initial joy.

Mandy saw the stiffness on Jake's face and felt ashamed of her churlishness. "Thank you," she muttered, still stinging over his interference. She was acting illogically, but it was all she could manage.

Pulling the lead line from her brother's hand, Mandy walked toward the stables with Pongo following behind. When she was several feet away, Mandy turned back to her brother and flashed him a bright smile.

"Thanks for bringing him, Ben."

"It was Jake's idea," Ben repeated, narrowing his eyes. "I agree with him that it's a good idea. You could be a little more gracious," he chided.

Mandy shrugged a shoulder, hating the feeling that her life was moving beyond her control. She looked up at Jake and met his gaze. Some of the tension eased from her body. "Ben's right. I'm sorry. I love having him here."

"There's plenty of room," Jake said flatly. He turned to Ben. "I told Mandy her horses were welcome if she wanted to move them out here."

When she moved out of earshot, Ben said, "I apologize if that's how Mandy's been acting toward you. I've never seen her so disagreeable, to say the least."

"We seem to hit the wrong chords with each other."

"Also, I thought Mandy knew about your plans for the house. I let it out of the bag."

"A few months makes no difference. I've converted a big box stall in the barn as a work area."

"It must be kind of crowded with all your tools." Ben's gaze strayed to his sister, who'd stopped to give her horse another hug. "So you and Mandy aren't hitting it off so good?"

"Sometimes yes, sometimes no."

Understanding lit Ben's face. "You don't have to tell me, I know how difficult she can be."

"Well, this time it's my fault. I probably stuck my nose where it didn't belong when I had you bring the horse. I still think it'll do her good to have Pongo to fuss over. Maybe she'll start riding.''

Ben nodded his head slowly. ''You might be right. Sometimes Mandy needs time to cool off and think things through. I hope she doesn't get it in her head to go too fast and hurt herself. Not that I dare tell her that. Mom and I have tried to steer her thoughts away from rodeo, but she's got her mind set on it. Have you tried to discourage her from going back to the circuit, Jake?''

Jake laughed, feeling hollow inside. ''Me talk Mandy out of rodeo? That's a joke in itself. No, our disagreements are nothing like that. She's let me know in no uncertain terms she doesn't want me looking out for her in any manner.'' The words cost Jake, pulling at that empty spot deep down inside him. He didn't want to be affected by anything Mandy said, but it bothered him nonetheless.

Ben looked at his friend speculatively. ''Mandy doesn't take kindly to any curb on her independence. It must be eating the hell out of her to have to go easy. I hope you're right that having Pongo here will make her happy. I want my sister back.''

''I haven't got a clue, Ben, what makes your sister happy.'' At one time Jake had thought he knew. He'd been wrong. He reminded himself it didn't matter in any case.

''She likes it here, but we all knew up front it was only temporary. I apologize, Jake, for tying you up like this. I'll keep looking for another place.''

Jake didn't answer. He was watching Mandy, and that tightness in his throat wouldn't ease up. His head was telling him not to let her leave again—that she wasn't ready to be on her own yet. But Mandy had always been independent. She hadn't listened to him the last time he had begged her to stay. He'd never beg her again.

Chapter Six

Mandy introduced Pongo to the horses in the large pasture. After the first initial kicking and squealing, the horses went back to grazing and ignored each other.

As she walked back toward the house, Mandy noticed cars in the driveway. Apparently Jake's football enthusiasts had arrived while she was occupied at the barn. The air carried the tantalizing scent of barbecue, making her mouth water, reminding her she hadn't eaten. Nevertheless, Mandy skirted the pool and headed for the door of her apartment. She was curious about Jake's friends, but she wouldn't intrude, even if Jake had extended an open invitation. Mandy knew it was probably unreasonable, since she was happy to have Pongo here, but she resented Jake taking the decision into his own hands.

"Hey, hang on a minute!" a female voice called out.

With her hand on the door latch, Mandy turned to see a slim girl in her late teens hailing her. She wore tight jeans and a bright pink halter top. The girl vaulted the steps to the pool area easily. Mandy felt a brief envy. At one time, she had taken such effortless movements for granted.

The girl held out a hand to Mandy with a big smile. Her dark hair was short and curly. Her somewhat familiar blue eyes told Mandy she could like her in a minute.

"Hi, Mandy! Don't tell me you don't remember me?" The girl's face fell.

Mandy studied her dark eyes and a smile welled inside. "Amy, Jake's little sister. It took me a minute...." Mandy reached forward spontaneously and enclosed Amy in a hug.

"Oh, Mandy, I'm so glad you're back with Jake—"

She pulled back. "Hold on Amy, I'm not back with Jake, not in the sense you mean." She drew a deep breath. The thought of belonging to Jake created all kinds of shivery feelings inside. "This is only temporary. I'm his tenant." Mandy almost felt amused by the chagrin on Amy's face.

"God! I'm sorry, I thought..." Amy opened her blue eyes wide and turned down her mouth. "I remember how romantic it was, you and Jake...."

"That was a long time ago. Now we're friends." If she said the words enough, would she start to believe that's all she felt for him? Mandy wondered.

Amy cocked an eyebrow. "Friends? You're as close-mouthed as Jake. My brother doesn't say anything unless he's forced to."

Mandy silently agreed. "How are your sisters and your mother?" she asked. She hadn't asked Jake much about his family. It had felt too personal.

"They're fine. With me out of the house Jake's finally getting a break." Amy gave her a gamine grin and in a friendly gesture urged her to the steps leading to the lawn below. "As you can see my oldest sisters, Janice and Luanne are here. Mom and the others live out of state. I came over to see if you'll join us. There's plenty of food, and you can play football if you like.''

She could see the tables loaded with food, lawn chairs scattered all about. Her stomach growled.

Mandy swallowed with difficulty, then said lightly, ''Um, thanks. I don't play football.''

''I remember you used to.'' Amy bit her lip. ''What I meant to say is it's a fun get-together.'' She looked out toward the playing field.

Curious despite herself, Mandy followed Amy down the terraced steps to the lawn.

''Everyone is dying to meet you. They're being polite and giving you space. As you can guess, I'm not the polite type.''

Mandy threw her a quick look. '''Giving me space?''

''Jake's phrase.''

Mandy looked at the other girl with raised brows. Jake had been talking about her to Amy?

Amy grimaced. ''I kind of walked in on a conversation he was having with Ben.'' She tossed her head back, her expression somewhat defiant.

''Jake thinks I need space?'' Mandy asked, tongue in cheek.

Amy caught her teasing smile. ''Jake says I don't think before the words come out. I know everyone would like to meet you.''

''That's nice of you to say so, but actually, I'm right in the middle of an article I'm writing....''

''I know you went to school for journalism, but I didn't know you had pursued writing.''

''My articles all have a rodeo slant. Unless you read those types of publications, you wouldn't be familiar with my byline. It's nice to have that second income when I'm on the road and the winnings are scarce that week.''

''Can't the article wait?'' Amy asked impulsively. ''From

what Ben's said about you, I didn't think you'd want to miss a party."

In the old days she'd never miss a party, Mandy ruefully admitted to herself. "Ben's been talking, too?"

"I probably know more about your rodeo days than I know about Ben."

Mandy looked out over the flat pasture, fixing her gaze on a lone, scrubby tree against the horizon. "That sounds like rodeo days, as in past tense." She felt tension invade her body. Was everyone talking about the mess she had made of things?

"I wasn't implying in the past," Amy said, flustered. "I heard Ben telling Jake about how you planned on returning, as...as soon as you got better."

"True," Mandy said shortly. "I guess the general consensus is I'd have better luck walking on the moon than returning to rodeo." She ran her fingertips down her leg.

Amy placed a slim hand on Mandy's arm. "That's not it at all. Jake admires your determination. Not one of the Miller women is what I'd call adventurous. At the slightest hint of a problem, we call Jake and let him take care of it." She let out a sigh. "We've all taken terrible advantage of my brother. I think he's never married because we've made so many demands on him over the years he hasn't had the time. What woman would tolerate that? I guess you figured that out a long time ago, Mandy."

She quickly shook her head, but then nodded. "When Jake and I split, I was just about your age." Memories flooded her. She had been so young. She confessed, "I was very full of myself, and it's true Jake had so much responsibility...." She let her voice trail off, seeing the keen interest in Amy's eyes. "It wasn't meant to be."

"If you say so," Amy said slowly. "But we've all made demands on Jake. It's time it ended."

"Is Jake seeing anyone?" After the words were out Mandy couldn't believe she'd said them.

"Jake's really closemouthed about his personal life, but I know he hasn't been seeing anyone for a while. I've noticed he's been different the last few months."

"How?"

"Jake's life is predictable. I have to say it—dull. I remember when Dad got sick and Jake gave up football. Everyone accepted that he'd take on responsibility for the family. We all benefited from the way he's made a success of the business, but enough is enough. My brother needs a life."

Mandy knew she had added to Jake's problems by leaving all those years ago. Should she have stayed? Jake had had all that responsibility and no one to share it with. Who had been there for him? Mandy felt ill, but she had to find out more.

"How do your sisters feel about Jake's lack of a social life?"

"They've never had a reason to rock the boat." Passionately, Amy continued, "It's time Jake thought about himself. That's why I moved out, though I wouldn't tell him that. He's making a name for himself with his wildlife carvings, and it's something he really enjoys. Otherwise he seems to go along in the same routine—no distractions or deviation from a set course. Get the picture?"

Mandy cringed inwardly. She had implied he was boring the previous day. She gazed out at the playing field, picking Jake out easily from the other players. "Jake's always been dependable. Family is very important."

"But now we can take care of ourselves. I've told my sisters to let their husbands tackle their problems. I worry about Jake being alone...not that he appreciates me saying so."

Mandy could understand that.

"My brother needs someone to love him passionately, above all else."

Mandy had loved him, but obviously not enough. She hadn't been ready to commit to marriage. Jake had talked about babies....

"These last months he's been distracted, which is not Jake. He's always on top of everything. When I was a kid it was darned unnerving. Even the family agrees Jake is not acting like himself."

"And by that you mean in a predictable way?"

"Right."

Mandy watched Jake intercept a pass. He leaped unbelievably high, his arms stretched upward, the movement pulling his shirt up to expose a width of tanned stomach. He had a look of such intense concentration on his face that Mandy found herself holding her breath, releasing it only when he caught the ball and ran with it. "Do you think Jake offering me this apartment is part of this new unpredictability?"

"That's Jake's normal generosity. I'm talking about when his picture turned up in the papers that night. You know…" Amy stopped suddenly and bit her lip.

"Jake's picture?" Mandy asked faintly. She had an intense need to know more. She had seen only one paper. She hadn't asked about others.

"The night you got hurt, Jake was there. As far as I know he hadn't been to a rodeo since you and he split." A few more steps brought them closer to the food table. Curious, despite herself, Mandy followed Amy as she reached over to a small table and grabbed a handful of chips from a basket. "I'm not surprised Jake reached you first. He takes charge."

Mandy clenched her hands together. Jake had gotten to her first? It was still a blur.

"He's been taking care of us so long it's second nature by now."

Mandy looked toward the football game in the field. Unbidden, warmth crept over her. Jake had turned his attentions to her. He thought she needed looking after; she intended to convince him otherwise.

Mandy watched the game with interest. As Jake ran and shouldered his way past other players, an odd sensation began inside, an unfamiliar burst of yearning. The old itch to be in the thick of things caught her by surprise. It almost felt...normal.

"Do you know why Jake came to that rodeo, Mandy?"

Mandy looked back at Amy. "No." She had wondered that same thing herself. "Jake used to go to rodeos." She accepted a handful of chips, wincing for Jake as he was grabbed around the knees and pulled to the ground. Fascinated, she watched as he disappeared beneath a mound of bodies.

Again she asked herself why Jake had been at the rodeo the night she got hurt. Vaguely, she recalled his air of calm. She had never depended on anyone to such a degree. Yet that night she'd felt as if Jake held her life in his hands.

Casually, she said, "I think I'm lucky your brother was there. I don't remember much, but I know he kept me focused."

Amy stared at her with a pleased smile. "Do you think you'd be interested in him again?"

Mandy raised her brows in surprise.

"I've always liked you, Mandy. I think you'd be good for Jake, loosen him up a little."

"Well, thanks for the compliment, I think," she said dryly. "You're an adult, Amy. You know relationships don't happen like that."

"I'll bet Jake went there to see you that night," Amy said stubbornly.

Mandy squashed the hope that rose within her. "No, Jake and I hadn't seen each other in years." There had been no contact, though God knows she had tried to keep the lines of communication open in the beginning. Jake had ignored her letters, had hung up on her when she phoned, then had gotten an answering machine. "You're wrong," Mandy repeated.

He couldn't have been there to see her. Why now, after all these years?

"Wrong about what?" Jake's voice came from behind them.

With a squeal, Amy spun around. Mandy turned more slowly, running her gaze over him. His hair was tousled, and he had a streak of dirt on one cheek, but he didn't look like he had broken anything under that pile of bodies. *Why, Jake? Why were you there that night?*

"Geez, Jake, don't do that—it's dangerous to sneak up on people." Amy playfully slapped her brother's arm.

Mandy took in his grass-stained T-shirt with cutoff sleeves, and the rip in the knee of his faded old jeans. Close-fitting, they hugged his legs, drew her eyes along their length. Her eyes lifted quickly to his face, and she found him watching her intently. She all but melted under that gaze.

"Has Amy revealed all the family secrets?" Jake asked.

He probably wouldn't like to hear his sister's theory about his love life or lack thereof.

"If Mandy's going to live with you, she needs to know what goes on around here," Amy said, lifting her chin.

"For the record, squirt, she's not living with me." Jake ruffled Amy's dark curls with a gentle hand. It was a simple gesture of affection, but it reminded Mandy of the old Jake.

As he looked down at his sister, Mandy gazed at his strong, decisive face, honesty and caring personified. She wondered how she'd had the strength to walk away from him. She was older now and maybe a bit wiser...or maybe not. She had wanted to succeed at rodeo ten years ago, and she still wanted the same dream. What had really changed? She had had plenty of opportunity to do as she pleased, but Jake hadn't had that. His life had been mired in duty, and her life had had a definite lack of it. Mandy swallowed hard.

"I promised to help flip hamburgers." Amy's voice broke into her thoughts. "Will I see you later, Mandy?"

Mandy hesitated, staring from Amy's bright eyes to Jake's watchful gaze. "I'll be here for a bit," she said.

"Great." Amy waved and walked to the other end of the food table where the barbecue grills were set up.

Mandy stared at Jake. His gaze made her want to melt in a heap. She wondered if she was crazy to stay here. She didn't know Jake anymore, but all the old emotions seemed to be there, right under her skin. Being away from him all these years and not knowing about his life had been easier than being in the thick of his life now. What if she saw women at his house, staying the night? She couldn't bear the pain. It would be worse than leaving.

With the hair falling over his forehead and a five o'clock shadow darkening his jaw, the man exuded raw energy, oozed sex appeal as if he had invented it. What she found really scary was the fact that although he still seemed unaware of his attractiveness, she wasn't.

"Looks like you've had a rough game," she said huskily.

"All in fun." Jake lifted a brow and his mouth curved with amusement. "What about you, Mandy? Are you having fun?"

She enjoyed the trickle of sensation making its way across her shoulders. Jake's intense gaze made her feel as if she were the only woman for a mile. "You know me, Jake, I never deny myself fun."

"Maybe I can add to it," he said softly, reaching out to pull her closer.

Mandy tensed with a mixture of desire and disappointment when his arm settled platonically on her shoulders. Surely she didn't want him to kiss her again?

"I'm glad you decided to join us," he said. "Come and meet my friends."

"I couldn't resist coming over." Mandy smiled with real amusement. "I had to see if you played football in a suit, since I've rarely seen you in anything else these last few days."

Jake's grin made Mandy want to lean forward and kiss his mouth. "You sound like Amy. She thinks all I know is work. I'm surprised her skill at digging until she hits a nerve hasn't scared you away."

"She thinks you need a love life."

Jake looked startled, then a guarded expression came over his face. "So she's been telling me."

"The consensus is you're secretly pining for someone." Mandy had always been one to stir up trouble. She couldn't stop the words.

Jake's light eyes pinned her. "Are you asking?"

"Yes, I guess I am."

Jake shook his head. "You were never one to back off, were you, Mandy? I have women friends." He stared at her as if gauging her reaction. "Some more special than others. Do you have a specific reason for asking?"

Mandy straightened her shoulders and gently twisted out from under Jake's arm. "Just curiosity," she lied, telling herself she didn't need to know more about him. "After all," she added lightly, "we have ten years to catch up on."

"Curiosity." Jake nodded his head, but his eyes seemed to be telling her something else. Mandy felt a leap of emotion. What did he really think about their past relationship? "What else could it be? We've been apart too long to go back."

Mandy forced herself to nod. "That's right, Jake. It's

been too many years. We both agree on that.'' For a moment she wished she could go back, could erase the old hurt and pain. From time to time she could still see it in Jake's eyes—the memories, the truth between them.

Just when she thought she would learn something from him, he pulled back. ''Never repeat mistakes,'' he agreed, his voice hard. He lifted his gaze to her. ''Come on. It's quite painless, meeting my friends. Not as bad as a trip to the dentist.''

Mandy hesitated. ''If you recall, we more or less agreed not to invade each other's privacy.''

''Sure. But one little barbecue doesn't mean we're sleeping together.''

Jake's derisive tone made the color flow into Mandy's cheeks. The words conjured a surprisingly sensuous picture in her mind. But the derision hurt.

She found her reaction alarming. Strange sensations assaulted her. The thought that Jake as a lover would be exciting and unpredictable insinuated itself. A shiver worked its way across the back of her neck. Don't go there, she warned herself. Trouble...delicious trouble.

''Come on.'' Jake held out his hand to her.

Mandy drew a fortifying breath. Slowly, she reached out and took it. Feeling his wide palm engulf hers, his fingers close gently but firmly on her own, became quite an intimate experience.

''On one condition,'' she said, holding back a moment. ''I'll stay for a little while, then I'll leave.''

''Done.'' His big hand squeezed hers. The smile he gave her warmed her from head to toe. They walked toward his friends, and Mandy knew it was his ingrained consideration that made him slow his steps to match hers. She held her hand stiffly in his, all too aware of the trembling of her arm. She had never felt such a sensation of walking into quicksand in her life, and all because a man was treating her carefully. A man she still loved, but who no longer saw her as anything but an old acquaintance.

Mandy knew then and there, for the first time in her life, that she would have to watch her step. Jake Miller was a dangerous man. A man who could hurt her, if she were careless. He cared about her getting well, but that was the extent of his interest. If she wanted to remain whole, she had better remember that.

Chapter Seven

Around eleven that night Mandy sat on the stone wall in front of the house with Jake beside her. She waved as the last car drove away, the red taillights disappearing onto the highway.

Jake turned to her, one brow lifted, a satisfied smile curving his lips. "So, on a scale of one to ten, how did meeting my friends rate?"

Mandy deliberately put her nose up in the air. "For such a pushy guy, you have amazingly nice friends."

Without thinking about it, she jumped off the stone wall, then let out a muffled groan as her leg began to collapse. Jake took a quick step forward and gripped her upper arms to support her.

"Easy there, or you'll end up in the rosebushes."

Mandy jerked her arms away. "I'm fine." Carefully, she walked sideways down the steps to the blacktop driveway.

"Tired?" Jake asked.

Mandy nodded stiffly, frustrated by her lack of control over her own body. "When I've been on this leg too much, it gets a bit sore. I've only been working with this a short time—my permanent limb, that is. By that I mean my prosthesis. I have to be careful. Negotiating this ramp sideways takes longer, but it's easier when the leg bothers me." It was the most explanation she'd offered to anyone since losing her leg.

Once up on the porch, Mandy turned and looked back at him. "Thanks, I had a good time. It almost felt like…" She paused, biting her lips. She had been about to say like old times, but that description might ruin the easy camaraderie they'd found.

"Home?" Jake suggested.

Mandy nodded. She was no longer the naive innocent of a decade ago. Jake wasn't the same man, either. There was a hardness to him she couldn't get past. It scared her, that shield he put up against her. Perhaps it was for the best; it kept them both on safe ground.

Jake's barbecue hadn't been anything like the parties she was used to. Today there had been a homey, festive air, despite some good-natured bickering between two of his sisters.

Mandy turned back to Jake. "G'night. Thanks, Jake."

Jake walked toward her. "I always see a lady to her door."

"Really, Jake, I can manage."

"I know. Call me old-fashioned."

Mandy looked up at his face, but the clouds passing over the moon kept him in shadow. She bit her lip again, then blurted, "Listen, Jake, about the rude things I said the other day—"

"Which time?"

Mandy gritted her teeth but then went on. "When I kind

of implied you were boring by teasing you about your box manufacturing business—"

"Are you going to take it back?"

"Will you let me finish?" she said between clenched teeth. He was treating this as a joke, and she felt only embarrassment over her behavior.

"Sure." The moon shone through the clouds, and Mandy caught his smile as he looked down at her. She was used to being at eye level with most men, but not Jake. She had always looked up to him. He managed to make her feel protected.

Mandy turned away abruptly and walked to her door. "Anyway, I'm sorry for what I implied."

"I think the word you intended was *boring,*" he supplied helpfully, leaning one hand on the dark siding of the house near her head. "Oh, sorry. I interrupted again, didn't I? But since I have, what made you change your mind?"

Now why did he have to ask that? Mandy thought, not having seen the trap. She was no good at this man-woman thing. Give her a fifteen-hundred-pound bull or a wiry mustang and she knew what to do. A man she loved, had never stopped loving—that was another story.

"I didn't say I'd changed my mind—well, I guess I have. Thing is, I'm sorry for my assumptions," she snapped, not used to being twisted up in knots. Jake never used to act this way. Sexual tension rippled through Mandy. She clenched her fists.

"Apology accepted." He said it with a mocking smile that wasn't all mockery. Mandy just wasn't sure what else was there. Perhaps a hint of tenderness? No, she was probably wrong. She drew a deep, fortifying breath. Damn, he was handsome.

Jake ran a fingertip lightly across her cheekbone, leaving a trail of fire. Mandy almost jerked her head back in surprise, then closed her eyes a moment.

"Since we're doing apologies, I'm sorry for riding you so hard by the pool last night. You're right, you're not seventeen anymore. I was out of line."

Mandy shrugged awkwardly. "Maybe it was something I needed to hear. I'm not saying it was," she qualified as she saw his slow grin. "I'm saying maybe. I'm still mulling it over."

"Then I'd say we're even and should call it a night before we disagree and get into a fistfight or something."

Mandy watched his face come closer, part of her afraid, the other part making her inch just the tiniest bit forward. This couldn't be happening again....

Gently, almost tenderly, Jake's lips touched hers, then slid away. The contact felt like a jolt from an electric fence. Before she could recover, his arms lightly enclosed her, his chest against her suddenly aching breasts. Mandy felt lost in the sensation, aware only of the feel of Jake's mouth on hers. So light, then deeper, his tongue swirling against her teeth, touching the inner softness of her mouth. The short bristle covering his jaw rasped across her skin, the slight sound pleasing, the contact sensuous. Jake began to pull away, his lips leaving hers slowly.

Boldly, Mandy pulled his head back down, her fingers clasped in his dark, silky hair. The only thing that mattered was having him close. All the years of loneliness, the pain of walking away, it all dissolved. Mandy wanted more from Jake. Her body trembled, but she was barely aware of it.

"Jake..."

"Shh." His finger touched her lips where his mouth had caressed. Mandy touched his finger with her tongue, and he stepped back. She tried to breathe normally, but felt as if she had run a marathon. He took another step back, his face devoid of emotion. Mandy dropped her arms slowly. Awkwardly, she rubbed her palms down her jeans.

"I guess this is where we say good-night," she murmured

lightly, throwing him a smile as she turned and pushed the door open.

"Mandy."

She ignored him this time. Slowly, she closed the door on him and collapsed into the nearest chair.

How had that happened? One minute they were almost friends, the next, close to taking a step toward an intimacy they had no right thinking about.

Mandy groaned, trying to think straight, but it felt impossible when she thought that Jake might be just outside her door.

She jumped up and paced the living room, an excess of energy gripping her. She felt keyed up. Mandy touched her fingers to her lips, closing her eyes as a shivery sensation fanned across her midsection. Why had Jake kissed her? More disturbingly, why had she let him? Did either one of them want to revisit old history?

Mandy shook her head quickly. It was crazy to worry about a little kiss. People kissed all the time; it meant nothing. It would never mean anything because they had nothing in common any longer. Maybe they had never had anything in common.

She walked into her bedroom, leaving the small light in the kitchen on. Her leg ached as if it were still there below her knee. The pain—phantom pain, they called it—wasn't as bad as in the first weeks in the hospital. Then it had been unrelenting, making her think she would go out of her mind.

Mandy undressed, unstrapped the leg and placed it on the bedside chair. Removing the special socks, she gently massaged the stump to ease the soreness. She had probably overdone it today, but it had felt so good to be back with the living. She had felt almost normal. There had even been moments when she had forgotten about her leg, and that hadn't happened since waking up in the recovery room. She felt kind of tingly, almost like a limb regaining circulation after being in a cramped position. Part of her that had felt dead since the accident felt vibrantly alive. All because of a kiss. One little kiss. *Not so little!* whispered a small voice. It had rocked her to her boots. She wondered how Jake had felt about it. Surely he had felt something.

Reaching into the old-fashioned washbowl beside the bed, Mandy picked up the hand soap and washcloth. Carefully, she wiped out the socket of the prosthesis and dried it, then proceeded to do the same for her stump.

The cheval glass at the base of the bed showed her reflection, but Mandy ignored it as she brushed her hair, then did fifty chin-ups using the metal trapeze bar at the head of her bed. She thought about the swimming pool going to waste most nights, and decided she would strike a deal with Jake about using it in privacy.

She had done her best to keep in shape in the last months, but sometimes, when doubt crept in, she wondered if she wasn't fooling herself. No one had come out and said she couldn't rodeo again, not even Mama, though Mandy was sure she wanted to. Mama raised bulls for the rodeo circuit, but she had always been fearful of Mandy riding them. A slight smile twisted her lips. Mama had been furious when she discovered one of the ranch hands had been letting Mandy ride the bulls her entire thirteenth summer. She had been grounded from riding her horse for a month. That had been the worst punishment of her young life.

Mandy had apologized to Mama for the terrible things she had said in the recovery room, but she still agonized over it. She knew it was her fault there was a strain between them. That's why she hadn't returned home. She needed to be on her own so she could recover her equilibrium. She needed to remain independent, and yet she had landed here, an imposition to Jake, an impediment to his plans. The knowledge bit at her. Dammit, she'd always prided herself on her independence. She couldn't depend on Jake's generosity forever.

Pulling on a light robe, Mandy picked up her crutches and moved over to the glass doors that led to a small deck outside her bedroom. After opening them, she tipped her head back, enjoying the cool breeze on her face.

She could hear the horses out in the paddock, whinnying softly to each other. Somewhere crickets were singing their night songs. Mandy saw a shadow in the yard beyond her small deck, and she stared curiously out into the darkness. Then she opened the screen door and stepped out onto the deck.

When Jake saw Mandy, his body was still humming from the kiss they had shared, his head reeling with thoughts he couldn't quiet. Why had he given in to the impulse to kiss her, taste her lips again? Dammit, what was this woman's hold over him?

"Still awake?" he asked her, stepping into the band of light spilling from her room.

Mandy turned sideways and leaned against the deck rail, the upright post shielding her leg from his view. Crutches rested under her arms, and her thin robe was almost transparent with the light behind her. Jake drew a deep breath and called himself a fool. He saw the outline of where her leg ended just below the knee, and he felt a deep, wrenching pain.

"I guess I'm keyed up."

Her voice sounded strangely breathless on the night air. Jake wondered if she wanted to repeat that kiss he couldn't get out of his mind. He stepped closer, pausing on the top stair of her deck. Watching Mandy, he leaned back against the railing and crossed his feet.

"Being out here must be quite a change from what you're used to."

"Actually, Jake, I like it here. I needed a break from the commotion." She gave a little laugh. "This is the perfect place to hide until I get better."

Jake stiffened and straightened up. "And then you go back," he said flatly. "After you're finished hiding."

"Of course. What else would I do?" A soft breeze played with Mandy's blond hair. Jake itched to run his fingers through the softness, as light and fine as a baby's. He struggled with the temptation. Mandy was no baby. He should turn around and haul his butt away from her. The night air, combined with her sweet scent, was too enticing for a man whose thoughts were stuck on decade-old memories. How much heartache could he tolerate? How many times did he have to have his pride stomped into the dust by size seven boots?

"Rodeo is all I know. You know me, Jake—I have a knack for landing myself in trouble. For once I'm trying to think ahead, look to the future. Sometimes it's pretty scary, looking ahead," she added, her voice almost a whisper.

Jake sensed her vulnerability. Maybe Mandy had changed. He'd never heard her asking for help as she seemed to be doing now.

"We all have to grow up," he drawled, refusing to be drawn in by her magic.

Mandy tossed back her hair. "I've always lived for the moment," she said, a challenge in her voice. "Up until now it's worked out fine."

Jake watched her fingers play with the folds of her robe. He heaved a deep breath. "Listen, Mandy, you don't have to hide from me. We've known each other too long."

"There are some things you never get over. I feel as if I'll never get over this self-consciousness about my leg. There's always someone staring at it to remind me. It's horrible…ugly."

Jake reached out and encircled her slim wrist with his

fingers. The bones felt so fragile, yet he had seen her competently handle animals many times her own weight. ''It will heal in time, inside and out.''

Mandy rolled her eyes at him. ''Maybe in ten years. Right now it represents everything I don't have any longer. Who would want to look at this leg?''

''You're a desirable, smart woman. Any man with an ounce of sense will see that.''

''I don't want any man, dammit!'' The words seemed to burst from Mandy. She threw him a wide-eyed glance, confusion written on her face as she stared at his fingers encircling her wrist. Jake stared at her bent head. He wanted to pull her close, take her inside and show her how desirable she was.

Instead, he made himself say lightly, ''Come on, Mandy, cut yourself some slack.''

''You're right, I should.'' She lifted her head and suddenly leaned toward him with a reckless grin. ''I find myself wanting to try that kiss again, Jake. What do you think?''

Jake felt his throat go dry. He wanted to kiss her, but it was probably the dumbest thing he could do—rekindle fires best left dead. Mandy's gaze remained unwavering. Desire tightened Jake's body. He moved closer, so close he could feel the heat of her own body, almost taste her scent.

Mandy's sigh feathered across his mouth. He knew he was playing with fire when her head tipped back and she opened up to him.

How had he let this woman go? Mandy looped her arms around his neck, the crutches clattering to the deck. It was a distant sound, and Jake didn't care. He felt enveloped by a haze, aware of the points of her breasts through her thin covering. He ran his hands over Mandy's hips, cupped her buttocks. He felt the tensing of muscle, then she leaned fully into him as they devoured each other, heat surely an aura of red-hot light encircling them.

Thoughts of the past exploded, leaving only dust. Jake explored the taste and texture of Mandy's mouth, the slim, supple length of her body. When he surfaced for air, he swept his tongue along her lips. Her responding shudder echoed his own.

She gripped his arms and pulled her upper body back, meeting his gaze, out of breath, hanging on to his arms and balancing on one leg.

"I guess that's about all the slack I can stand for now," she muttered.

Jake started laughing. Mandy lifted her brows and he shook his head. "Only you, Mandy, would say something like that."

She smiled slightly. "You used to love my unpredictability."

Jake put up a hand and gently threaded his fingers through her hair. "You're right. But back then we were kids. What did we know?"

"What are we doing, Jake?"

The words seemed to spill from her lips. He felt her tense against him, as if prepared for a blow.

Jake stared at her wordlessly. What *were* they doing? What were they thinking? "Maybe we're just finishing up old business, Mandy, so we can both get on with our lives."

He knew it was the right answer for both of them, but he felt weighed down by a heavy ache. How could he want things to be different?

"I guess you're right." Her voice was tinged with sadness. "We're not the same people." Mandy stepped away from him so they no longer touched. She pulled the fluttering material of the robe against the residual limb, then indicated her leg with a sweep of her hand. "Too much has changed to go back."

Jake stifled the protest inside him. Part of him wanted to go back, wanted to try and fix what had gone wrong. But

the rational part of his brain told him it was impossible
"Someday you'll realize your leg won't matter to anyone
who cares about you."

Mandy gave him a bright smile. "I know you're right
Good night, Jake."

Mandy wanted to damn the consequences and invite Jake
into her bed. She entered the apartment alone, feeling
drained. In Jake's company, she felt almost light, freely giving of herself, until the reality of her situation smacked her
in the face.

Mandy deliberately stared into the mirror at the stump
which she hated to look at.

Mandy recalled its swollen and discolored appearance
right after surgery. She had never considered herself squea-
mish, but that first time she had seen her amputated leg had
made her sick. Blood had roared in her ears, and a cold
wave came over her. It had been frightening.

Such a loss of control terrified her. How many times had
Daddy imprinted in her mind you had to stay in control of
a situation? If you lost control you had to know when to
bail out, whether it was a bull you were riding, or life.

Day by day Mandy felt she gained a better grip on her
life. Setbacks occurred, but she had to move steadily forward. She felt confused as to why she was hankering after
the past, with Jake. It was over and done with.

Returning her attention to her stump, Mandy noticed that
the line of stitches had faded. It didn't look nearly so gro-
tesque. Everything had smoothed out rather well.

She lay down on her back. Ever since the amputation she
felt off balance, when she rolled over in bed at night. She
had to be careful when she slept that she kept the stump
straight, so it didn't seize up on her. She had learned how
to sleep on her stomach.

Continuing her nightly ritual, Mandy reached for the elastic bandage and wrapped the stump, wondering if she could ever ride again. Maybe she'd never regain her center of balance. She took a deep breath and told herself it was a miracle she hadn't lost both legs.

She had cracked her ribs, knocked some teeth loose and suffered a mild concussion. She was lucky to be alive.

For the umpteenth time, Mandy pondered the question Amy had raised. Why *had* Jake been at the rodeo that night? Could he have come looking for her? No. They hadn't had contact in years. Why would he seek her out after all this time? Deep inside, Mandy knew she wanted that to have been the reason, but it was a foolish wish at best.

Jake had made a success of his life, but he had not married. Mandy wondered why.

She knew why she wouldn't marry. She was like her father. Daddy had tried ranching, tried settling in one place, but he had left again, declaring rodeo was in his blood.

Mama had bred the best of the bulls used in rodeo. Times had been hard, but Mama was strong. Mandy recalled many an evening when Mama sat on the front porch swing, humming a song only the night would hear, or a child up later than she ought to be. Daddy hadn't been around to keep a woman's heart from aching. Rodeo was rough on family life when you pursued it six days a week.

Mandy had been consumed by rodeo until she met Jake. Mama had convinced her to get a degree, see what else the world offered before she decided to pursue rodeo full-time. It had been during one of her spring breaks that she had met Jake. She'd had all summer to fall in love with him.

Mandy hugged her arms around herself, her mind filled with lost dreams. She hadn't felt anything but a passing interest in other men since Jake. How could she, when a part of her had always loved him?

Trying to ease the worry and old pain, Mandy relaxed each muscle and concentrated on her breathing. She couldn't get Jake's kisses out of her mind. What did he think about them? It was no big deal; they were old friends—at least that's what she told herself. But she was burning up inside, remembering the feel of Jake's mouth on hers. She wanted more than kisses.

With a groan, Mandy told herself such dangerous thoughts didn't bear thinking about. She'd get sidetracked. It was best to remember she had no home, that she was a roamer. She didn't belong here; she'd just taken a slight detour. Strangely, that empty stretch of rodeo road didn't have quite the appeal it used to. The glory of rodeo paled when all you came home to were your horse and buckles.

She didn't know what lay ahead, but she was a fighter. Maybe she should start by returning her friends' calls. Mandy wondered if it was time to reconnect with her past.

She looked at her leg, the feelings of uncertainty insidious. It had healed fine, but inside herself she knew there remained a gaping emptiness, a fear that wouldn't let go. Mandy still felt as if she was in a dark tunnel. Would she ever reach the end? Would her life feel complete if she could return to rodeo?

She needed to recharge. Perhaps bringing her friends back into her life would fill that empty spot.

A party would liven things up and help her get back in the groove of things. Then life could resume some normalcy. Mandy knew there was no going back, no fixing the life she had thrown away ten years ago. But how she wished time could be turned back! She wanted a second chance with Jake.

Chapter Eight

Mandy stood in the doorway of her apartment and watched Jake's black pickup truck disappear down the driveway. She rubbed her damp palms together. Her hands shook slightly. The time of reckoning, so to speak, had arrived. She had wakened early this morning and deliberately planned the day right down to the last moment of daylight.

That thought gave her a moment's pause. She had never planned anything to the minute in her life. She had always acted impulsively, not worrying about consequences or ramifications.

With a disgusted grunt at her own meandering, Mandy walked to the door with determination. Jake was off to work. The ranch was her playground, and she intended to play.

In the small mirror beside the front door she caught sight of her own reflection and saluted herself. ''Welcome back, Mandy Thomson, it's been a while.''

First stop: the barns. Today she would climb onboard

her baby, Pongo. She hadn't ridden in three months. Luckily, Ben had brought her favorite equine. Of her four horses, Pongo had the most patient and gentle nature. He could race and raise hell with the rest of them, but he would stand for hours, if that's what was asked of him. Only last year at the county fair he had been the center of attention, patiently allowing kids of all ages to crawl over, under and around him. Nothing riled him.

With a deep and quivering breath, Mandy feared that's what she might need. Back to square one, as if she were learning how to ride all over again. Pushing aside the self-doubt before it could grip her, she left the house. She would allow only positive, upbeat thoughts today.

As she walked around the pool she looked longingly at its clear depths. Already the day held promise of being a warm one. Mandy relished the thought of sliding into those refreshing depths after her ride. Lightly, she said, "I've got a date with you later."

She made her way to the barn, trying to walk without feeling awkward and ungainly. Her therapist had told her it might take time to move naturally and without effort, but she felt impatient with how slowly things seemed to be progressing. Some days went along fine, other days did not. She never knew when her knee would suddenly give way and she would fall down. It happened less frequently than in the beginning, but now and again she was caught off guard.

By the time she visited her doctor for her follow-up visit, she wanted to be able to tell him she was well on her way to reclaiming her life.

Entering the barn, Mandy found the stalls were empty. Jake must have fed the horses, hers included, and put them out in the pasture.

Standing at the edge of the pasture, Mandy leaned against the wooden rail and whistled for Pongo. She would talk to

Jake. She didn't expect him to take care of her horse as well as his own. For the short time she was here she intended to pull her own weight.

Pongo whinnied low and cantered toward her. Tibald and the other two horses watched, but stayed where they were.

Mandy unhooked the chain and went through the gate. Pongo stood patiently while she slipped the leather halter over his ears and adjusted the brass buckle.

Mandy pulled several carrots from her back pocket. While Pongo munched them, she looked him in the eyes. "Well, buddy, this is an experiment of sorts. You're going to have to be patient with me. Do you remember the first time we went riding when my ankle was broken a couple years back?" She grimaced as he dipped his head as if in understanding. "Well, keep that sloppy performance in mind."

Mandy fancied Pongo was paying attention. "It's going to be a bit like that time, only probably worse. So if I kick you in the ribs or thump you on the butt, just be your usual good-natured self and put up with it. I promise you some extra carrots." Pongo's ears twitched forward. "Carrots...the magic word. I knew you'd relate to that."

Mandy led him into the barn. She had noticed earlier the cross ties hanging from the solid beams in the center of the barn aisle. She snapped the ties on either side of Pongo's halter to hold him in place.

Mandy briskly rubbed the brush over Pongo's back and across his ribs, her mouth curving as she remembered the countless times she had ridden his wide barrel of a back without a saddle.

"No bareback riding today, my beauty. We'll save that for another time."

Mandy placed her cherry-red saddle pad and then her roping saddle on his back. Once the girth was tightened, she unsnapped the cross ties and slipped the bridle over his ears.

"Come on, old boy, here we go."

Taking a fortifying breath, Mandy led him outside. It was now or never. She beat back the fear that she wouldn't measure up, and placed her left foot in the wide leather stirrup.

Mandy swung herself onto Pongo's back and settled in her familiar comfortable saddle. She had a problem picking up the right stirrup because she couldn't angle the prosthetic foot. Impatiently, she leaned down and pushed her boot into the stirrup leather with her hand.

"Don't give up," she muttered, refusing to be daunted. "Let's walk, buddy. Just remember, if I fly past your head, don't let it bother you."

They walked along a dirt path that skirted the fenced pasture. It looked as if it went on forever through the short, stubby grass.

"God, I have missed this." Mandy felt her confidence rise, and urged Pongo into a trot over the uneven ground. Almost immediately her body listed to one side. She stiffened instinctively and Pongo slowed to a walk. Mandy wiped the moisture from her forehead. Leaning down again, she shoved her boot back into the stirrup. Damn! The last time she'd had a problem keeping her feet in the stirrups she'd been four years old. She could still hear her daddy yell, "Mandy girl, put your weight in your heels!"

Now she knew for sure. She needed to work on the basics of riding. Her balance wasn't right.

Mandy reined Pongo around, heading back toward the barn. God knows what would happen if she tried a lope or a run.

"I'd probably end up eating dirt," she muttered. Stubbornly, Mandy urged Pongo into a trot once more, trying to put more downward weight into her prosthesis.

The second time went better. At least her foot didn't slip out of the stirrup. But with mounting frustration, Mandy realized she was tilting to one side.

She left the path and trotted over a bare, sandy area. She

practiced circles to the right, then the left, determined to find her point of balance. Gritting her teeth, she straightened herself as she again slipped to the side. She couldn't feel her foot, so unless she kept looking down, she wouldn't know if it had fallen out of the stirrup.

The sun had grown warmer while they were out in the field. Mandy glanced at her watch. Ten o'clock. Sweat ran from her hair, dripping down into her eyes. Impatiently, she wiped it away with an arm. Pongo was likewise streaked with sweat along his neck and shoulders.

"Okay, buddy boy, you know I've never been patient. Let's try one more. Just for the hell of it we'll do a short run. If I fall, I fall." Mandy gently nudged the horse with her left heel. Pongo's ears perked forward and his front end lifted as his back legs settled into his rocking-chair-smooth lope.

As they moved across the ground, the warm breeze dried the moisture on Mandy's face and neck. She felt exhilarated and confident. They had done it!

She circled and trotted past the barn. To her surprise, out of the corner of her eye she saw Jake standing in the doorway. Something in her faltered, hesitated. Mentally squaring her shoulders, Mandy said to the horse, "One figure eight, Pongo. We've done it hundreds of times." The horse never hesitated. Smoothly, they circled to the left. When it came time to circle to the right, Mandy abandoned leg aids and used neck-reining alone, placing the reins flat across his mane. Pongo responded beautifully. Triumph filled Mandy like sweet success. Grinning, she reined Pongo over to the barn where Jake stood.

"Looked pretty good from where I'm standing," he said encouragingly. He shaded his eyes with one hand and stared up at her. Mandy could see the tiny lines beside his eyes and read the pleasure on his face.

"Thanks." She felt uncharacteristically shy, her insides

tightening in reaction to his nearness. Into her mind flashed the remembrance of his body against hers. "My trot's a little rough—my balance is off."

"I was watching. I thought you did great for the first time out. Maybe if you used a breakaway strap on the stirrup leather to keep the boot in position—"

Mandy clenched her jaw, her fingers tightening on the leather reins. "I've been riding long enough to know how to keep my feet in the stirrups. I can do it without straps."

"All I'm saying is if you use a strap until you figure out your balance, it would be one less thing to worry about."

Freeing her boots from the stirrups, Mandy let her legs hang down. "Do I look worried, Jake? I'm just a little rusty. I don't need straps. I said I would ride again and I'll do it my way."

Mandy turned Pongo and urged him into a trot, away from Jake. She blinked hard, telling herself the glare of the sun combined with some dust had filmed her eyes with moisture.

What did Jake know, anyway? He rode for fun. He'd never been interested in entering a riding competition in his life. If you wanted to win in rodeo, you had to be better than the competition. How would he know if she was doing it right or wrong? Mandy resented the fact that he was supposed to be at work, yet was here intruding on her private time.

Having worked herself into an irate frame of mind, she was determined to find her center of balance at the trot. She and Pongo did circles, serpentines and figure eights. Finally, feeling satisfied and knowing they had both done enough in the rising heat, Mandy stopped the horse in front of the barn again. She didn't see Jake anywhere. She swiped the sweat from her forehead, annoyed that he hadn't stuck around to see what she'd accomplished.

"The second half of that went much better, Pongo."

Gripping the saddle horn in case her leg buckled, Mandy threw her leg over Pongo's hindquarters and dropped to the ground. Quickly, she unfastened the girth and placed it on top of the saddle. "I think I saw a hose somewhere. I'll give you a cool reward for that wonderful ride."

Tying Pongo to the rail with baling twine, Mandy pulled the saddle from his back and turned to carry it inside.

Jake was suddenly behind her, making her catch her breath in surprise. "What are you doing?" she gasped, her glance straying to his mouth. He stood very close. A fluttering began in Mandy's stomach, her stray thoughts heating her cheeks. Would Jake kiss her again? Maybe she should kiss him. Mandy felt an unfamiliar softness creep over her.

"I'll take that." Jake reached for the saddle.

Almost instinctively, Mandy jerked it back. "I can handle this myself." She shook her head in exasperation and turned away from him. Didn't Jake know she could take care of this on her own?

Jake, seeing the residue of temper in Mandy's eyes, let out a laugh. "Lighten up, Mandy. Before you get a notion to tear into me, let me make it clear I've got other things to do than follow you around." He took a step back. "I'm working on a commission piece, and my workbench is out here. I'll take the saddle while you hose him down." Jake pulled the saddle from her hands before she could protest again. He stared at her, daring her to argue.

A frown appeared between her brows. "I'm not trying to be difficult, Jake, but it's been frustrating, having to start riding all over again. Besides, I'm used to doing things on my own."

Jake nodded in agreement. "Yeah, so what? Is there a rule somewhere that says you can't have help once in a while? If you'd told me you were going to ride I would have stuck around earlier."

"The last thing I need is an audience," she muttered, slapping the dust from her jeans.

Amused, Jake lifted a brow. "Do you know something? I think you just like to jump on anything I say. I was going to suggest we take a ride together."

She stopped slapping at her jeans and straightened. "Ride together?" She made it sound like a foreign notion.

"Why not, if you feel like having company sometimes? I don't ride as much as I used to. But I have these horses here and all they do is eat."

Mandy lowered her gaze and bit her lip. "Oh."

Jake carried the saddle into the barn and dropped it on the saddle tree. When he walked back outside he handed her the hose. As she began to hose down the horse, Jake gave her a hard stare. "Why in hell are you so ready to jump down my throat? If everything I say rubs you wrong I'll make sure I stay out of your way." Exasperated, he spun around and walked away from her. It was either that or kiss her, and she didn't look like she was in the kissing mood. Not like last night, when she'd been all soft, warm and willing. He muttered under his breath.

"I guess it's my natural reaction when someone tries to tell me what to do," Mandy called after him. "Daddy always said I had a problem with authority figures."

Jake threw a glance over his shoulder at her. She stood with one hand on her hip, the hose in the other hand. "Do you see me as an authority figure?" he asked incredulously.

Mandy looked startled, then a wash of color flooded her face. Watching her with interest, Jake wondered what her thoughts were.

"I've never seen you in that light," she said in a husky voice. Mandy bent over and directed the hose through her hair. "Mmm, this water is icy. It feels good."

Jake felt his stomach muscles tighten. Was she doing it

deliberately? Damn! Mandy still had the power to excite him.

"J-Jake…" he heard her call out. Jake looked back once more. She had pushed her hair back and now it dripped onto her shoulders, soaking into the white fabric.

"I'm sorry. I would like to go riding with you sometime, if—if you've got time, that is," she stammered. "I just feel really inadequate right now, and I'm taking offense at every gesture. It stinks to have been riding all these years only to find out I have to relearn it. I apologize for laying that on you. I'll try to keep my temper under control."

Jake took her apology at face value, pretending he didn't see the trembling of her lips. He tried to ignore the heat pooling in his stomach as he stared at her. She looked damned vulnerable, but he knew she wouldn't welcome him saying that. He wanted nothing more than to step close to her and pull her into his arms. Man, that would feel great, and he'd probably get a punch in the gut for it. Jake had the notion it would be worth it.

"There's no reason you should feel inadequate, Mandy. You've always been a good rider. Maybe I'm easily impressed, but that last bit of riding you did without your stirrups wasn't bad. In time, you'll get your brash nerve and confidence back. When that happens," he drawled, "look out." Jake knew that, at that point she'd leave.

As if she took pleasure in his compliment, Mandy smiled tremulously. Jake let his gaze hold hers steadily until she looked away.

"I appreciate you taking care of Pongo, Jake, but I want to help out with the feeding. I can't let you take that on. Also, I need to work out a board fee for keeping him here. It'll be extra cash, and surely everyone could use extra cash."

Jake saw the determined line of her jaw, and once again her eyes seemed to challenge him. He remembered that was a lure he had thrown out that first night to keep her here. He'd said he was strapped for cash.

Slowly, he nodded his head. "Sure," he said easily. "If you want, you can feed the horses at night. I'll take care of the morning feeding. As far as the board, we'll work something out."

"Good." Some of the tension seemed to ease from her. Jake knew she had been ready for a fight, but he was determined to avert it. It was no sweat off his back, feeding one more horse, but he could understand her need to pay her own way.

"I was surprised to see you back so soon," Mandy said slowly, spraying the water over the horse's back. "I thought you'd left for work."

Jake looked away from her vibrant face, gazing instead at the distant, orange-brown hills. "I'm taking some time off work this week. I have a few carvings that need to be completed." He began to think that if she didn't take those blue eyes off him, he was going to do something stupid, like grab her. He hoped Mandy didn't have an inkling as to his thoughts. He wanted to pull her against him and kiss the hell out of her. He wanted their closeness of last night all over again. Only more. They could make love in the straw....

Impatient with himself, knowing it was years too late, he grabbed a plastic scraper and started removing the water and sweat from Pongo.

A few moments later, Mandy led the horse back to the pasture gate and released him.

"One last thing," Jake said. "Anytime you want to use the pool, feel free to do so."

"I'm glad you brought that up, Jake. I'd like to make arrangements with you to use the pool. It's—swimming is one of the best exercises for my rehabilitation." She drew a deep breath and rushed on. "But I'll need some privacy."

Jake walked toward her. Pushing a hand through his hair, hoping he could keep to his promise, he assured her it wasn't a problem. "Just tell me the times and I'll stay out of your way," he told her easily. He'd like to join her in the pool. A long ago memory flashed into Jake's mind. They had gone swimming. It had been a family picnic, before everything turned upside down. Mandy running from the water toward him, her face laughing, eyes lit with what he had thought was love....

She spread her hands in front of her, then dropped them. "I feel really awkward about this. This is your home—"

"Mandy, if it helps your leg, I'm all for it. If you want privacy while you're swimming, that's fine, too. Don't apologize or feel like you're being unreasonable."

Mandy nodded. "I'd appreciate the pool from eight until nine most nights, unless you have something going on."

"Settled." He grinned at her. "See? That wasn't so hard."

"Here," she said, pulling the hose away from him as he began to coil it up. "I can do that."

Jake saw it coming, but the import of her actions didn't register until he felt the icy-cold water shoot across his neck and down the front of his shirt.

"Mandy!"

She began to laugh. Jake stood stock-still. It was the first time he'd heard her really laugh again, like old times. He wanted to hear it again but she was backing away, the hose now on the ground, water pooling around his boots. Mandy ducked into the barn and turned the hose off. Jake still felt the aftershocks of seeing her laugh, just as he remembered. A sinking feeling started in his stomach, but he didn't understand it.

Mandy smiled at him as she came back outside. "You look like you're in shock. Honest, that wasn't on purpose."

"Yeah, right, like I believe you." She had a devilish

gleam in her eye. Jake pulled the wet shirt away from his chest. "It'll be great unloading the hay I'm expecting with a wet shirt."

"Oh, don't be such a wet blanket." She made a face at him.

Jake swore he heard her snort.

"I'll turn the hose back on, Jake, and you can get *me* wet. Then you'll feel better."

Jake eyed her, noticing the thin T-shirt she wore, which was wet from the water still dripping from her hair. The blond strands hanging around her eyes made her look even more sexy. He stifled a groan. Mandy might be up to a wet T-shirt contest, but he sure as hell wasn't. God knows what would happen…

"I owe you one, Mandy," he muttered, knowing it was better for his sanity if he left the barn. He did so, unbuttoning his shirt and pulling it off in the process.

Mandy hurried to catch up with him, and he slowed his steps.

"Jake, I'd really like to see some more of your carvings sometime, if that's all right."

He hesitated, wondering if he wanted to let her into that part of his life. His carvings were a part of him that even he didn't understand sometimes. The ideas came from deep within. He worked at them until his thoughts took shape.

"How about right now?" he heard himself say. He saw the instant delight on her face.

"I would love to."

Jake cursed himself for letting his body's reaction to her override his common sense. He jerked a thumb toward the barn interior. "Come on, then, I have a few minutes." He would give her five or ten minutes of his time. She could look and then leave.

Jake led the way to the makeshift work area he had set up in a double box stall. He had moved everything he needed out here; all his tools were close at hand. He slid open the stall door and stood back to allow Mandy entrance. Reaching up, he hung his wet shirt on a hook to dry.

Mandy halted in the doorway, her mouth opening on a small sigh, then she stared up at him. She was so close Jake could see the dark flecks in those blue irises. He breathed deeply of the lemony scent that clung to her hair.

"This is your private sanctuary. This is where you work on your carvings." A simple statement. Jake had a feeling he was letting himself in for a load of trouble by showing Mandy his work area, but it was too late now. Her fingertips lightly touched his bare chest. Jake held himself very still, glad when she finally stepped back.

He released his breath. "This is it, until I rig up something else."

Mandy moved toward a long table where several elk and moose antlers lay, partially carved. Jake didn't move from the doorway. It was all he could do to stand still as Mandy picked up a small set of horns, turning it this way and that, her fingers lovingly caressing the lines he had chiseled. Jake's gaze was transfixed as she continued to caress the horn where several horse heads had begun to emerge. She turned sideways and looked at him, the antler pressed to her chest.

"Jake, this is extraordinary. What an expression of art you've created. I've never seen anything like it."

He pushed himself away from the door. "Luckily, others share your sentiment. The orders come in so fast I have to turn a lot of them away."

"I imagine you could ask premium price for these." Carefully, she put the antlers back on the table. "You've really made a success of your life, Jake." Those blue eyes met his again. "I envy you."

Jake frowned. "We all follow the path we choose, Mandy. You've had your own measure of success."

"You're right Jake. I just seem to stumble more often than not." She shrugged. "When I'm old I'll be able to say I tried everything I set out to do, win or lose." Her voice dropped to a thready whisper. "I'm so glad you've decided to do these carvings. I always loved the wooden animals you made for me."

Jake felt a tightness in his throat. "You still have them?"

"Of course. I love that little hedgehog you made. But I had no idea you were so serious about this."

"I needed something to fill in the nights I sat with my father." As soon as the words were out, Jake wished he could recall them. They felt too private to be sharing them.

Mandy wore a frown. Hesitantly, she said, "Was it so bad, Jake?"

He drew his shoulders back. "My dad lost the will to live, to care. You knew what he was like before, how vibrant. You can guess what hell it was, seeing him so apathetic. My mom needed a break, so I stepped in."

"I'm so sorry, Jake."

"Actually, my dad was the one who encouraged me to expand my carving. He mentioned idly one time that he had seen a set of moose antlers someone had carved. I decided to try it myself. I found some antlers in a box in the barn when I bought this place. I didn't even know what I was going to carve, until the head of a bear took shape."

"The one I saw that first night in your house?"

"Yes."

"You've really developed your talent."

Jake stared at Mandy, but she had turned away and was studying another carving. He tried to slow his breathing, but memories hit him broadside. *Mandy laughing up at him, a small wooden figure he had carved held tightly in one of her hands. She held it to her breast, tears glistening, yet not falling. The small hedgehog had fit easily in her palm....* It had been his first gift to her. Jake closed his eyes, willing the memories away. He had moved on with his life. Mandy had moved on. They were different people.

"I've got to lock up," Jake told her abruptly. He felt a confusing mix of anger and want. His guts felt tied up in knots. Mandy was doing this to him.

Immediately, she placed the carving she held back on the table and walked out the door. "Sorry, Jake. I know you have other things to do. I appreciate you letting me see these. I wish you every success."

The soft words made Jake feel like a heel, but he had to get away from her. The damned memories were bombarding him. He needed some space. This whole thing was getting too comfortable, and it was only temporary. Mandy would be gone when she was well, and that was that.

Chapter Nine

As they left the barn, Mandy averted her gaze from Jake's chest. Jake's business might be manufacturing, but he kept himself in superb physical shape. Watching him play football had told her he was still an athlete. He put his whole heart into the game. In all her life, Mandy had never been attracted to another man the way she was to Jake. He had ruined her for other men. As a teenager, she might have been too young to know what real love was about, but she was feeling the pain of it now…regretting the lack of it in her life.

Mandy closed a mental door on that thought. Despite their mutual desire, she knew Jake had no real interest in her. Surely she had more sense than to pine after a man who did not want her.

She pulled herself out of her foolish daydreams. She and Jake had agreed to be friends.

Man, she must be loco to be thinking of Jake in romantic

terms. She was the one who had put an end to their relationship. If only Jake weren't so attractive.

Unfortunately, Mandy hadn't been able to get their kisses, the closeness that had felt so very real, out of her mind. His mouth, the touch of his hard body, had felt so right against hers. Last night was a fluke. She might have had the same reaction to any man, given the same set of circumstances. She couldn't get sidetracked. She had to get well, not fall in love.

Restlessly, Mandy turned away. "I guess I'll head back to the house. I'm working on an article."

"Ben told me you take freelance jobs sometimes. What's the article about?"

"It's one I started before—before I got hurt. I'm researching women in rodeo. It covers the financial aspects of rodeo, the effect on family life, that kind of thing."

"I imagine rodeo life must play havoc with a woman who's got a husband and kids."

"A woman has no business dragging kids on the rodeo circuit," Mandy said flatly.

"So you're really dead set against marriage?"

Mandy threw back her head, wary of the question. "As long as I'm rodeoing, I know there'll be no husband or kids. You know how I grew up, Jake. Daddy was hardly ever around. I'd never want my kids to think rodeo meant more to me than they did." After the words left her mouth, Mandy felt appalled. Quickly, she added, "Daddy loved us. We knew that."

"It must have been hell on your mother."

Mandy looked at him quickly, then nodded. "It was tough on Mama, making a go of it alone." To get past the emotion in her throat, Mandy blurted, "You must wish things were different. You had a great football career lined up, Jake. You were really good. How much it must have hurt you to give it up."

He pulled on a pair of leather gloves and slowly turned to face her. His face looked emotionless. Mandy felt as if she was up against that wall he sometimes put up.

"That was a long time ago. I was a kid."

"I'm sorry," she said quickly, "Maybe I shouldn't bring it up, but everything went so wrong, didn't it, Jake?"

A frown hung between Jake's dark brows, and his eyes didn't meet hers. "Let it go, Mandy. It's old history. It doesn't hurt anymore."

"It wasn't that long ago," Mandy protested. He was wrong—it still hurt.

"It's almost eleven years." Jake slid his gaze to her. "It seems like another life. I've made a success of my business. I really like being my own boss."

Mandy couldn't let it go. "You were ready to go professional."

"Yeah, but real life gets in the way. My parents needed help, my sisters were dependent, I couldn't let them down."

"You gave it all up and worked to support your family." Mandy's throat felt dry. She didn't think she had ever known someone so unselfish. How could she have been so blind back then?

"Something like that."

"I wish…" Mandy let her voice trail off. She couldn't put her wishes into words. She wanted Jake's love again.

"What, Mandy?" There seemed to be an urgency in his voice.

"Nothing, Jake," she said softly, feeling like a coward. "There's no sense in rehashing the past. I guess I'm just missing rodeo." At least she had been out there doing it all these years.

"I missed the football in the beginning," Jake admitted in a low voice. "I'm too old to play professionally now, but I've always tried to keep up with the game."

"Is that why you have Sunday games here?"

"Partly. It's also a good way to keep in touch with friends."

"What are you going to do with this place?"

"Why do you ask?"

"It's big enough that you could do just about anything. The barn alone would hold twenty horses."

"Actually, I've got plans to raise horses."

Mandy's eyes sparkled. "Really? I've always wanted a barnful of horses. I've settled for four because I was on the road so much. It seemed foolish to have more than that and have them sit idle at Mama's ranch."

"Well, that's the major plan."

"How come you haven't done it before now?"

"Time. When I took over from my dad, the industry was undergoing a major change. Luckily, my dad's manager was really great, otherwise I'd have sunk the business. We had to figure out a way to go with the changes and come out on top. He retired about a year ago. I've hired a new manager and it frees up some time for me now. I've also been doing a lot more carving these last few years."

"Have you had any shows?"

"Right now I'm looking for a place to hold a regular, ongoing show."

"You're lucky, Jake, that you've found something that will satisfy you." She looked around. "This will make a wonderful horse farm."

Jake moved closer, and Mandy sensed a new intensity in his gaze. "What about you, Mandy? Have you found something that will satisfy you?"

You. The answer came instantly into Mandy's brain. She could feel the heat from his body, the magnetic aura that attracted her to him against her better judgment.

She moved closer, touched a finger to the skin of his neck, traced the line of his collarbones. His warm chest was an expanse of muscle. The tanned flesh seemed to beckon to her, making her want to touch him. "I'm still looking." She swallowed hard and attempted to make her voice flip, knowing she had to protect herself and keep her defenses up. "There's so much out there."

His eyes slitted and his jaw clenched as if he were displeased with her answer, maybe even angry. Mandy saw him draw off the gloves, and then his hand came up to curve behind her neck. He urged their bodies closer, his grip almost rough. Where they touched, fire ignited and burned.

"Why look any farther than here, Mandy?" His murmur seemed to indicate impatience. His scent swirled around her. Mandy closed her eyes as his mouth touched hers. She needed to concentrate on each unique sensation: the scent of Jake, the touch of his big hands, the sound of their mingled breaths, the taste of lips against lips. Some of it felt so wonderfully familiar. A groan let loose from her throat, startling her with its connotations of intimacy.

Mandy felt as if her legs were wobbling, and the notion was reinforced as Jake's arm settled on her waist and pulled her close, steadying her. She angled her head so she could feather a kiss across his. There was no denying it, Jake made her feel special. Being close to him gave rise to emotions she had all but buried.

Jake leaned down and lifted her off her feet. Mandy murmured in soft protest as she clutched his shoulders, feeling the bunching of muscles. He nuzzled his face in her neck a moment, carrying her a short distance. Then he let her feet touch the floor, and followed her down to a bed of loose straw.

"We shouldn't be doing this," Mandy murmured, knowing she had to say the words. Her own protest seemed to mean nothing as she sought his mouth once more, winding her arms around his neck, then pressing them down his long back to the base of his spine. He felt so good! She liked the weight of his body along hers. It had been so long.

"Yeah, we should." Those huskily uttered words tore through Mandy like jags of lightning. Her desire turned her body warm and boneless. Jake touched his tongue to her lips, then sought her inner warmth.

Heat such as she'd never known uncoiled inside Mandy, snaking to the very core of her. God, they fit so well together.

Vaguely, she realized Jake's legs were wound around hers, one hand gently cupping the seat of her jeans. Mandy became even more aware of his strength, the hardness of his body. She splayed her fingers along his ribs, traced the contours and hollows.

Suddenly, Jake shifted his weight away from her, but Mandy pulled him back. He looked down at her, his cheekbones touched by a faint flush, his eyes steady with purpose.

"You're a beautiful woman, Mandy. To this day I've never seen hair like yours, the color of deep gold straw." He picked up a handful of loose straw, then let it slip from his fingers. He leaned forward to kiss her eyelids, gently trailing kisses across her jaw and down her neck into the warm, heated opening of her blouse. He pulled two buttons through the holes, and Mandy quivered beneath him.

She was tongue-tied. She wanted to tell Jake how she felt, but she couldn't. She pressed herself to him instead, reveling in the feel of him against her, though his hands on either side of her in the straw held some of his weight off her.

She would sort out the sensations later, she decided. Meanwhile, she felt bombarded by his every touch, and breathing became more difficult. Jake's body moved heavily against hers, and she felt protected, but so hot. She wanted to say the hell with everything and damn the consequences. Wild thoughts raced through her mind. She wanted more than Jake's chest naked against her; she craved the weight of his body against her own. *Now*.

His hands moved up under her rib cage, the long fingers stopping just short of touching her breasts. Mandy caught her breath, waiting for them to move upward, sensation piercing her to the core when those hands gently cupped the sensitive flesh. A deep, shuddery breath escaped her lips. She swallowed quickly, watched him lower his head and kiss her pale flesh above the vee of her blouse.

Mandy pushed her fingers through the fine silkiness of his hair, needing to touch him. She pressed his head to her, fingers frantically tracing the back of his skull. The tremor that coursed through his body urged her to move closer still.

"This feels so good, it should be illegal," Mandy murmured, opening her eyes to stare up at him. She knew her hair probably lay in a wild, tangled mess, but she didn't care.

Jake smiled, one brow going up. "We'd be great together, Mandy." His gaze dropped to her mouth, and she shivered, lifting her face to seek his lips.

Mandy wondered fleetingly if she were brave enough to take things one step further. Three months ago, before her accident, she might not have hesitated to make love with Jake. Now she let the thought sink in, let it stiffen her into emotional paralysis. Was that all this meant to Jake—physical gratification?

With his long legs twined around hers, Mandy understood the crystal clear implications of letting this continue. Intimacy lingered a step away. Her body wanted to feel him against her, yet her brain urged caution, breathing fear and uncertainty into the situation.

Her withdrawal was slight, but Jake must have felt it. Looking down at her, he narrowed his eyes and seemed to read her hesitation.

In that split second, her reasoning reasserted itself. An emotion akin to panic flared in Mandy. Her earlier eagerness dissolved, hardened into an attempt to draw back. "This is a bad idea," she said shakily. Damn! Why had she let things go this far?

Twisting away from Jake, Mandy sat up and swiped bits of straw from her jeans. She chewed at her lips. When had she turned into a coward? Fear made her draw away. "I'm sorry, Jake," she muttered, unable to look at him.

"Are you hurt, Mandy? Did I put too much weight on you? Is it your leg—"

She stumbled to her feet with a laugh, ignoring the hand Jake held out. Self-directed anger and disgust tore through her. She felt ready to snap. "Yes, it's my leg, but it's not my leg in the way you mean. I'm not hurt."

"Then what—"

"Please don't say anything more. I know this is a big letdown. Well, suffice it to say it would've been a bigger mistake if we had continued. Luckily, I came to my senses in time."

Jake grabbed her wrist as she tried to turn away.

"Don't!" Mandy jerked her wrist away and half ran from the small room back into the main barn. She heard Jake's steps behind her. If sound was telling, she figured he was royally ticked at her. "Let's not talk it to death. It's just not a good idea. We can't go back."

"I'm not trying to go back. Maybe we can go forward."

"This might be a normal occurrence for you, Jake, rolling in the hay." Angrily, Mandy slapped more straw from her jeans. "It's not for me. I don't take this lightly."

"What are you implying? I've never taken intimacy for granted."

Mandy choked on a sob. At least he didn't say "sex." That made it sound so base, as if there were nothing else attached. No human emotion. With a self-derisive laugh, Mandy realized she was caught up in an excess of emotion. Maybe it was just sex and maybe she was the guilty one here. The thought left her cold. Was she the one in it for instant gratification? It seemed she had wanted Jake for so many years, why not take what was offered? But no, she couldn't handle exposing her body, her leg.

Knowing she needed a defense against the emotion Jake stirred in her, she snapped out angrily, "I can figure out what you thought. Mandy Thomson, party girl, hopping in and out of men's beds. I've heard it all before." Hurt more than she cared to admit, Mandy hurried from the barn. She had to get away from Jake before she gave in and went back into his arms and finished what she had started. Her body throbbed, reminding her she wanted to do just that. She had lost all control over her emotions; all she could think about was what her body was crying out for. And it was crying. Mandy knew instinctively she was missing something really wonderful. The feelings she had had for Jake as a young girl were no comparison to what was happening now. Now felt so much more real, so much stronger. But her life was a mess; she couldn't involve Jake any further in it. It wasn't as simple as falling in love and showing that love. Mandy looked down at her hands. They were shaking.

Jake came up behind her. She saw him standing there out of the corner of her eye, hands on his hips. "You're wrong, Mandy, that's not what I thought."

"I think neither one of us was thinking, Jake." Mandy pushed past him. The ache in her leg told her to stop, but she kept walking. She shouldn't have been so curious to explore the sensations Jake evoked in her. Intimacy involved body parts. No way did she want to expose herself, not when she felt so deficient. A small voice, the rational part of her, said she wasn't lacking, but she couldn't convince her heart.

As Mandy walked, emotion twisted inside, making her hurt. Why did she still feel this way about Jake? Why did making love with him fill her thoughts to the exclusion of all else?

"I wasn't intending a roll in the hay!" Jake insisted, not

bothering to follow her. "Dammit, I didn't plan on this happening."

Mandy didn't turn, but his words ripped through her. "I didn't plan it, either," she said, but in a whisper she didn't intend for him to hear.

Jake cursed, feeling lower than a snake. He had hurt her—he had seen it in her face. In her present state, at this fragile stage of her rehabilitation, she certainly didn't need him messing up her mind. Jake realized then that he didn't want to settle for a lukewarm relationship, he wanted fire and unpredictability. God help him, at some unknown point he had decided he wanted Mandy. The rational part of his brain told him he was asking for god-awful trouble, but the rest of him didn't give a damn at this moment.

Jake muttered a string of curses. For someone who'd grown up around women, he seemed to do all the wrong things around Mandy. Maybe he shouldn't have touched her, but man, his brain and body had gone into overload.

With a determined glance at Mandy's straight back, Jake wondered if there was a way to get through to her. Should he risk it and see if she'd give them a chance?

He couldn't just let her walk away. He wanted to be more than a friend. Friendship was ludicrous between them after the history they shared.

Jake looked up at the cloudless sky, the heat of the afternoon seeping into his bones. He clenched a fist. He might as well admit he'd never stopped wanting Mandy, even with all that had happened.

He stopped kidding himself. He needed to finish this thing with Mandy for good. She wasn't a woman who would hang around, or who wanted to set down roots. She would never change. Jake needed to get her out of his system and get on with his life. But how?

Chapter Ten

Mandy swam once more to the end of the pool and back, then floated facing the star-dappled sky, a sense of peace settling on her.

In the two weeks she had been here at Jake's ranch, she had finally settled into a semicomfortable frame of mind. The bouts of depression had eased, and for the first time since the accident, Mandy actually felt no urgency about returning to the rodeo. It was always there at the back of her mind, but the feeling that life was passing her by had abated.

She had begun writing again, more frequently than ever. Her outline on women in rodeo had been submitted to a magazine editor, who had expressed interest in seeing the article in its entirety. Mandy's life was coming together. She didn't feel quite so much at loose ends. She had begun to scope out other writing opportunities.

She regretted that she didn't see much of Jake, but that

was the way she had wanted it. He had been keeping his distance, and they saw each other in passing. A part of Mandy yearned for what could have been. The rational part knew it was her own fault. What she perceived as her physical deficits kept her at a standstill. Mandy knew she had to work on that part of her life, and maybe the rest would fall into place. Even so, she knew, sadly, that there would be no future for her and Jake. They'd had their shot at happiness years ago.

Yesterday Mama had driven Mandy's sport-utility vehicle out to the ranch, and to prove to Mama and to herself that she could handle her four-by-four, Mandy had driven them into town for lunch. Afterward, she drove Mama the twenty miles back to the ranch. It had turned out to be a pleasant afternoon, and some of the hurts had started to heal.

Having her own vehicle gave Mandy a renewed sense of freedom. Now she could schedule her doctor visits without worrying about depending on others. She almost felt like her old self.

She rode Pongo daily. She had reached a point in her riding where she felt confident of her skills once again. She compensated for the prosthetic leg by using simple hand signals on Pongo's withers to indicate turns and changes of gait. The inability to use leg pressure on her right side left her no other choice. Mandy felt satisfied with both her progress and Pongo's. She had also seen the wisdom in Jake's suggestion about using a breakaway boot strap to keep her foot in place in the stirrup. However, she had not yet shared that fact with him. An ache of regret pulled at Mandy. She missed Jake.

She swam lazily toward the side of the pool, then pulled herself out to sit on the curved edge, enjoying the night air on her skin. There was nothing in the world like a warm, Oklahoma night. She had always taken it for granted. Now she didn't. Mandy realized nothing should be taken for granted. Too bad it had taken the loss of a limb to teach her that lesson.

It was midnight, hours later than her usual swim time, so Mandy had not turned on the overhead floodlight. As she sat there, she suddenly sensed another presence. Nervously, she kicked her foot through the water.

"Is that you, Jake?"

"Mandy?"

Relief flooded her. "Yes. I didn't turn the light on in case it bothered you."

"The light wouldn't bother me." There was silence.

Mandy sensed he stood on the opposite end of the pool.

"It's pretty late," he said.

"I'm all keyed up. I couldn't sleep." She had been too excited to sleep. She and Pongo had made such good progress, she couldn't get it out of her mind. She wanted to share it with someone.

"I'll leave you to your swim, then," Jake said.

Mandy didn't want him to leave. She had to share her news or burst. Even if Jake thought her a fool for getting excited about something so simple, she had to tell him. She needed him to know of her progress. In part, some of her progress was due to him. He had had the foresight to have Pongo brought to the ranch.

"Jake, that's all right. I don't mind company. Did you come out to swim, too?"

"No, I've been going over my quarterly figures. I thought I'd come outside to clear my head."

"Everything okay with work?" Mandy wanted to tell him she felt embarrassed about their last encounter. She had acted out of character, almost childish. The incident in the barn had been days ago, but it was still fresh in her mind, teasing her.

"Yes. We've got it pretty much down to a science now."

"How's Amy? I haven't seen her in a while."

"She was here last Sunday. I didn't see you around."

Mandy had made herself scarce purely out of a sense of self-preservation. She wanted to see Jake, be in his company, so she had deliberately stayed away. Why cause herself unnecessary heartache?

"Amy has a new job working at the local elementary school."

"She's working with kids? I always liked kids myself."

"Yes, she's training to be a teacher's aide." Mandy heard a sound like a chair toppling over, then Jake's muttered curse.

"You can turn on the overhead light if you want," she said slowly, gearing herself up for the glare of the lights. Why have him stumbling in the dark just because she was shy of anyone seeing her leg? It would be exposed. For some reason, the thought didn't bother her quite as much as she thought it would. She held her breath, then looked up as the soft light flooded the area. Her crutches lay beside the pool. She could stand and move anytime she wanted.

Jake stood across the pool from her, facing into the light. He had on a dark shirt, unbuttoned and tucked into the waistband of a pair of faded jeans. His flat stomach and muscular chest drew her eyes before she forced herself to glance away, trying not to stare. She wanted to keep looking at Jake instead of pretending she wasn't. Although he needed a shave, Jake looked better than ever. Her brain conjured up the warm feel of his body beneath her fingertips. It might have been minutes ago, instead of more than a week since he had held her.

Despite the light, Mandy willed herself to remain still. Her first instinct had been to cover her stump. If Jake wanted to see her leg, or what was left of it below the knee, maybe she could be brave enough to take that step. Perhaps that time had come. Maybe she needed that shock factor to harden her, so she wasn't so sensitive out in public. The

thoughts were easier than the actual fact, though. Mandy bi
at her lips and her fingers tensed as Jake moved toward her

She began to speak tensely, quickly. "I've made som
real progress with Pongo. We've been riding every day.
work each day on some simple hand signals. It's pretty easy
He caught right on."

Jake pulled a chair up and straddled it, his eyes on her
"You're using hand signals?"

Mandy nodded. "Yes, simple ones. He neck-reins reall
well, but I wanted to teach him the hand signals for mor
fine-tuned riding." She drew a deep breath, then admitted
"After shortening my right stirrup a tad, I also took int
consideration your suggestion. I'm using a breakaway stra
to keep the boot in place."

"Have you ever thought about teaching others to ride?'

Forgetting about her leg and her self-consciousness
Mandy twisted around and faced Jake fully. "Teach riding'
To tell you the truth, I haven't thought about that."

"I'm sure there's a need for it. Think of the confidenc
builder riding would be. Look what it's done for you."

Mandy laughed. "Me? I'm the least confident person
know right now. Isn't it silly to be so excited about some
thing so simple?"

Jake shook his head. "It's not simple. This represent
your progress. You're a different person from when you firs
came. Maybe some of the hurt and confusion is still there
but you're working past it. I've got plenty of space here i
you decide you want to tackle something like that…givin
riding lessons." His glance swept over her and he smiled
as if he liked what he saw. Mandy felt happy suddenly, bu
she remained cautious.

"What are you saying, Jake? You know I can't stay here
You've got plans, I've got plans. This whole deal is tem
porary." She had to remind him of that, and keep he
thoughts in line against rising hopes.

"We can work around it." Jake shrugged, and hope surged foolishly, perhaps, into Mandy's heart. "It's another option, if you decide it's something you'd like to do. I have the room."

Mandy made herself breathe slowly. She had to face reality. "I won't be staying, Jake," she told him firmly. "I just haven't found another place yet." She took a deep breath. "On a lighter note, I never did tell you how much I appreciate you bringing Pongo to me. It was the right thing to do. It seems like I'm forever apologizing for the way I've acted, but I am sorry."

Jake's smile melted her insides. Mandy wanted to fall into a heap at his feet. She swallowed hard.

"I'm glad it's working out."

Mandy looked down over her one-piece, black bathing suit. The neckline plunged to expose part of her breasts; the legs were cut high on her hips. Suddenly, she saw her leg. It ended abruptly below the knee. It looked so different and out of place. Despite her earlier moment of braveness, she pulled her legs closer to her body.

"Don't," Jake said, his voice low. "There's nothing to hide, no reason to hide. You've got beautiful legs."

Incredulously, Mandy protested, "Are you kidding—"

"You do," he insisted. "You've kept yourself in shape, and both your legs are beautiful and sleek. Look at your residual limb. Even the kneecap is the same size as the other one."

Mandy did look down, seeing her stump objectively, perhaps for the first time. Jake was right, her legs were finely muscled, and the right knee looked the same as the other one.

"Even if you hadn't kept yourself in such good shape, believe me, you're not lacking. Only in your own mind. You've got a lot to offer, Mandy."

Mandy took the compliment and digested it, hugging

close the warm glow it created. She narrowed her eyes playfully and quipped, "So now you're saying my mind is lacking?"

Jake gazed at her, his eyes half-closed as he surveyed her from head to toe. "Nope." His mouth curved sensually. "I'd take you, mind and all."

"Thanks," she said with affected dryness, trying not to put too much weight into his choice of words. They were words, that was all, but her heart beat faster in her chest.

"So here's fair warning. If I give you a hand now and then, don't take offense. It's not because of your leg, it's because you're a beautiful woman, and we're friends, remember?"

"You're full of surprises," she replied breathlessly, elation gripping her. She felt as if she needed to dispel the seriousness of their conversation. "But now I sense male chauvinistic tendencies."

That sexy-as-hell grin split his face. "You don't know the half of my tendencies."

Taking up the challenge to get everything out in the open, Mandy admitted slowly, "About that day in the barn, I guess I just got overloaded on emotion. Do you think we can start over?"

Jake nodded, his eyes never leaving her face. "As far as starting over, honey, we can start anywhere you want."

It wasn't quite the answer she had expected, but coming from Jake, she didn't know what to expect anymore. One moment he donned the attire of a successful businessman. Other times he wore sexy-as-sin jeans, bringing to mind the Jake she used to know.

"Well, considering how we began, maybe the best way is to go back to the beginning," Mandy said breezily, pushing herself to stand on her foot. She grabbed her crutches and stood straight, no longer trying to hide, but still watching his face. Her breath came quickly, but when he smiled, she felt the tension in her shoulders ease.

"We can do that," Jake agreed, moving closer. "Or we can go back to the middle. Myself, I favor the middle."

"What do you consider the middle?" Mandy asked boldly, watching him pull his shirttail from his pants. He shrugged the material from his broad shoulders and let it drop to the ground. He stepped closer still and startled her by reaching forward to run a gentle fingertip along her jaw.

"Right about here, where you and I kiss and make up," he murmured.

Mandy leaned heavily on the crutches, aware of the reaction of various parts of her body to his words, and to the heated look that came with them. She felt totally enveloped by a rush of want and need. Jake. She wanted Jake. He was so close, the scent of him around her, in her nostrils. She drew in a deep breath.

"All right." Mandy threw him a daring smile. "You proceed from the middle and I'll tell you if I like it." Some part of her acknowledged that eventually she and Jake would be lovers. She wanted it, craved it, knew it was inevitable. A delectable little shiver raced across her bare back. Mandy could hardly wait. She ran her tongue over her lips. She didn't want to wait.

Jake saw the imp surface in Mandy. He felt as if the years rolled back. This was the Mandy he remembered. Did she realize how fascinating he found her? She had guts and a liberal amount of nerve. She was getting on with her life, instead of letting it pass her by. Her courage touched him. He had loved her when she was a teenager. But now she had matured into so much more than he remembered. For a moment he regretted that time had erased their love. Jake wished he knew how to handle the newly rekindled desire he felt.

"Proceed from the middle? I don't want to scare you now. I know how skittish you can be."

Mandy smiled, and it lit her eyes. "Do your worst."

Jake's body reacted instantly. She looked perfect. His hands itched to trace the slimness of her waist, the rounded curve of her buttocks. She appeared to be in a happy, daredevil mood, yet he sensed a tenseness about her, as if she was afraid he would stare overlong at her stump. Jake couldn't help his curiosity about the changes she had undergone. He wasn't sure himself how he felt about the absence of her lower leg. In the end, he knew it didn't matter how he felt about it. What mattered was that Mandy regained control over her life and accepted herself for the way she was now.

With a strong measure of restraint, Jake leaned forward and placed a deliberately chaste kiss on her lips. To his amusement, she looked chagrined. "Am I going too fast?" he asked, making a show of stepping back.

"Maybe it's the company you keep. Let me try," Mandy suggested, moving closer until the thin layer of Lycra was the only thing between her skin and his chest. Jake drew a deep breath at the contact and held himself rigid. He wanted to crush her close to him, but he held back. He was a grown man. He could control himself. For the moment, he let Mandy set the speed.

Her tongue traced his lips, then delved inside. Jake felt the weight of her suddenly in his arms. He stepped closer to her, his arms enveloping her. He lifted Mandy up against him as she turned her face into his neck. Jake groaned as her lips nuzzled there. He struggled to keep his head as her slim hands ran quickly, tantalizingly along his back. He bit back the groan of pleasure building in his chest.

After several moments, he let her drop back down to her toes. Vaguely, he felt his chest heaving, as if he had run hard. "Now that's what I'd call middle ground. We should meet on it more often," he said, his voice rough with desire. Jake held her head against him, feeling her wet tongue run along his jaw. "Geez! Mandy."

She gave a gurgle of laughter and did it again, then rested her face against his collarbones, her warm breath fanning his skin.

"I concur," she said in a husky voice. She rubbed her cheek against his chest. "You smell good, Jake, but your skin is hot. I think we should go into the pool and cool off."

"Mmm." That was about all Jake could manage in reply as he lifted her hair and kissed his way across the sensitive skin of her neck. Her immediate response was to melt into him, and the hot awareness in Jake built to a powerful need. Not sure he wanted to follow blindly where this was leading, he pulled himself up and out of the seductive aura that Mandy exuded.

"How about that swim?" he said briskly.

Jake could almost see the wheels inside her head working. He knew the situation could go either way. She might be hurt that he had pulled away, or she might be thinking of the next step in their relationship. Jake wanted to make love to Mandy, wanted it with everything inside him. He wished it wasn't so, but there was no denying the truth.

"You're right, Jake," she murmured. "A swim is the solution."

Jake watched as she tossed her hair back. He had tried like hell to keep his distance these last few weeks. Part of him knew he was asking for trouble big time. He and Mandy had had their shot years ago. Another part of him wanted to race ahead and take the decision away from both of them. He wanted to go on gut instinct alone. Instinct was telling him to claim what Mandy offered and not let go. They were adults, not kids.

"Come on, last one in is a loser. And I'll warn you I

don't intend to lose!'' Mandy pushed him away from her. Jake saw her hop back when he put out a hand to catch her. Off balance, he fell backward into the pool. Before the water closed over his head he saw Mandy jump in beside him.

They surfaced together.

''You're going to pay for that,'' he warned, treading water.

Jake read the exhilaration on her face, the sheer glory of living. She threw her head back challengingly and laughed. ''Do your worst...or best, Jake Miller,'' she invited throatily. ''But make sure you do a good job of it.''

Staring at her through slitted eyes, Jake pulled himself from the pool and stood on the edge. Very deliberately he unzipped his jeans and yanked them down, knowing his boxer shorts didn't leave much to the imagination. If she was going to back away, Jake intended to give her the opportunity right now.

Mandy couldn't tear her eyes from Jake, her gaze stuck on his lower anatomy, so starkly outlined by his wet shorts. He turned and threw the jeans onto a chair, giving her a perfect view of his trim backside. It was a cowboy behind, to be sure, the kind that looked perfect in jeans or just about anything. Or nothing, she realized, gulping water. She coughed and gagged, holding on to the side of the pool. Drawing a ragged, embarrassed breath, Mandy tried to inhale past the chlorinated water in her airway.

Somewhere above her she heard Jake laughing softly, and she knew he wasn't fooled by her. He knew he'd caught her off guard.

''This boring old boy caught you by surprise, eh, Mandy?''

She didn't answer. She had seen a naked man before, brief glimpses, but never frontal, personal, someone she knew.

Never Jake Miller. She had wanted to make love with Jake ten years ago, but he'd held back each time when things reached fever pitch. Maybe he had known she was too young to handle the consequences back then. They had both been too young.

A splash told her he had reentered the water. Mandy twisted her head around, once more able to breathe normally. He was behind her, not touching, but there, smiling, challenging her to continue where they had left off.

Mandy kept her eyes on his face, wondering if for once she had bitten off more than she could chew. Had she met her match in this man? Maybe some of her doubts showed on her face, or in her eyes, because Jake swam away, then around her in circles.

"Ever skinny-dipped before?" he asked lightly.

Mandy considered his question. "Will you believe me if I say never in mixed company?"

"I didn't mean to shock you." His words mocked her.

She could tell by the glint in his eyes he was lying. Mandy would have laughed, maybe, if he wasn't so close. "I'm not easily shocked." Was she really a prude? She considered the question. "I never thought of myself as a prig, but on the other hand," she admitted truthfully, "I've stayed away from relationships with men for a while."

"Are we having a relationship?" Jake asked curiously. He reached out his hand and let the strands of her hair float atop his upturned palm.

"There's a possibility, isn't there?" Some of the tension eased inside Mandy, and she took a reviving breath. "I'm not very experienced at this," she told him flatly.

"I'm not one for casual flings, either."

Mandy began to feel chilled. She pulled herself from the pool and dangled her foot in the water. "Casual or otherwise, I've tried it…getting seriously involved. The leaving is more agony than it's worth when two people want different things.'' She threw her head back and pushed her wet hair away from her face. ''You know what I mean, Jake. Look at our history.''

''I would like to think we've moved beyond who we were as teenagers.''

''In some ways, of course we have, but some experiences...'' Mandy shifted sideways. ''There's no sense pussyfooting around. What I'm trying to say is my experience is pretty narrow,'' she finally blurted. ''Despite my reputation, all the partying...I've never been with a man. I'm afraid you're going to be in for a big disappointment if you believe everything you've heard about me.''

Chapter Eleven

If Jake found her admission startling, he didn't say a word. Instead, he swam away from her. She watched his arms cleave the water as he circled back toward her. He rested his elbow on the pool edge beside her thighs.

Gently, he pulled her close, urged her face down to his. Their mouths met, and Mandy slid into the water against him, moved down his wet body, her leg twining with his. It felt good, until her residual limb bumped against him with the movement of the water. Mandy felt her eyes widen in shock. Her gaze latched on to Jake's face as she tried to gauge his reaction. Would he show distaste, revulsion?

Jake ran a fingertip down her nose, his mouth curving slightly in a smile. "When I'm with you, Mandy, we're on equal ground. I feel as inexperienced as any kid."

Mandy licked her lips, trying to breathe normally. She felt her spirits lift. He hadn't pulled away from her, from her leg. She wound her arms around his neck, feeling the pool water push her up against him. The contact was her undoing. She needed more than his water-cooled skin against hers. She had missed him the last week. A part of her yearned for him. The feeling had grown steadily, but she had determinedly filled the hours by riding, walking, exercising, all the while knowing she didn't want to stay away from him. All the while knowing she would soon be leaving.

"Maybe we should be inexperienced together," she whispered, using two fingers to push the hair from his eyes. She reveled in her freedom to touch him. It might not last, this freedom, but it felt wonderful in this moment.

Without a word Jake put his hands on her hips and pulled her through the water with him, to the opposite side of the pool. At the ladder, he lifted her out, then followed, pulling her upright. His hard, muscled arms carried her to the cushioned chaise in the shadows, where he let her stand once more.

Lifting the cushions, he positioned them on the pool deck, then helped her sit on them. Knowing Jake watched her, Mandy crossed her arms and very slowly slid one bathing suit strap down, then the other. She felt incredibly sexy. For the first time since her accident, she didn't feel self-conscious about her body and the changes it had been through.

Jake knelt beside her, one hand reaching forward until, almost reverently, it seemed, he cupped her breast. His head moved closer and she caught the glint of his eyes, his face so serious, before his hot mouth dropped to her skin, his lips moving to heat her flesh. The feel of his mouth on her cool skin was erotic, mind-blowing. Mandy cupped the back of his head. Feverishly, her fingers traced the bones of his skull, sensitive to the silky texture of his hair. She dropped her head back, concentrating on all the sensations. Jags of awareness vibrated through her, one after another. Never had she been so aware of her own body's needs. She had ignored those very needs for a long time.

His hands wiped the droplets from her skin slowly, sensuously, as if he liked touching her. Mandy watched Jake's face, so serious and intent, as his hands continued to trace her arms and shoulders. Leaning over her, he grabbed a towel and slowly dried her body, the material semi-rough and titillating against her ultrasensitive skin.

Pulling the towel from his hands, Mandy did the same for him, enjoying his muscled body beneath her palms. She rubbed the cloth over his broad chest and watched the dark hair spring back. Gently, she drew the towel behind his neck and rubbed it over his hair. Lastly, Mandy dried his shoulders, then moved the towel aside so she could touch the warm brown skin with her mouth. She couldn't resist that glorious temptation.

Abandoning the towel, Mandy lay back and reached toward Jake as he hovered above her. The light was behind him, throwing his face into shadow. She traced a finger along his lean cheek to the corner of his mouth. Jake turned his head and nipped her finger, then licked and kissed it. He placed a hand on either side of her. Mandy felt so strung up with desire, she didn't care if she ever moved.

"I'm a patient man, Mandy."

"That's a strange choice of words," she murmured. "Right now I don't want words, Jake." She placed her open palms on his chest, curled her fingers into the springy hair and felt the delicate quiver of muscle. Jake wanted her as much as she wanted him.

"Sometimes the words have to be said."

Mandy placed her hand flat against his ribs. "What are you telling me?"

One of his own hands captured hers, and his long fingers twined with her own. "I'm saying we've got all kinds of time."

"I'm impatient by nature," Mandy admitted, smiling. She'd always lived for the here and now, damn the consequences.

Jake smoothed her hair out, spreading the wet strands over the cushion. "Believe me, I feel the same way."

"But?" Mandy tensed, a slow spiral of emotion settling in the pit of her stomach.

He let out a deep breath and his gaze met hers. "Maybe we're not ready to take this step."

The words were a dash of cold air on the hot emotions surging through Mandy. She tried to stay calm, but a certain hurt wended its way through her.

"If you're having doubts, Jake, just come out and say so." She moved to sit up, but his hand cupped her shoulder and held her still.

"Hang on a minute, don't get riled up."

Mandy felt a sting inside, an abrupt coil of tension. "Well, what do you suggest? I'm ready to take this further, but you're not."

"Oh, no, you've got that wrong, sweetheart. I'm ready to go as far as you need." His voice was calm, the words slow and measured, lessening the sting Mandy felt. "But I want you to consider that we've barely spoken to each other this last week, hardly even seen each other...and here we are, suddenly, with nothing between us but some words." His gaze moved over her bare breasts as if to emphasize his words.

"We ignite, and right now that feels like enough. I want to find out where it can go. I'm ready to take that step." Mandy felt like a defiant teenager. She took a deep breath and tried to get a grip on her feelings. She had never been good at containing emotion.

Jake put a fraction more space between them and gripped the back of his neck with one hand. "I don't want the mere fact of passion bringing us together." He shook his head in irony. "Geez, I can't believe I'm saying this."

Mandy bit on her knuckles. "Let's cut to the chase. The fact is neither one of us can forget what happened before."

"I'm not trying to forget anything. All I'm saying is if we get involved, we're both adult enough to realize it's a matter of body chemistry." Jake gave an exasperated sound. "Hell, I don't know. Call it unfinished business. Maybe we both need to carry this to the next step, and then it'll be played out like it should have been ten years ago."

"So you're saying we should have an affair, get this thing that's plaguing both of us out of our systems." Mandy felt a piece of her heart shrivel. Her skin felt clammy, the night air suddenly too cool.

"I'm not sure what I'm saying. You mean a lot to me, Mandy, otherwise this situation here and now would never materialize. You've always gotten under my skin. I'm the type of man who can't ignore that."

Mandy bit back the cry of despair that wanted out. "You make me sound like a sliver you need to extricate." She put up a hand and pushed herself back from Jake. "I take life one day at a time, Jake, even more so since the accident. But even I draw the line at a relationship that sounds so cold and clinical."

Blindly, she reached for a towel. With shaky fingers she pulled her bathing suit back into place and wrapped herself in the towel. The air had a bite in it. Damn! She felt like she was back to square one, vulnerable and exposed.

"There's nothing cold and clinical about any relationship we'll ever have," Jake said dryly. He stared at her until Mandy met his gaze. Heat leaped up her neck and into her face. She knew he was right, but now the mood had changed.

He stood up and disappeared into the shadows. When he returned, his jeans clung to his damp, lean legs. Mandy watched him, a feeling of sadness overcoming her. He had been right about one thing—they would have been good together. A part of her ached because she knew that wasn't going to happen. He wanted something she couldn't give. A promise to walk away and not want more. Wasn't that what he was outlining in black-and-white? Sleep together, get rid of this bothersome desire and then they could each go their separate ways. Six months ago Mandy might have pulled that off. Taken what Jake offered and walked away with head held high. But not now. Lies and deceit had a way of coming back to you. She had seen it firsthand with her own family. She couldn't pretend she didn't love Jake.

He walked over to the pool and retrieved her crutches. As he handed them to her, Mandy smiled regretfully, hiding her pain.

"I do have to admire you, Jake. Any other man wouldn't have thought twice about taking what was offered." Her heart didn't want any other man.

"The door isn't closed, Mandy."

The words caused a shivery sensation to shoot down her back, but she made no move toward him. She couldn't tell him she loved him. She'd feel like she was pleading for him to make love with her. Obviously, he no longer loved her. It was years too late for her to have come to her senses.

Draping the towel over her shoulder, Mandy made her way to the door of her apartment. On the threshold, she threw him one last glance. "I can't believe you're doing this," she said. "I can't believe I'm letting you."

Jake groaned and muttered, "I can't believe it, either." But he stayed where he was on the opposite side of the patio.

Mandy closed her door, shutting him out as he stood there, silhouetted against the overhead light.

With a muttered curse Jake stood by the pool, staring at the gentle ripples on the water. With things so hot between him and Mandy, why had he brought them to a grinding halt? Making love with her was what he wanted. Once he and Mandy were together, he could get her out of his system. Why delay the inevitable?

Jake unbuttoned his jeans again. He needed to ease the stiffness in his shoulders and the regret in his gut. Now more than ever he had to deplete the adrenaline still pumping through him. He would swim until exhaustion made him stop. How many nights had he swum out here since Mandy arrived? Jake had lost count. Damn! He must be seven kinds of a fool. Hadn't he learned his lesson the hard way? Mandy might like to play, but when it came time to pay, she was out the door.

He had put a stop to their lovemaking because he didn't want her hurt. But Jake felt as if he himself were in danger—of getting too wrapped up in her life. It had happened once. How could he think about caring for her again? When she was ready, she'd leave. History repeating itself.

Maybe he was too old-fashioned, but he had been brought up to believe women needed and wanted to be taken care of. His sisters were prime examples. He had been taking care of them for so long, it was second nature. It suddenly struck Jake that in the last several weeks, however, his sisters hadn't asked him to solve any problems. He had talked to them at various times, but they hadn't asked him for a thing. Strange.

Mandy wasn't anything like his sisters; she had made that abundantly clear. She was determined to make her own decisions. She didn't welcome his help over the rough spots. Jake knew she wouldn't hesitate to walk away again. She hadn't changed. She would return to the rodeo. That had always been the plan.

Jake wasn't going to be the one hurting this time. He would go into this affair with his eyes wide-open. No expectations, just take what was offered and enjoy it for the time it lasted, two weeks or two months. If it came down to the wire, he could handle it. He'd get two things: Mandy Thomson out of his system and his life back. After all, that's what he'd wanted all along.

Several nights later Mandy looked out her front window for what was probably the hundredth time, then walked through the living room and into the kitchen. Nervously, she scanned the bags of pretzels, chips and party mix on her kitchen counter. Then she pulled open the refrigerator and looked again at the bottles of soda and six-packs of beer.

Letting the refrigerator door swing shut, she turned and leaned against it, clasping her shaking hands together. "This is ridiculous," she muttered. "I'm a basket case, all because I haven't seen my friends in umpteen months, and now they're all going to be here tonight." She pushed herself away from the solid support of the refrigerator and walked across the living room. "They're my friends, for God's sake! It's not like they're suddenly an unknown entity. Why am I acting like this?"

Mandy was disgusted with her clammy hands and rubbed them down the sides of her jeans. Why be nervous? She had decided, in true Thomson fashion, to invite all her friends back into her life at once. It had taken only a couple phone calls to start the process. An open invitation had been extended to her friends to come to her place for a get-together. She had kept them at bay for months and months, but now she felt the time was right to let them back in. She had to face them, answer their questions if necessary, and get on with the business of living. Mandy supposed her nervousness stemmed from the fact that she had deliberately kept them away and she wasn't sure now if they'd even show up.

She jumped when a knock sounded at the front door.

Before she could turn the knob, the door swung inward and she heard a familiar voice exclaim, "Mandy! It's been so long!"

Her friend Denny Moran moved forward and threw her arms around her. Having dreaded and looked forward to this moment for so long, Mandy felt a tightness close around her throat as they hugged, the embrace light and quick.

Denny stepped back, her dark eyes running over Mandy. She met her gaze once more and gave her a big grin. "God, you look good, Mandy. It's seems like forever since we've been together...." Her voice trailed off, and Mandy knew immediately she was thinking of the night of her accident, the last time they had seen each other.

"I know," she said lightly. "I've missed everyone so much. I'm so glad you came tonight."

Another friend, Lynn Barr, rushed in behind Denny. Short and sassy, Lynn made up in enthusiasm what she lacked in size. "A party! I told Denny you'd be back in the swing of things!" she said happily. "I knew you couldn't stay away."

"It's great to see you guys," Mandy said affectionately. She brushed Lynn's red curls lightly. "I heard you won big last week?"

Even though she didn't participate in rodeo right now, Mandy made a point of keeping up on the news. There was an awkward silence, then Lynn nodded, her eyes dropping down Mandy's jean-clad leg. Quickly, she looked back up to Mandy's face.

"Yeah, no big deal. If you'd been there, I wouldn't have had a chance at the big money." Quickly, she added, "Do you think you'll ever come back, Mandy?"

Mandy saw the way Denny dug her elbow into Lynn's side. Mandy shrugged her shoulders and laughed, surprised to realize it didn't hurt as much as she had feared to hear such a question. A twinge of regret, maybe, but not a real angry hurt, not the way she had felt after the amputation.

"Well, who knows? My prosthetist hasn't given me an answer on that one yet, but there're all kinds of possibilities. Right now, I'm concentrating on getting back into the swing of daily living. I've started riding again, and everything seems to be falling into place. Any news I should know about?"

A small grin appeared on Denny's face. "Maybe."

Lynn moved closer. "I knew she couldn't wait to spill her guts. She's seeing a guy—"

"Lynn, don't you dare tell," Denny said hurriedly, twisting sideways to clap a hand over Lynn's mouth.

Lynn gave Mandy a slow wink, then pulled Denny's hand away from her mouth.

"What shouldn't she tell?" Mandy asked, curious.

"I'm seeing someone," Denny admitted.

"And that's big news? What happened to Johnny?" It was no secret that Denny was a woman who loved men.

"He ran out of money in Tulsa and I told him I'd had enough. I got tired of taking second place to his rowdy habits, so I split."

"I know our Denny here changes boyfriends more often than a horse changes leads," Lynn interjected, "but this is different. She still hasn't brought this guy around to introduce him to the crowd." Lynn rolled her eyes dramatically. "She did promise she might invite him along tonight, but he hasn't shown yet."

"He doesn't rodeo. He's different from the rest of us," Denny said defensively. "I wanted to wait awhile before he got a handle on the rodeo scene. I don't want you all to scare him away."

Mandy got an odd feeling from Denny's words. Was Denny in a similar situation to herself—attracted to a man from a totally different background? How could she expect it to work out? Denny's childhood had been similar to Mandy's. Her family had been involved in rodeo from the word *go*. It had been her way of life while growing up.

Throat dry, Mandy asked lightly, "Is he someone I know?"

Denny shook her head. "I don't think so, but you'll meet him soon enough. We're still getting to know one another and I don't want to ruin it. You know how I louse up relationships and get hooked up with the wrong guy. There're other considerations, too. His wife died and he's got a little girl. I really like him, so I'm going to take it very slow."

"He must be special." Mandy cleared her throat, forcing a smile. She felt guilty over the dart of envy that pricked her. "Good luck. Let me know how it goes," she told Denny sincerely.

"We'll know more tonight...if he shows up," Lynn quipped.

Others began to arrive and the house quickly filled up. Mandy had forgotten how many people she had invited on her spur-of-the-moment phoning around. Her earlier anxiety receded as she talked to more of her friends.

The country music was loud and satisfying. Several couples danced on the living-room floor; others were out on the front deck. Mandy had invited Jake, as well as his sister. Amy was in the midst of the crush of bodies and appeared to be having a good time. After introducing Jake to her friends, Mandy had lost track of him.

She checked the drinks, made sure the ice buckets were full and then replenished the snacks. She chatted with everyone, even new acquaintances that had arrived with old friends.

There seemed to be an initial awkwardness, as if her friends didn't quite know how to treat her. Mandy managed to get past that and began to feel like she had never been away from the old crowd. She even reminisced about rodeo meets. She had a keen interest in who was competing and what the standings were. She didn't want her friends to feel as if they had to be careful of what they said in front of her.

Mandy had already made the rounds when her eyes settled on Denny's animated face across the room. There was a difference in her friend, a definite glow about her. Denny had always been a love-'em-and-leave-'em type of girl. Had she found the right guy? Was she finally ready to settle down? An inexplicably heavy feeling settled on Mandy. Apparently Denny wasn't afraid to swim out of her element and take a chance.

Needing some fresh air, Mandy moved to the edge of the crowd, then opened the patio door and stepped out into the pool area. She had told her friends to bring their bathing suits, but no one had wandered out here yet. Mandy wondered where Jake was. She wanted to find out how he felt about her friends. It was suddenly very important to her.

As she perched on the stone wall beside the pool area, she reflected that there was a lot to be said for reconnecting with old friends. Yet the longer she sat there, the more her doubts began to prick at her. She had thought bringing back certain aspects of her past would fill the puzzling gaps she felt in her life. Always gregarious and fun-loving, Mandy suddenly felt tired. It was barely ten o'clock, she was with a circle of friends she'd thought of as her extended family, and still she was dogged by a niggling dissatisfaction.

Listening to her friends tonight, she wondered if she had always been so single-minded, concentrating only on the next rodeo, the next beer and where the best parties were.

Her friends and fans had been extremely supportive, and her intrusive thoughts made her feel ungrateful. The cards and letters hadn't stopped the entire time she had been in the hospital and rehabilitation. Now that everyone was gathered here, she was staring at the stars and feeling out of place. What was the matter with her? She hated feeling out of her element. She had never sat on the fringe of a party in her life. She could fit in anywhere. Why did she feel as if she were the odd one out? Where did she belong?

"Nowhere," she muttered.

Hearing a sound, the scrape of a foot on stone, Mandy looked into the shadows behind her. She wasn't alone. Jake stood silhouetted against the overhead floodlight some six feet from her, his hands in his pockets. She sensed he was looking at her, but she couldn't see his eyes.

"Catching a quick breather, Mandy? Looks like the party's a hit. Everyone seems to be having a good time," he said.

"Yeah, everyone's having a great time," Mandy said lightly. "I have a reputation to uphold, you know. I'm known as one of the better party-throwers."

"You rodeo with each of them?"

"Most of them, yes. They've been good friends, but then that's how rodeo people are. They're always willing to help out and offer support when you need it."

"They seem like a good bunch. So why are you out here?" His question seemed deliberate, as if he knew something she didn't. Could Jake have guessed she was feeling out of place?

Mandy looked away, lifting her shoulders in a careless shrug. "I just wanted a breath of fresh air. The smoke-filled room started bothering me. Do you know something, Jake? They're still my friends, but it feels different."

"Maybe you treat them different, expecting them to treat you that way. Do you always sit on the outskirts of a party by yourself?"

"No, usually I'm in the midst of it, making the biggest noise. I always liked being the center of attention." She gave him a wry smile. "Of course, I'd never admit that to Ben. He claims I'm an exhibitionist, and he said it comes from being the youngest. He insists I sucked up all the attention.''

She heard Jake's soft laugh. ''I probably told my sisters the same thing.''

''I don't feel like that anymore. I don't want that attention.''

''What do you want, Mandy?''

She expelled a heavy breath. ''What do I want?'' Mandy shook her head, giving the question serious thought. ''That should be an easy question, don't you think? After the accident, all I wanted was to be alone. When I had that, it still didn't feel right. I'm not really sure. I needed this party to get back in touch with my friends....'' Mandy felt swamped by confusion. ''I feel kind of like a stranger to myself. I'm sitting here—I know it's me—but the old urges aren't there. I haven't had a beer since the accident. I haven't wanted one.''

''I wouldn't say that's a big deal.''

''It is for me. I feel so changed.''

''That's understandable. You're going through some major adjustments in your life. You've got to expect things to change.''

''I'm not so sure I want to party and be rowdy anymore. The lust for that is gone. But I'm not going to sit in a corner, either,'' she said emphatically. ''I'm just not sure how to deal with this sense of uncertainty.''

Jake came closer. For a fleeting moment Mandy longed to lift her hand and run her fingers through his hair, then trail them over his hard jaw. She recalled the last night they were together. An ache tightened the back of her throat. Maybe it just wasn't meant to be, she and Jake.

She tipped her head to stare up at the sky, mocking herself. He was Mr. Right, she the undomesticated Mandy Thomson. Hadn't she proved that years ago? She couldn't settle anywhere for long if her life depended on it. She had hurt him once. Why should he ever forgive her and take another chance? Jake was a forever kind of guy. The marrying kind. Mandy didn't kid herself. She wasn't the marrying type.

The thought intruded that if Denny could do it, why couldn't she? When Denny had talked about the new man in her life, Mandy had sensed something different and wonderful in her friend. Denny was as much of a rolling stone as she was. Mandy was ashamed to have felt envy. Of all her friends, Denny deserved a good man in her life.

The door opened and the party in her living room spilled out onto the deck. Mandy smiled as her friends' hooting and hollering broke the quiet of the night.

"It's a good thing I have a lenient landlord." Mandy laughed, enjoying her friends' antics. The night breeze touched her hair, gently pushing it back from her face.

"It helps when you invite him to the party," Jake said dryly. He reached up a hand and smoothed his fingers lightly over her cheek. "I'm sure your motive was to keep the peace between us."

The tenderness of the gesture caught Mandy by surprise. "I've never been one for seeking peace," she assured him gravely. "You should know that, Jake."

"Some things never change," he said with a slight narrowing of his eyes.

"Oh, I wouldn't say that. Sometimes changes are so subtle we miss them at first." Mandy knew she had changed, she just wasn't sure how to deal with all of it yet. "By the way, Jake, I have some news." Mandy saw the sudden wariness on his face. "I heard of a new place in Oklahoma City that's looking for different art exhibits to display."

"Really?" Wariness gave way to surprise. "I've been scouting around but I haven't found a suitable place yet."

"Well, I was talking to a friend of a friend tonight. This new gallery has just received a sizable grant, and they're setting up a permanent display area. The news should hit the papers this week. And they're taking applications. I know you're interested in a place to have your carvings on display. This might be the perfect opportunity.''

"So you've been networking on my behalf," Jake said slowly.

"Sure. That's what friends do." Mandy deliberately used the word *friends* to gauge Jake's reaction.

"And are we still friends?" he inquired, one brow raised.

"I hope so, Jake." Fervently, Mandy hoped they could remain friends, if nothing else.

Jake didn't answer her right away. Mandy felt anxiety flash through her at his hesitation. "I'll bet your friends were glad to see you back to your old self," he said finally, his gaze intent on her face.

Mandy drew herself up. "Well, not quite my old self, but a close second. It was kind of awkward at first. They tried not to stare at my leg."

"It's human to be curious. I bet you handled it just fine."

Mandy laughed with genuine amusement. "I surprised the heck out of them by rolling up my pant leg and letting them see my Star Wars technology." She had surprised herself. A month ago she couldn't have done that. "I believe I owe that in part to you, Jake."

He started to shake his head, but she touched his arm. "Yes," she insisted. "If you hadn't treated me so normally, I might still be ultrasensitive about letting anyone see it. I'll never forget that day I fell in the pool and you dried my prosthesis like it was nothing out of the ordinary. I think that's when I started to heal a little bit." Self-conscious after having admitted so much to him, Mandy turned to watch her friends, and couldn't help but smile. "In a minute somebody will find the pool," she murmured. "That always happens. They'll all be in it."

On more than one occasion she had led the pack to a

moonlit pool. Mandy stood up, for a moment coming heart-breakingly close to Jake, breathing in a touch of aftershave and the unique scent that was his.

"I guess I'd better move back over there in case of drowning." Her voice came out oddly breathless, but then Jake had that effect on her.

"I'll come with you."

Mandy intended to step away. Her feet didn't move. She reached out a hand and tentatively placed it on his chest. "I think I'm stuck," she said weakly, looking up at him. *Stuck on you, Jake Miller.*

"I've got the same problem. Maybe we should make the best of it and find a common solution," he said huskily. Jake's head dipped toward hers. His warm breath fanned her lips.

At five-eight, Mandy had never felt short in her life, but with Jake looming over her, she felt dainty in comparison.

His mouth pressed against hers, the contact electric, jolting through her entire body. It was just like she remembered, only more intense. The feeling concentrated in the pit of her stomach, then spread outward until the very tips of her fingers and toes tingled. Strange, but she swore she felt the sensation even in the toes she knew were missing.

Mandy drew a quivering breath. She needed to touch him. Her fingers crept up to his collar and into the back of his hair. Hungrily, she wound her arms around his back, felt each hard, contoured muscle. They were connected, breast-bone to thigh. It felt wonderful and so right. Jake was holding on to her as tightly as she wound herself around him. Mandy's breath came in short spurts. She missed being this close to Jake.

The sound of splashing water drove them apart. With a groan, Mandy rested her forehead against his. "Sounds like they found the pool."

"Yeah."

This time, reluctantly, they turned and moved out of the shadows toward her side of the house. Mandy walked slightly ahead. Trying to breathe normally, she stepped into the beam cast by the overhead halogen light.

Amy came running toward them, using her arm to wipe water from her face and neck. Her short black dress was plastered against her body; a high-heeled shoe dangled from each hand.

The face she lifted to Mandy held excitement. "There you are, Mandy!" she exclaimed. "Wow! What a great party. It's the first time I've ever gone swimming in a dress." Amy looked at her brother as he stepped into the light. "Uh-oh. Hello, Jake. I'd better get dried off. Mind if I run over to your place?" Without waiting for a reply, Amy ran on. "See you guys later," she called over her shoulder. "Thanks for the invite. I've never had so much fun."

The yells and squeals from the pool grew louder. To Mandy, it sounded as if someone were drowning. She rushed forward, her gaze skimming the heads in the pool to see if someone really was in trouble.

A flurry of activity drew Mandy's attention. She turned to see Jake discard his boots, whip his shirt off and dive into the water. Someone was in the deep end, arms flailing. Mandy hurried toward that end of the pool, grabbing a towel off a chair as Jake hauled a man to the edge.

Somewhat subdued, several others rushed forward to help pull him from the pool. He lay on his back with his eyes open. It was Marty, a young, promising bull rider. Sheepishly, he grinned at Mandy. "Sorry, I guess I had too much to drink."

"Are you all right?" she asked anxiously.

"Yeah." He coughed a few times, but kept nodding his head. "Yeah, I'm fine. Give me a minute."

"Well, I'm glad you're okay." She handed him the towel and quickly turned to walk over to where Jake sat on the pool's edge. She leaned down to peer into his face. "You okay, Jake?" she asked.

He looked up at her and pushed his hair back with both hands. Mandy tried not to stare at the water running in rivulets into his chest hair. Man, but this guy was sexy!

"A bit damp around the edges," he drawled.

Someone pushed a towel into her hand. She placed it on Jake's shoulders, her heartbeat beginning to slow. Everyone was fine. "Thanks," she told him.

Everyone had quieted. Even the CD music blaring in the living room had cut off.

Mandy straightened. All eyes seemed to be on her. And Jake. Clearing her throat, she felt an imp of mischief take over.

"Looks like somebody died," she commented to no one in particular. She sat down on the pool deck next to Jake and rolled her pant leg up. Quickly, efficiently, she proceeded to undo her prosthesis straps.

"Mandy, what are you doing?" Denny asked, clearly bewildered.

Minus her prosthesis, Mandy grabbed Denny's hand and pulled herself upright. She looked down at the young cowboy who had almost drowned. "Marty, I think it's a good idea if you stay right where you are. We don't want anyone drowning tonight."

Mandy looked around the patio and read the surprise on her friends' faces. They had stuck with her through the years, and they had all helped each other out when times got rough. "To the rest of you I'm throwing out a challenge. The last one in the pool is a one-eyed, one-armed, flying purple-people-eater..." With a screech of joy, Mandy hit the water first. She was never one to lag behind on any challenge.

Chapter Twelve

"I'd say your party was a success," Jake stated later that night. They sat in chairs on the back lawn. She rested her head on the back of the chair and stared at the fog now hovering in the air.

"I found out what I needed to know," she said softly. She felt incredibly relaxed.

"What is it you needed to know?"

"I needed to find out if I still fit in. Even though I'm not quite in touch with my life, my friends came through for me."

"Sometimes it takes time for life to fall into place. Your friends obviously care about you. That's not going to stop because your situation has changed."

"I knew that but I guess I didn't know it. I had to see it for myself."

"There's a long line of people who care about you, Mandy," he said quietly. "I still care about you."

Touched at the depth of feeling in his voice, Mandy jerked her head sideways, her gaze meeting his. "I think we'll both always care about each other, Jake. Too bad life isn't that simple." If it was, she would be in his arms now and never leave.

"It can be."

Mandy went very still. Surely Jake could hear her heartbeat. "There's been a lot of years and living since we were together."

"On both sides."

"There are things you don't know about me," she said warningly. "Times have been hard. I can't say I'm proud of all I've done, and I've managed to do some pretty dumb stuff. At this point in my life I still feel like I'm growing up."

"We all do things we regret. Hopefully, we learn from the mistakes and go on."

"That sounds pretty magnanimous." Mandy stood, then walked toward the house and the door to her apartment. She looked over her shoulder at Jake as he remained seated. "Would you like to come in?"

"Sure."

Mandy looked around the now empty apartment. Beer cans sat on the tables and counters; ashtrays needed to be emptied and washed. Popcorn littered the area rug in the middle of the room.

"How about I help you clean up while you tell me about it?" Jake offered.

"No, that's okay. Tomorrow the maid comes in," she quipped lightly, then she grimaced. "Find a seat." She waved a hand around the room, then walked back to the sliding glass door and opened it. Some fresh air would disperse the stale smoke in the room, and she needed a moment to figure out how to tell him what she wanted him to know.

Perhaps sensing her hesitation, Jake said, "If you're not

sure about this, maybe it's better if you don't tell me. Contrary to popular belief, confession isn't always better for the soul.''

Mandy sat down next to Jake on the couch, leaving a couple of feet between them. He sat forward, his hands between his knees. Mandy wanted to sit closer and curl herself against him, but knew the truth had to be told. Jake had to know the woman she had become, the woman she was still trying to define.

"There's no easy or pretty way to say this. I always liked to party and have fun, but a few years back I lost control." Mandy pushed herself deeper into her corner of the couch. "I went overboard. For about six months, I didn't know where I was half the time after six o'clock." She looked sideways at Jake, a grimace of disgust flashing across her face.

"I got into a real partying habit, and I'm not even sure why. I had broken my ankle, and of course I couldn't ride in the finals. That year had been my best yet." She shook her head. "I'd been so sure I'd be in the top ten, but I had to pull out. If I hadn't had a couple bad rides toward the end of the season I might have been able to pull off the last few rodeos. But I was in a streak where I couldn't seem to win. I began to get desperate.

"When I was a kid that's all Daddy talked about—about how I could win big, and that I was the best darned rider he'd ever seen."

"His wild child."

Mandy smiled slowly. "He always called me that. I guess I got that idea stuck in my head, and I've been trying to make the grade ever since. When I didn't, I couldn't handle it.

"I'd been seeing this bronc rider on and off, but it was nothing really serious. He had a bad rep. He'd been in and out of jail." She shrugged. "I just thought I was above it all, you know—too smart to get caught in a bad situation. I flirted with danger.''

Mandy drew a deep breath and continued. "One night he found me in a little bar, a regular hangout. I was drunk, dancing on the tables, ankle cast and all. I didn't care. Nothing mattered. I thought I was having a good time.

"When this guy came in I kind of fell into his arms…maybe I pushed myself into his arms, I don't know. He was putting me into his truck when, luckily, my friends Lynn and Denny showed up. I had passed out by then. They managed to get me out of there. The next morning I had an unbelievable hangover…I wanted to die. Lynn told me what had happened. It really scared me, especially since I didn't remember any of it. Anything could have happened that night if my friends hadn't come along. About a year later this same guy was arrested for murdering a hitchhiker he picked up.'' Mandy felt a shiver as the memory crept over her. "I was lucky. I also wised up. Eventually luck runs out.''

Mandy looked at Jake, wanting him to say something, anything, even call her a fool. She saw the movement of his jaw, but he didn't speak.

"I stayed away from that guy, but I did see him at rodeos after that. On one occasion he called me everything he could lay his tongue to. I'd never lost control to that point. I was terrified by the total memory lapse. I felt I had hit the bottom. I decided I didn't want to be there ever again.''

Mandy swallowed hard. This was the hardest part. "I had to face up to my life. Mama just about ran over me with a steamroller, and when Daddy got wind of my partying, he threatened to beat me black-and-blue if I didn't get my life in order. By that time I had already realized I couldn't go on the way I was.'' Mandy gave Jake a straight look. "I'd be in a pine box before I hit thirty.''

She looked down, pressing her fingers together, distressed

when she saw Jake's mouth was a grim, white line. "I suppose you're disgusted with me for being dumb enough to allow my life to get out of control."

She couldn't imagine him letting his life get to such a point. He was always in control, taking care of every aspect of his life and his family's problems with precision and honor. Amy was a fountain of information regarding Jake's support of his family through the years.

Taking a deep breath, Mandy met his blue eyes. "I'd never deliberately hurt anyone, Jake, but I've got a pretty wild reputation, some of it deserved."

Jake let out a deep breath, then leaned forward and gently touched her hair, letting his hand slide down behind her ear. "I know about you. It doesn't matter what they say in the papers."

Mandy sat up straight. "Really?"

"I've read about you through the years, Mandy. You're not telling me anything I haven't already heard."

"Jake, I have to know why you were at the rodeo that night."

He looked at her warily before answering. "I came across a picture of you in some boxes I was packing away. It was like an omen or something. Amy had moved out, my mom was settled with my sister, I was alone for the first time in ten years and I come across your picture." Jake drew a deep breath, and Mandy felt her own breath squeeze from her chest. She was afraid of what he would say next. She clasped her hands together tightly. "I was packing away some old things, and your picture was right there, staring up at me. It was like the years rolled back."

"My picture?"

"You were on Pongo, your legs hanging down past the stirrups. I guess the photographer caught you by surprise. You were turned in the saddle and I could almost see the startled expression on your face. I felt all the old anger well up inside. The anger and a ghost of the old feelings.''

Mandy felt pain lance through her. ''Old feelings.'' In the past. Not something he felt anymore.

''I put the picture on my desk. I saw it every time I went into my office for about a week. I knew you would be rodeoing that weekend, since it was one of the big rodeos that count toward the finals. I decided I had to come and see you. It was time to put the past to rest. I figured I had to see you again to do that. Then it would be over.''

''I don't recall that picture.'' Mandy shook her head, not wanting to understand what he was saying. Dread pooled in her stomach. She ached with it. ''So, you really came to say goodbye?'' She didn't want to hear this, but she had to know all of it, no matter how hurtful.

''Yes. I came to the rodeo to see you, to say goodbye. I don't know that I actually intended to talk to you. I just knew I needed some kind of ending. I wanted closure on this anger that I'd hidden for so long. My life had gone on, but the emotional aspects seem to have stalled that night ten years ago.''

''Jake...'' Mandy couldn't express in words the pain she felt in him.

''Then you had your accident.''

''And you were there. Why did you come that night and not before?''

Jake looked away, but finally he said, ''You were always on the go, one rodeo after another. I stayed away deliberately. Why would I pursue you when you'd walked away?'' There was a glint in his eye. ''You made it plain that last night that you wanted out. You wanted rodeo.''

Mandy swallowed hard. ''It seemed the best solution at the time. I—I was frightened. Everything seemed to be happening all at once.'' She tipped her head back. ''God, I was so young!''

"You walked away at the worst time, when things were so bad."

"It was the best solution." Mandy felt as if she was still trying to convince him, and maybe convince herself.

"For you, Mandy. You wanted the rodeo more than you wanted us."

She felt the hurt of years ago come to the surface. She felt his pain and remembered her own numbing agony. "Neither one of us walked away unscathed." Defiantly, she added, "I did what I thought was right, Jake. I've always loved the rodeo, you knew that. You had so much responsibility. At seventeen, you don't always see the whole picture. We'd talked of spending forever together. When you spoke about going to the courthouse for a marriage license, it was suddenly more than talk, it was real. With rodeo, I knew what to expect. Marriage..." She let her voice trail off. "All I knew of marriage was the mess of my parents' life."

"So you chose the rodeo instead."

"I've always had that, always knew it would be there. I don't know what else I'd do if it wasn't there. It was something I could do."

"You didn't give us a chance."

Mandy felt her shoulders slump. "At the time, I thought I was giving us the only possible chance. It didn't work that way."

"No, it didn't." His face looked hard, and he'd put up that wall again. She would never scale it.

"I have made mistakes," she admitted. "But if I had stuck around, who knows we wouldn't be divorced by now? After my parents' failure at marriage, I was scared as hell."

"You're a strong woman, Mandy. If you set your mind to something, you'll succeed."

"I don't feel strong."

"You've carved your own niche in this world. You'll do it again."

Mandy felt shaky and uncertain as she stared at Jake, studying his dependable face, the hard set of his shoulders. She wanted to scoot over to where he sat, but stayed still. "I didn't mean to hurt you all those years ago, but I know I did. I hurt, too. I had to tell you this so you'd understand about me." She curled her fingers tightly, holding herself stiffly as Jake moved closer.

"Anybody can change if they want to," he said in a low voice. "I recall liking you back then as you were."

Mandy leaned toward him, letting his voice sink to the very marrow of her bones. "Not always," she whispered, doubt gnawing at her. With a heavy frown, she shook the hair back from her face. "Jake, I know about choices, some right, some wrong. I won't hurt a family the way my dad did. He was never there when it counted. He missed so much." She sighed. "My life's already been set in stone, and I carved it. I'm my father's daughter through and through. I'm afraid we'll hurt each other again."

Jake lifted his hand and gently cupped her throat. "You're not your father. If we go into this with our eyes open, no one has to get hurt."

Mandy swallowed hard, wetting her lips with her tongue. Was that true? Could they both walk away without getting injured? "I—I don't know, Jake. I don't want to be hurt. I don't want to hurt you."

"I'm a grown man, Mandy. Let me worry about it. With that said, right now I need to touch you." Gently, he traced her mouth with his. "Can I touch you?"

Mandy nodded her head slowly, mesmerized by the desire she saw in his face, the narrowing of his eyes. Jake's touch sent tremors of sensation straight to her inner core. It caught her off guard, starting that impossible yearning again. How she wanted Jake! Some things never changed. Right now everything felt hazy, her body charged by his touch, his scent in her nostrils.

"We're not rushing into anything," Jake murmured. "When we make love, it'll be the right time, the right thing to do."

"Oh, God." Mandy opened her lips, wrapped her arms tightly around Jake's hard body. His talk about making love did strange things to her. She leaned into him, willingly overcome by emotion and feeling, her fingers gripping his arms. She wanted Jake. He made her burn, made her want to let go of the past, the fear of not measuring up. Right now past mistakes faded into dust.

Jake felt the urgent press of Mandy's slim body against his. Dropping his hands to the small of her back, he traced his palms over the slight curve of her hips, felt the bones beneath the soft, responsive flesh. He drew her quivering reaction into himself, felt his own body tremble. He'd wanted her desperately, but he had to go slow and make sure it was right for both of them. He didn't want any doubts clouding this moment. They had both come so far.

Jake groaned. How much longer could he hold off? He wanted her so badly every muscle of his body was tensed and there was a roaring in his ears. He lowered her to the couch cushions, his body covering hers. Mandy's leg came up, curved around the back of his, her body tight against him. She gave him everything she had, all the intensity of emotion stored inside. Jake felt as if he were in a twister, emotion pulling at him, trying to rip him apart. The past tried to hold him in its grip, but he pushed that aside. All he thought of now was this moment with this woman. A woman he had lost once, but now held in his arms. They had each other, for however long it lasted.

Trying to slow down, Jake held her face with cupped palms, kissed her deeply, the fragrance of her skin winding round him. He slid the blouse from her shoulders, let his mouth plunder soft skin, run lovingly over the hollows revealed. She felt so good! He wanted to explore each sensation, each part of her body. Mandy tried to be tough, but Jake felt the trembling in her limbs. He sensed the vulnerable core inside her. He wanted to find it, touch it, hold it.

Mandy moaned as if she liked the feel of his mouth on her soft breasts. Jake traced his tongue over her flesh, following the delicate veins under the skin of her throat. Her fingers pulled at the hair on his chest. She splayed her fingers and touched his nipples. Jake dropped his full weight on her, and her hips thrust against him.

It seemed to Jake they played a dance without music. Words, too, were unnecessary.

"I want you with me, Jake."

Mandy's whispered words smashed his last bit of self-control. He abandoned the idea of going slow, and pulled his shirt over his head, then slanted his mouth over Mandy's soft lips. He kicked his boots off, yanked his jeans down, saw Mandy fumbling to do the same with hers. When her fingers couldn't pull open her jeans snap, he gently pushed her hands aside. Slowly, driving himself closer to the edge, he watched the button come through the slit, then slowly, tooth by tooth, he lowered the zipper on her jeans. It was torture—pure, wonderful, slow torture.

"Jake." Mandy gripped his hands tightly, then pressed them to her flesh. "Don't torment me."

He watched the deep intensity on her face, and for a moment, he thought he saw fear. He felt uncertainty touch him. Was he doing the right thing, letting Mandy into his life? What if she left again? *Not what if,* Jake reminded himself, *when she left.*

He didn't want to doubt that what they were doing was right, not when he felt so involved, so connected to this woman. Mandy arched up against him as Jake splayed his

fingers across her belly. He dropped his mouth to the sligh
hollow of her stomach, kissing a path across the smooth
skin.

Mandy writhed beneath him. He soothed her with kisses
his mouth on her skin as he knelt above her, drawing ai
into his lungs, trying to catch his breath. Her blue eyes
clouded with passion, told him what she wanted, and he
knew it was what he wanted, too. It seemed like they had
waited too long already.

"Slow," Jake said hoarsely, hardly recognizing his own
voice. "Go slow. I love your skin, so soft, so soft...."
Sweat beaded his brow. It took a tremendous effort to go
easy, not to engulf her. Jake's hands shook, and he felt like
this was his first time. He almost wished it was. He was
struck with wonder and reverence for this woman. So
fiercely independent, so dependent on him now...

He let his hand slide down her thigh, gently traced sca
tissue, then smooth muscle, feeling the goose bumps rise a
his touch. He gently traced the straps. Mandy's trembling
hand covered his, but she didn't stop him. She seemed to
grow still, waiting for his next move, her body suddenly
transmitting fear.

Jake held himself quiet, knew in the next few second
there would be no going back. He felt the weight of the
responsibility he had undertaken. Mandy's scarred flesh was
there for him to see. Gently, he traced the slightly pinkish
skin, drew her quivering response into himself.

He didn't want to hurt Mandy.

He feared he would.

Slowly, carefully, knowing she watched him, Jake undid
the straps. Giving both of them time, he removed the arti
ficial limb and rolled down the socks.

Mandy watched Jake look at her stump. This was what
she had wanted, to be loved and touched by Jake, but now

she waited, almost afraid to breathe. Would he be repulsed, distressed? Could she bear it if he got up and walked away? So many questions crowded her mind. The vulnerability she felt terrified her, and she wasn't someone who ran scared. Never had she depended so much on another human being's thoughts and reactions. Mandy prayed that if Jake walked away, she could handle it. She watched him, biting her lips anxiously, emotion tight in her chest, as if something vital hinged on his reaction.

As if he sensed her fears, Jake lifted his eyes to hers. "It's okay," he said in a low voice, perhaps guessing at the tumult twisting her insides. "It's okay, Mandy."

Some of the coldness receded. Mandy felt heat return to her cheeks, her face. A shudder passed through her, chasing some of the tension away. Gathering her courage, she decided he might as well see everything. She needed to know Jake's reaction to this most vulnerable part of her body. It took precedence over everything else at the moment, even the heat of their lovemaking. She wanted to be emotionally connected to Jake, not just physically. He had seen her leg before, but now they were so much more intimate, his reaction was so much more vital to her.

Jake's gaze left hers and he looked at her leg. Gently, he traced his fingers over the sensitive flesh. Mandy drew in a quivering breath, her knee jerking involuntarily. She was surprised by the sensitivity of her skin to his touch. The limb near the incision had always felt vaguely numb of feeling.

Solemnly, Jake said, "You're a strong, beautiful woman, Mandy. This only makes you more so."

Mandy felt the tears come to her eyes. How had Jake found the right words to say? He made her feel special, strong and loved. She tipped her head back, closing her eyes as Jake ran his mouth over one thigh, then the other. Heat began to rise again. Mandy ignored the wetness that burned under her lids as she pulled Jake's mouth to hers. How had she gotten so lucky, finding Jake again? She'd be crazy to let him get away. Crazy! The tears gathered force and collected in her throat, but she swallowed them.

"Now, Jake. I want you now," she said, her voice deep throated, demanding. She wanted to give him all of herself. She was so full of emotion and want. Jake's tenderness had increased those feelings tenfold.

"I understand the want—my body's saying the same. But I don't have any protection—"

Mandy watched him pull away. She shook her head, feeling light-headed. "Don't leave."

"Damn! We can't—I won't take a chance."

"In—in my bathroom cabinet, there're some packets." She touched his shoulder with her lips. "I like to be prepared for any eventuality. I bought them last week." She'd bought them hoping Jake would make love to her. She had seen those packets every night when she brushed her teeth, and each time, regret sliced through her that they hadn't used them yet.

Jake grinned at her. "Last week, huh?" He dropped a quick kiss on her mouth and, with a fluid movement, lifted her up against his chest. Jake carried her into her bedroom, pushed the covers aside and lay her on the bed. He turned and walked across the room. Mandy put her head back on the cool pillow, watching him through heavy-lidded eyes. His body was big and well muscled. Soon, it would be hers. She shivered, rolling over to watch him as he walked back into the room, apparently undisturbed by his nudity. Mandy tried not to stare at the most interesting part of his anatomy, but she got caught. She felt the color flood into her cheeks.

With a big grin, Jake slid down beside her, the single mattress giving beneath his weight.

Wide-eyed, Mandy watched him toss all but one of the packets onto the bedside table. A slow grin lifted her lips as he tore open the foil. "Oh, my, all those?" she murmured.

"I'm optimistic," he said, leaning down to nuzzle her neck.

She forgot about the foil packets as she and Jake touched skin-to-skin once more. "Now, Jake."

Clenching his jaw, he thrust forward. Mandy stiffened slightly as pain streaked through her, and she felt Jake freeze.

Dropping his forehead to hers, Jake closed his eyes. "Mandy." He began to pull away.

She gripped his arm, her nails biting into the muscle. "No, Jake, don't. It's okay."

She drew a deep breath.

Jake felt it all the way to his toes. "You've never been with anyone. Damn, you told me that, but..." He hadn't really believed her.

Mandy put her mouth to his, silencing him, silencing his inner demons. Slowly, their lips met and played.

Jake held very still, but Mandy ruined that by arching up against him, her eyes closed, her lips parting in a sultry smile. "That feels good, Jake...so good."

He looked at her, at her flushed cheeks, her sultry eyes. Then he leaned down to kiss her brow, nuzzling her cheek. She was so giving, so warm. She continued to move and tantalize him. Jake gritted his teeth.

Mandy suddenly went still. She looked up, holding herself locked against him. "Did I hurt you?" she whispered.

Incredulous, Jake made himself focus on her face. "God, no. It just feels so—so fantastic."

Mandy began to smile. "Then don't stop. No thinking allowed," she murmured. Dropping back to the mattress, she lifted her arms to pull him down. Carefully, he moved forward until they were as close as possible, thigh to thigh.

Jake twisted his hips, feeling her body, and his, shaking with reaction—one so hard, the other yielding. An exquisite sensation began to rock him.

He closed his eyes, wanting to hold on to the feeling of having Mandy so close. They filled each other, emotionally, physically, fully, again and again.

Gradually, the ripples of desire receded, leaving Mandy quiet against Jake. They clung tightly to each other, and Jake pulled the sheet up over them, chilled by the night air on their sweat-dampened bodies.

Mandy turned her head to look at him, with wonder in her eyes. ''Wow,'' she said simply, then allowed a big smile to light her face.

Jake returned the look, putting up a hand to brush the hair back from her smooth forehead. ''I second that,'' he agreed, attempting to come to grips with what had just occurred. Making love had felt so right with Mandy, as if they were connected on all levels. Had she felt the same?

''Why, Mandy?'' Jake shook his head in bewilderment. ''I can't believe you've given me something so special, so precious....''

Mandy ducked her head as if to avoid his scrutiny. Jake frowned, placing a finger under her chin and urging her face upward. He had to understand what was going on inside her head. It seemed vitally important to know why she had remained a virgin.

''Mandy?''

She shrugged. ''Time and circumstances just never seemed right before, Jake.''

He swallowed hard, his mind reeling from the knowledge that he was the only man to know her intimately. ''You're a beautiful woman, Mandy. I just wish I could claim the same innocence.'' A sudden realization hit him in the face, and he felt his jaw go slack. He meant it. He wished, for that moment in time, that he could turn the clock back. Jake thought back to all the years full of responsibility. And yet he'd kept himself empty of this type of emotion. That strange feeling of emptiness had intensified when he saw Mandy again; beginning to grow from the time he'd found her picture. Had he suppressed his feelings all these years? Work, family, obligations…

A slight chill touched him. Mandy was recovering from her accident. He could see her confidence increase with each day. He'd helped her along the road to recovery, but soon she would move out. What did she truly feel for him? Jake wasn't sure what he felt for her. But the idea of caring for her again filled him with hope, and at the same time, despair.

He knew Mandy's reticence regarding commitment, knew her love of rodeo. She'd made no secret of her preference for a single lifestyle. She was still the same woman she'd been ten years ago.

"Maybe we should have gone slower, Mandy." He felt her stiffen beside him. The dreamy look hovering in her eyes changed, and Jake stifled a groan of impatience at his inability to accept things as they were.

"Let's not have a postmortem here, Jake. Why can't we just enjoy what we've found together again? It doesn't have to be anything more than that."

"You're right," he said, feeling the old anger wind around him.

Jake knew Mandy was an independent woman. A woman who had gotten along fine without a man in her life. She apparently hadn't felt the need to be in a relationship until now. Why had she chosen him as her lover?

"Jake?"

Hearing the uncertainty in Mandy's voice, he tightened his arm around her shoulders. "Are you okay?" he asked in a low voice, pushing aside his own concerns. They had both gone into this with eyes wide-open. Too late for regrets. What was done was done.

Lifting one brow, Mandy indicated the unopened foil packets on the side table. Giving him a brash smile, she snuggled closer into his chest.

Jake felt the heat rise. How could he ever think of pushing her away?

"I feel more than okay," Mandy said, voice sultry, one brow raised provocatively. "I'm resting up for the encore."

There was nothing else for Jake to do but pull her closer. How could he resist? He'd wanted her for what seemed too long. He'd never satiate himself in one night, but he could try.

Jake stayed the entire night with Mandy. They held each other close in the single bed. Early in the morning, before he left for work, Mandy stirred, wakened by fleeting kisses along her shoulder. She and Jake made love slowly, as if it were the first time all over again, only much better. She knew what to expect now. Jake was a generous lover. Just thinking about him made her shiver with aftershocks from their lovemaking.

Long after he left, Mandy couldn't stop thinking about him. Their time together had been like hot, molten fire. She'd never wanted to be so close to another man the way she yearned for Jake. He gave her something essential, filling that empty place inside her. Despite the pain of the years in between, the wait had been worth it. Never could Mandy have guessed they'd end up lovers after the misery of their parting a decade earlier. Had she subconsciously been waiting for Jake? Mandy shook her head. That was too crazy, but it also felt too close to the truth.

She hugged herself, pulling the soft sheets up under her chin. Jake was as clear as water; there were no ulterior motives to his caring. He didn't give two hoots about her career, the money she had made or the brief walk of fame she had enjoyed.

Mandy looked at her prosthesis, which was lying on the bedside table. Jake hadn't been repelled; he had removed it without flinching. Through his care and sensitivity, he had helped her restore a measure of wholeness, something she hadn't felt since the accident.

They hadn't discussed what had happened between them…what would happen in the future. Mandy wasn't prepared to talk about an involvement until she had had time to put some thought into this new phase of their relationship.

She experienced a certain queasiness when she thought about love and forever. Her unconventional upbringing got in the way. Mama had loved Daddy unconditionally, and had been hurt time and again, until Daddy finally left. Even as a child Mandy had understood that Daddy was involved with other women. What was to keep any man from going elsewhere? Jake cared about her, she knew. Maybe he loved her, even though he hadn't put it into words.

The thought of walking away from Jake was unbearable. Mandy Thomson, daring and audacious, knew she had to take this seriously. Love and relationships were topics she needed to do some real soul-searching about.

She and Jake could take it one day at a time, see how things developed. She didn't want to make the same mistakes again.

Chapter Thirteen

Mandy watched Jake skim the pool's surface with the nylon net. Lazily, she admired the smooth line of his bare back, the taut pull of his cutoff shorts against tanned, muscular legs. She hadn't seen him in a suit and tie in days. In fact, she hadn't seen much more on him than the shorts he wore now, and sometimes far less than that. He had stayed home from work almost the entire week. She was a bad influence on him, but he didn't seem to mind. They spent a lot of time beside the pool, and it felt like they had created their own world.

As Jake turned, Mandy's gaze snagged on the dark hair covering his chest and flat stomach, dreamily recalling its firm texture against her breasts and belly when they made love. Just thinking of making love with Jake caused Mandy's heart rate to increase.

She was minus her prosthesis, and amazingly, she felt more and more comfortable to be around Jake this way. He had seen her without it each night since that first time, almost a week ago, when they had made love. It had somehow managed to become less significant in her mind.

Feeling like a kid with her first crush, Mandy allowed her eyes to trace the smattering of freckles across Jake's shoulders. They had gone horseback riding last evening. It had been a companionable ride, and they had let the horses walk the entire time while they talked. When they returned to the barn near dusk, Jake had laughingly half pushed, half carried her up the narrow loft stairs. On a scratchy wool blanket they had made frenzied love near the open haymow door. Mandy knew the scent of fresh green hay would forever be imprinted on her mind when she thought of Jake.

Mandy couldn't ever remember feeling so happy or content, not even the summer she and Jake first fell in love. She knew her feelings for him had much more depth now than they had then. She recognized the difference in her own maturity, but if she allowed herself to dwell on the past, she began to feel anxious. They had a good thing going, a wonderful wholeness together, and she didn't want to mess it up. Mandy stared hard at Jake. She knew her time here was growing short. When would it end?

Jake slowly turned his head, a quick smile lifting his mouth when he saw Mandy watching him. She had a serious expression on her face, but he recognized the hint of desire curving her lips. His body reacted instantly to her interest. Mandy was dynamite in his arms, displaying the same gusto she brought to every aspect of her life. He'd never met anyone with such a passion for living.

"Thirsty?" Mandy asked him now, holding up a glass of iced tea. Jake saw the slight flush of color in her cheeks and lifted a brow, certain where her thoughts lay. Mandy was a sensual woman, although she surprised him by her reticence during the times they weren't making love. Memories of the last week they had spent together rumbled through Jake. He didn't want it to end. He wanted to ride this out indefinitely. Right now it was a glorious time for both of them.

"Sure, what have you got?" he asked lightly.

"I've got a variety of selections," she retorted with a saucy, daredevil grin, running a fingertip down the droplets coating the glass. "You get to pick your favorite."

"I don't play favorites," he told her, deliberately dropping his voice.

This last week in each other's company had amazed Jake. There had been no disagreements, no discord; things had flowed smoothly. Especially their physical relationship.

Jake dropped a kiss on her shoulder. Mandy's lightly tanned skin felt warm under his lips, and he breathed in deeply. He didn't recall ever noticing a woman's particular scent before, but Mandy's wound around him, pulling him in closer. A hint of lemon, a tantalizing suggestion of spices, the scent he associated with Mandy alone... Jake reached for the glass she held out to him, deliberately putting his fingers over hers. Dropping beside her on the deck, still holding her fingers captive, Jake tilted his head back. The tea felt icy going down his parched throat.

Slowly, he rotated the glass toward himself, pressing it and Mandy's captured fingers against his chest. He watched her lazily, fascinated by the way the blue of her eyes appeared to deepen. He heard the small sound she made in her throat, and he lifted a brow.

"Want me to put some lotion on you, Mandy? It looks like you're getting burned."

"Burned?" she murmured, her voice a caress, as was the gaze that ran over him like quicksilver. "If you like." Mandy lifted her hair off her shoulders. "I don't usually burn."

"We're not taking any chances."

Jake unscrewed the cap and poured cool lotion on the

light gold of her skin, watching her shiver. Slowly, he spread it over her shoulders, then lower, over her back. Looking at the soft vulnerability of her exposed neck, he placed a chaste kiss there. Her quiet sigh came to him as he gathered the warm weight of her hair into his hands and moved his lips along the side of her neck and up her jaw. Jake wondered again how long this could last—this accord he felt with Mandy, this close harmony.

"Mandy?"

"Hmm?"

"Have you ever thought about what you'd do if you didn't return to the rodeo?"

Jake felt an immediate tensing in the muscles beneath his lips, but she didn't answer.

"Have you, Mandy?" he insisted. It was something they hadn't talked about. Jake knew he might be starting a fire here, but it couldn't be ignored. He had to know if she had considered the possibility she might never return to her former life.

Mandy twisted in the chair, her eyes dark and unhappy. The sultry look had vanished from her face. Drawing a deep breath, Jake acknowledged that he had to finish what he had started. He pulled back and stared at her until she moved uncomfortably in her seat.

"Let's not fight," she entreated, running a hand up his arm, lightly brushing the hair until Jake put out his hand and grabbed her fingers.

"We're not fighting," he told her firmly. "I asked you a simple question. It can be answered with a yes or a no."

"We'll fight if we talk about this," Mandy said, suddenly impatient. She slipped her fingers from his. "There is no simple answer. You know rodeo is my life, Jake. Nothing has changed. I never tried to make you think other than that. It will never go away."

Jake bit back a mutter of disgust. He ignored the niggling

sense of disappointment. What had he expected—a decla-
ration of love from her? "I don't expect you to change,
Mandy. All I'm saying is you should consider the possibility
that rodeo might, at some point, not be an option."

"Rodeo will always be there, so get used to it. I'm not
giving it up just because—just because we're having sex."

Put like that, in such bald terms, their relationship
sounded much less than Jake considered it. He felt something bleak and cold curl around him. Was she using him,
filling in the time until she left? Was this a replay of ten
years ago? He hardened his heart. It didn't matter. They had
both entered this relationship knowing it had to end.

"Good sex," he said bluntly, his tone sarcastic.

Mandy touched his hand immediately, her face apolo-
getic. "Jake, I didn't mean that the way it sounded. I say
stupid things when I get scared. You know how it is with
me. It's not just sex."

Jake stood up. "I think you meant it, Mandy. It's been
fun and convenient for us, but when you're ready to move
on, you'll go without a backward glance. This brief interlude
is just another rodeo stop. Hell, it's what we agreed on,
going in, more or less." He didn't know why he felt so
mad, but he did.

"That's right, Jake. We've always known how it would
end. We always said my stay here was temporary." Mandy
looked away from him, her shoulders hunched.

He felt like he was losing her again. "At least we know
where we stand." He knew with certainty where he stood.
He wanted Mandy longer than she was planning on staying,
but it wouldn't matter. He *knew* that.

Mandy suddenly leaned close and encircled his neck with
her arms, pressing against him. Jake stared into her eyes, so
close to his.

"Let's not talk about it, Jake. It's not important now,"
she whispered entreatingly. "Let's be grateful for any time

we do have. This last week has been fabulous. I've never felt like this about anyone. It's almost like I'm seventeen again.''

"God forbid," Jake said, uttering a small laugh. He felt his body's immediate response to Mandy. It was always like that. He wanted to forget about the words they had exchanged, but knew they would remain there between them. "We'll take what we have for now." Stiffly, he opened his hand on the warm flesh of her waist, moved it down the rounded contours of her bottom. The smoothness of her skin beneath the pads of his fingers made him want to devour her. Desire rode him hard. Jake didn't stop what was happening. He would lose himself in Mandy, but only temporarily. He would deal with the hurt later. It was easier to do when she wasn't near him. They would use each other until they were all used up.

Mandy slid into his arms fully as he bent his knees to keep his balance. Jake's breath whooshed from his body as the sun-heated skin of their bellies touched and burned.

He heard the lotion bottle drop to the ground, but by then his arms were fully around her and he was lifting her back onto the lounge cushions.

Jake slid the thin straps of Mandy's top down, deliberately trapping her arms in the material, dropping his mouth to her breasts as she arched upward with a soft sound. He moved to capture her lips, breathing in the soft, breathy sounds she made. Undoing the tie at her back, he tossed the bathing suit top aside.

He knew her body by heart, yet he still wanted more. He hadn't tired of her yet, even though they'd been together every day for a week. He peeled the skimpy bottom of her swimsuit down her hips and felt her trembling hands doing the same for his cutoffs. Her hands on his body started him shaking, skittering close to the edge. She had learned how and where to touch him to make him lose control. He had no defenses against Mandy when they made love. She was as untamed as the rodeo horses she vowed to ride once more.

The air around the pool remained hot, almost airless. Jake welcomed the slide of Mandy's skin across his. He wanted to give in to his own urgency, but he took his time, as if they had nothing but time. Behind Mandy, Jake saw the sun reflecting off the water, blinding him.

Mandy squeezed her eyes tightly shut. Making love with Jake was always different, always exciting. Sometimes a whirlwind, other moments agonizingly slow. Mandy felt as if she couldn't get enough of him, which in saner moments scared her. She held a secret fear that this man would change her life forever, whether she wanted it or not.

She couldn't think about the future, when they would once again be strangers. She knew if they talked about it, their remaining time of joy and discovery would come to an abrupt end. She wanted it to go on, wanted to be with Jake, be loved by him. Wanted to enjoy the physical aspects of their relationship. She couldn't think past that right now. If she did, the old fears would rise to the surface.

Mama had loved Daddy so much, and he'd left. Mandy knew what the loss of love felt like. She had seen it her entire life and lived it. She couldn't bear to leave Jake again, but knew she would. Jake would tire of her, put the past behind them once and for all. She couldn't stay when that happened.

Mandy stifled the sob that rose to her throat. She kissed Jake desperately instead, emotion a raw ache in her chest. Their lovemaking felt different yet again, their coming together urgent and necessary. A strange intensity clutched at Mandy as Jake filled her, and tears clung to her lashes. She dashed them away, gripping him around the waist and letting him take her up and up, and then slowly down, leaving them both breathless, satiated for the moment.

When their heartbeats slowed, and the sounds around them once more intruded, Jake shifted to give her more room on the lounge chair. Cupping her face with his big palms, he gently pushed damp tendrils from her face. Now Jake was tender with her, and it was what Mandy wanted. Despite her independence, and her determination to keep her heart locked away from him, she craved these moments of tenderness. She needed to store them up.

Watching his face, Mandy experienced a fleeting moment of anxiety. How long could this last, these wonderful, idyllic moments where they filled each other and the world seemed to revolve around them? Jake's earlier question about the rodeo showed that reality was already intruding. Mandy knew she couldn't bury her head in the sand any longer.

"Jake, we have to think about what's going on here." The words spilled from her, despite her intention to keep quiet. "I mean—what's really going on."

"We ignite," he murmured, his gaze deep and probing. "We knew it would be like this."

"Yes, I guess we did," she admitted. "We'll ignite until we burn ourselves out." And then she would leave, because she wouldn't be able to bear the indifference on Jake's face. The way she felt right now, she couldn't bear for their feelings to burn out.

Jake's eyes were more gray than blue right now. "I know we've avoided serious conversation all week, but I never stopped caring."

She looked away, licking her lips, frowning down at her hands. "I care about you, too, Jake. But sometimes—"

He put a finger to her lips, not letting her finish. "Let's not get ahead of ourselves."

Mandy bit the inside of her cheek, then nodded. "Maybe

you're right. There's no sense worrying the situation to death.''

"If things are moving too fast for you, Mandy, say the word and we'll slow the pace.''

"Is that what you want, Jake? To slow this down?'' Mandy paused uncertainly, then blurted, "Or are you like me? I want to ride as fast and hard as we can, crazy as that may be, and see where it takes us.''

He stood up, and she immediately missed the contact. She watched him reach for his shorts and pull them on. As her body responded again to the sight of him, she hurriedly picked up her own bathing suit pieces and donned them.

Jake's gaze was steady. "It's not my usual style, rushing along at breakneck speed. But with you, Mandy, that's exactly what I want to do—ride fast, hang on and damn the consequences.''

Mandy slung her towel over her shoulder. Despite her earlier misgivings, she said, "Then we have nothing to argue about. Our relationship is perfect.'' Standing, she reached for her crutches. Jake handed them to her and gripped one of her hands.

"How about we ride into Oklahoma City? The gallery is seriously considering my exhibit under the umbrella of their grant. We could go there and I'll show you the place. The architecture is great.''

Mandy threw her arms around his neck. "Jake, I knew they would love your carvings. I am so happy for you.''

His arm came around her and held her close to his side. "I owe you for this, Mandy,'' he stated.

"You would have found out about it. I just got you there quicker.''

"There's also a carnival going on all weekend. Maybe you'd like to stop there, too?''

"That sounds like fun,'' Mandy exclaimed, glad to drop the serious side of the conversation. She watched a lock of dark hair slide down over his brow. Balancing her crutches in one hand, she carefully wound her fingers through the silky strands. "I've always felt comfortable in a carnival atmosphere."

"I remember how you liked to go on all the crazy rides," he said with feigned resignation.

She lifted a brow, knowing they were on safer ground. "I still love those rides, Jake. You've got yourself a date."

Mandy drove into town early the next morning for her doctor's appointment. She arrived early, only to discover the doctor was out on an emergency.

Jake had offered to drive her to the appointment but she knew she needed time to think about this past week with him. Mandy felt like she was walking a couple inches off the ground. It was a new feeling for her, one she was careful about exploring. Having a man look out for her made her feel special...cherished. She felt kind of strange, associating those words with herself. Surprisingly, the old fears about relationships were calm today. She and Jake could take all the time they needed to find out about each other. Despite her usual style of jumping in feetfirst, she was treading carefully.

Mandy shifted in her seat in the waiting room, staring at the kaleidoscope of colors reflected on the pale walls. Crystals hung in every window of the office, throwing light in all directions.

"When it's late in the afternoon, I sit over here and the rainbow colors are all over my arms," a child's voice said.

Mandy turned her gaze toward a young girl, the only other occupant of the waiting room. The child sat in a wheelchair.

"Do you come here often?" Mandy asked, trying not to stare at the child's thin arms and tiny, misshapen legs.

The little girl, about ten, nodded her head, causing her

two red plaits to bob on her shoulders. "Just about every week."

"I love the bright colors," Mandy said with a smile.

"My mom's going to put some in my hospital room."

"It'll be nice to see those rainbows on the walls." Mandy wondered why this child would be talking about a hospital room. She had a mischievous light in her green eyes, but looked very frail.

"I'm Emily. I know who you are. You're Mandy Thomson."

"You know me?" Mandy asked in surprise.

"I love rodeos. My mom takes me when there's one close by. I think you're the best I've ever seen."

Mandy felt touched. "Thank you. That's nice of you to say so."

"I wasn't there the day you got hurt, Mandy, but it was on the news. I'm glad you're okay."

Mandy expelled a slow breath. "I'm kind of taking a vacation right now."

Emily nodded, her eyes direct. "You're rehabilitating," she said matter-of-factly. "I'm going to have two new legs, you know. Then I'll be able to walk. Maybe even horseback ride," she added wistfully. "I hope I can walk as good as you after my operation."

Mandy felt touched straight to her heart.

Leaning closer, Emily lowered her voice. "Mommy's real worried, but it's kind of exciting, you know, thinking I'll be able to walk. I'm always in this dumb wheelchair on account of my legs are all twisted. The blood supply is bad, so they have to operate."

Gently, Mandy lifted Emily's thin fingers. "You tell your mom to let me know when you have your operation, Emily. I'll come see you."

"Would you really?" A grin split Emily's face and her

freckles stood out on her small nose. "My friends will never believe it."

Mandy walked over to the reception area and wrote down her name and phone number on a piece of paper.

"Ms. Thomson," the nurse behind the counter said, "the doctor will see you now."

"Okay." Mandy gave Emily the paper. "I want you to give this to your mom."

"Thank you, Mandy."

"Good luck, Emily. I'll be seeing you."

As Mandy followed the nurse down the hallway, she thought about how brave Emily was, and recalled her own anger and subsequent depression over losing a leg. Emily had never known anything but a wheelchair. She hadn't been able to ride every day, as Mandy had taken for granted at that same age. Faced with an amputation of both legs, Emily was looking forward to getting her prostheses and learning to walk on new legs.

Talking to her made Mandy feel as if she had wallowed in self-pity. She had never been as strong as that little girl. It gave Mandy an entirely different perspective on her own situation. She began to realize how selfish she had been, how centered on herself and her own wants. She wondered if she were capable of making a difference in someone else's life. Maybe some changes were in order.

"I'm riding again," Mandy told Dr. Winans after he'd examined her leg and watched her walk through her strengthening exercises.

"You're making good progress, Mandy, but I still want you to be careful not to overdo it," the doctor cautioned. He looked up from her file, his deep brown eyes studying her. Mandy liked him. She had liked him from the first moment she had met him in the hospital. He was young, and seemed very interested in her progress.

Mandy lifted a paperweight of heavy crystal and turned

it this way and that. "What's to be careful about? I'm doing
what I set out to do. I've opened the door to living."

"Which is all well and good, but I have to wonder if
you're trying to prove you're better than all the two-legged
people out there?"

Mandy jerked her head up to stare at him, then carefully
put down the paperweight. "You sound like you're telling
me to give up or something." She couldn't help the anger
that rose. His words put her on the defensive.

The doctor shook his head. "No, not at all. I'm glad
you're doing so well. Believe me, a lot of amputees don't
adapt as quickly as you seem to be doing. Some struggle
all their lives. I'm merely saying take it easy. If you overdo
it, you're going to end up with blisters and soreness, then
you'll be back on crutches or in the chair."

"Of course I know that. I'm careful, but I'm not stopping
for anything."

"I guess I ought to know you by now, Mandy. You're
like a steamroller when you decide on a course of action.
But think about what I've said."

As Mandy prepared to leave the office, the doctor waylaid
her. "There's one other thing I'd like you to consider. I try
to get active amputees like yourself interested in talking to
new patients. Would you be willing to do that?"

Something inside Mandy stiffened, and she began to
shake her head.

"Do you remember Doris, the girl who came to see you?
How did you feel after she spoke to you?"

"Yeah, I recall Doris." Mandy wrinkled her brow. "I
was depressed when she came to see me." She didn't like
thinking about that early time in the hospital. Mandy had
thought her life was over. Slowly, she admitted, "Near the
end of our meeting, Doris said something that really hit
home. She told me I could work hard and resume a normal
life, or sit and stare at the walls. Since I'm not yet thirty,

that might be quite a long time staring at walls. At that moment, a pinhole of light pierced the darkness.''

"Wouldn't you say talking to someone who experienced amputation makes a big difference?"

Mandy gave the doctor a doubtful look. "You really think anything I say could make a difference?"

"I do. You've got a lot to offer, Mandy. I want you to think about it. Your determination would be an asset. Another thing I wanted to mention, since you're a horse person, is that you should check out the riding clinic in Riverdale."

"Riverdale? That's not far from where I'm living now." Mandy looked at the doctor doubtfully. "My riding is coming along. I'm doing pretty good on my own."

"I didn't mean for yourself. It's for disabled kids. Maybe you could donate your services. It's a nonprofit program, so there's not a lot of money."

"It's for kids with disabilities?"

"All types of disabilities. Riding is a great confidence builder, for kids and adults."

Mandy left the doctor's office with the riding clinic's address in her pocket. On the way home, just out of curiosity, she drove down the back road where the riding stable was located.

Parking her vehicle beside a small red barn, she walked around the back of the building, following the sound of voices to a small fenced paddock.

Two boys and a girl, each about ten years old, were riding horses in the enclosed area. Several adults watched from outside the arena as a tall woman wearing skintight riding breeches and leather boots gave instructions to the mounted children.

The children wore safety helmets. Three teenage girls on foot led a horse each, while another person walked beside each horse.

"Okay, now everyone bring your horse to a halt." The

instructor appeared to be in her early thirties, with dark hair tucked up under a wide-brimmed straw hat. Briefly, she glanced at Mandy, then back at her students. "Michael, pull gently on the reins and hold them steady. Very good. Everyone give your horse a pat for a job well done. Parents, you may come into the arena now. The girls will help each child dismount."

As the children began to dismount with their helpers, the instructor turned to Mandy, an inquiring lift to her brows. When Mandy looked at the woman fully she could see how striking she was. She had a creamy complexion, slim dark brows and a full, sensuous mouth.

"Hello, my name's Mandy." She held out her hand.

"I'm Samantha Evans, the manager here." The woman took her hand firmly, then gave a sigh. "Sorry, but if you're looking to get a child into this program, we can't handle any more."

"No, actually, Dr. Winans from Oklahoma City told me about this place. I thought I'd check it out." Mandy made a sudden decision. "He thought maybe I could help you out, Samantha."

"Call me Sam. So Dr. Winans sent you? Do you know anything about horses?" Sam asked immediately, her eyes lighting with interest.

Mandy smiled. "I grew up with them."

"Really? I'm liking you already. We can always use extra help. Right now, though, that's the least of our problems. It looks like the funding for this program is drying up, which means that will be the end of it. We'll know in a few weeks, maybe less. The outlook isn't good."

"Is there another program that can take these kids?"

Sam turned to wave as one boy and his parents left the arena. She shook her head. "No, not in this area. We're having trouble meeting the program expenses this year. The lease on this property is almost up and it doesn't look like it will be renewed.'' With a grimace, Sam threw Mandy a glance and asked jokingly, ''You look familiar…you're not somebody rich, are you?''

''Sorry, I can't claim that.''

''The loss of this program will be a blow, it's such good therapy for the kids. We've had to cut down on our class size, but at this point I'm happy for any extra help.''

''What does it cost to run an operation like this?''

''There're a lot of small costs that add up. The director could answer that question better than me. Why, do you know someone who could help?'' The note of hope in Sam's voice was all too clear to Mandy. She felt guilty shaking her head and dashing the other woman's optimism.

''I was just curious. It seems a shame to discontinue a worthwhile program.'' Mandy wasn't really sure why she had asked.

''Well, the biggest thing is the red tape involved. You have to follow certain guidelines if you want to be a certified instructor, and you have to keep up with the CPR training, your certification. It's getting tougher to find volunteers.'' Sam waved her arm to indicate the teenagers who'd been helping the children in the arena. ''Annie, Mira and Jen are about the only ones I can count on anymore to show up when I need them. I get a break on the riding insurance costs, but the program equipment that we use is in need of replacement, not to mention some of the horses are getting too old. We've got nine healthy horses, but with feed bills and routine veterinary and farrier visits, donated money doesn't go very far.''

''What about private donations?''

''Some trickle in, but we lack an administrator to get our name out there—that would involve another salary. We don't have the funds to hire someone to bring in the money.''

''It sounds like a vicious circle.''

"You hit the nail on the head. However," Sam said with a smile, "on a brighter note I'm determined to keep going until, and if, they close us down."

Mandy stared at the remaining children. The little girl, now in a wheelchair on a ramp beside her horse, was tenderly patting the animal's neck. Mandy swallowed hard, touched by the obvious happiness on the child's face. "I'd love to help. I don't live that far away, just the other side of High Flats."

"High Flats—I have a friend who lives there. Jake Miller. Do you know him?"

Mandy's throat felt dry. "Yeah, I know Jake. That's a funny coincidence. I rent half of his house."

Sam gave her an interested look. "What did you say your last name was?"

"I didn't, but it's Mandy Thomson."

Sam widened her eyes the slightest fraction, then slowly nodded in confirmation. "I thought I recognized you from somewhere. Am I pleased to meet you! Just about everyone around these parts has heard of you. I was sorry to hear about your accident. You must've had a rough time. It was a big waste when rodeo lost you."

"Well, it hasn't lost me yet. I plan to go back," Mandy said lightly. "Right now I'm looking for something to fill in the time while I recuperate. I think this might be just the thing, if you think we can work together."

Sam quickly said, "I don't think we'll have any problem working together. I appreciate anyone who's willing to donate time." She took off her hat and fanned her face and neck. "So tell me, how is Jake these days?"

"Fine. I'll tell him you asked about him. Have you known Jake long?"

"I've known him for years. I've hauled his horses a few times."

Mandy felt a hard lump in her throat. "You knew him when he played football?"

"I met him some time after he quit. It was terrible that he had to give it up. A lot of guys would have turned their back on the family responsibility and taken the scholarship, but not Jake."

Mandy hadn't known Jake had finally been offered the scholarship. She had left before that, and Jake hadn't mentioned it. Her heart ached for the young man Jake had been; she hurt for him and all he had lost. She knew she had added to his hurt. How could she ever make it up to him?

The admiration in Sam's voice made Mandy begin to wonder about a lot of things, like about a past relationship she might be stumbling onto. The thought of Jake with another woman speared through her, leaving a burning pain in its wake. It was only natural there would have been other women in the intervening years. Mandy knew she should probably leave it alone, but she couldn't.

"Maybe I'm being nosy but I'm going to ask, anyway. Jake and I are seeing each other, so before you and I work together I should probably know if you two have any past history."

Sam looked momentarily surprised by Mandy's forthrightness, then she laughed. "No, we weren't involved, but not for want of trying on my part. A few months ago Jake needed a horse trucked to the vet, and since I do horse hauling on the side, he called me. I hadn't seen him in a while and we got reacquainted, but I gained the impression he was seeing someone else." Sam gave her a wide grin. "It must have been you, Mandy. How did you hook up with Jake?"

"Oh, uh, he's a friend of my brother, and we knew each other as kids. Ben set it up so I could rent the apartment in Jake's house."

"That was a lucky break for you, Mandy, but anyway, Jake and I have never been more than friends."

Months ago Sam had thought Jake was involved with someone else. That would be right around the time Mandy had had her accident. With a frown, she wondered if Jake had been seeing someone else the night he came to the rodeo.

A nasty thought insinuated itself. What if she'd just appeared at a convenient time? Maybe she had caught Jake in between women. It was a terrible thought, but possibly true. Jake knew of her inexperience where men were concerned, but he hadn't disclosed any of his own personal history.

Mandy had made it clear she didn't want or need any commitment from Jake. Even so, she realized she had taken it for granted that Jake was heart whole and wanted an exclusive relationship with her, for as long as it lasted. Why hadn't she thought of that before?

Several cars pulled into the parking lot just then and dust rose in the air. Sam squinted through the whirling cloud. "My next students are here," she said. "If you want to stick around, I'll show you the ropes. I guess I won't need to check your credentials," she said with a quick laugh. "Your reputation can stand on its own. If you're serious about helping, you can start off leading one of the horses. I have a feeling this could work for both of us."

"I hope so. I'd like that," Mandy said. A feeling of excitement wound through her. For the first time in her life she felt as if there were many possibilities open to her. It was an empowering moment, and she couldn't exactly understand why, since she had always had the freedom to make her own choices. For the first time, she contemplated doing something for someone else, not for herself. Maybe that was the difference. It made her feel lighter inside.

Pushing back her shoulders, Mandy concentrated on

Sam's teaching style. Later, she helped saddle the horses, then watched the routine the children followed during each lesson. A new sense of purpose filled Mandy. These children needed this program, and maybe she needed them.

Chapter Fourteen

Several hours later Mandy drove up to the ranch and stopped her vehicle next to the deck ramp. A sense of excitement gripped her, and it hadn't abated since she had left the riding school. She had spent the entire afternoon there, much longer than she had at first anticipated. Right now she needed to share her news with Jake. Lifting her wrist, Mandy glanced at her watch. Jake should be home by now. It was well after six.

Without thinking twice about it, Mandy hurried toward Jake's side of the house. Gripping the brass knob, she swung the door open and burst into his living room, but she found it empty.

"Jake!" She didn't see him, but it didn't deter her from walking through the house. "Jake? Jake! Where are you? Wait until I tell you what's happened!" Mandy moved down the short corridor to his office. It was empty, but seeing the pile of boxes in one corner, Mandy was reminded of her earlier promise to find another place to live. Jake's renovation plans...that brought her up short. Jake's plans had not changed, had they? Those boxes were one more reminder that she lived here for a limited time.

Impatiently, she looked across the hall into the bedroom, but he wasn't there, either. Then she heard Jake call out her name.

Mandy walked toward the kitchen. "Jake, you'll never guess what I did today."

"Out on the back deck, Mandy."

Mandy rounded the corner of the kitchen and saw him standing at the sliding glass door that led out to the pool deck. "Hey, Jake!" With an exuberant lunge forward, she reached him and looped her arms around his neck. Standing on tiptoe, she planted a noisy kiss on his whisker-shadowed chin, then ran a string of kisses down his throat. He steadied her when she deliberately leaned her weight against him, her fingers pulling playfully at the buttons on his shirt.

"Ooh, you didn't shave today...didn't you go to work?" she asked with a laugh, noticing his worn jeans. Without waiting for a reply, she rushed on. "You'll never guess what I did. First of all Doc Winans gave me a clean bill of health, and then he told me about a program that teaches disabled kids to ride. Remember that idea you had about the same thing? Out of curiosity I drove out there...and one thing led to another. I'm going to help out...."

She suddenly realized he hadn't said a word, and his hands held hers still on his shirt. Mandy went motionless, then looked past his shoulder and noticed for the first time the man who stood on the patio. Hands on his hips, he tipped his cowboy hat back and watched her.

Freeing her fingers, Mandy dropped her arms to her sides almost guiltily. "Daddy!" she exclaimed, running her palms down the sides of her jeans. Unaccountably, she felt a flush mount her cheeks.

"Hello, Mandy girl," Lanny Thomson said quietly. His graying hair was brushed back as usual, but there seemed to be more lines in his face. He looked tired, and something about her father's voice alerted Mandy, something that she remembered as a child. She braced her shoulders, a strange foreboding filling her. Quickly, she banished the thought. This was her father. He cared about her and she loved him. He had never knowingly hurt her.

"I was in town for a spell so I thought I'd stop by to see my little girl." He watched her with a questioning look in his eyes.

Almost defiantly, Mandy placed her hand on Jake's shoulder, feeling the tensing of the muscles beneath his shirt. She glanced into his face, but his expression gave nothing away. She gave him one more quick peck on the cheek and turned. Awkwardly, she took a step forward, for the first time that day feeling as if her artificial limb weighed her down. "I didn't see you standing there, Daddy."

"I figured that, Mandy." Her father moved forward to meet her and enclosed her in a one-armed bear hug, then held her away from him as he studied her, his eyes narrowed against the sun.

Mandy felt as if her cheeks were on fire. She knew her father would have questions about the way she had greeted Jake. Luckily, she hadn't done anything to be really embarrassed about. With a toss of her head, she gave him a bright smile. "So what brings you out here? I thought you'd be somewhere down in Texas right about now."

"I was supposed to be, but I wasn't feeling up to par, so I thought I'd look you up, seeing as how we haven't seen each other in a long time."

Instantly, Mandy became concerned. "Are you feeling okay, Daddy?"

He gave a gruff laugh. "I'm fine, I'm just not as young as I thought I was."

"I'm glad you're here." She wanted to avoid the questions in his eyes. Her relationship with Jake wasn't something she planned to discuss with anyone, least of all her father. It still felt too new, too full of unanswered questions.

"I'll leave you two alone to catch up," Jake said from behind her, speaking for the first time.

Mandy turned to him, not wanting him to leave. "You don't have to go, Jake," she protested, extending her hand. She stared hard at him, willing him to stay with her. Jake hesitated, and his glance strayed to her father.

"I just need a couple minutes, Mandy," her father said. "We need to do some serious talking."

Mandy swallowed, a cold feeling settling in her chest at his almost somber tone. "Daddy, don't be silly. We've got more than a few minutes. I don't have any plans and I expect you to stay awhile."

"I'm going out to feed the horses," Jake said. "You two catch up on the latest with each other." With a reassuring smile at her, he strode across the deck and down the steps.

Mandy turned back to her father. "You could have waited until Jake left, Daddy. You made it plain you didn't want him to hear what you had to say."

Her father made a snorting sound. "A little plain talking never hurt anyone. I think that boy's drawn a bead on you, Mandy."

She released an exasperated sigh. "I'm not a creature to be sighted in and hunted, Daddy. Before you say anything else, what's between Jake and me is not up for discussion."

"I'm your father, Mandy. I have a right to know what's going on. I have a right to know if you've taken up with that boy again."

Mandy swallowed her immediate retort, remembering all the times her father had not been there when she and Ben were growing up. She had thought she'd put that bitterness behind her, but now it threatened to swell and close up her throat.

"We're adults, Daddy, not kids any longer. We both know our own minds."

"I have a right to know if you're happy or not," her father continued. "You and Jake looked a might cozy from where I was standing. So are you picking up where you left off way back when?"

Mandy looked up at the sky, counted to five and then said patiently, "If I am, Daddy, it's really not your concern." She didn't want to argue with her father, but she wasn't willing to discuss her relationship with Jake. She tried to soften her tone. "So what happened that you decided to take a few days off rodeoing?"

Lanny stared hard at her. "I care about you, Mandy, and I'm worried. I was there, remember. I know the state you were in when you and he split up."

Mandy deliberately lowered her voice. "I was the one who walked away, Daddy. It wasn't Jake's fault. And it was a long time ago. Now, what brings you to town?"

Her father turned and sat on the edge of one of the deck chairs. "My leg's been aching me something fierce."

"Your leg?" Mandy moved over to him and touched his shoulder. "Have you seen the doctor?"

"It'll ease up on its own."

Mandy found his reply too evasive. "It's been bothering you for years, but I don't remember you ever taking time off."

Her father shifted on the chair. "I'm thinking of quitting."

"Quitting?" Mandy repeated. She couldn't have heard him correctly. "Quitting for the year?"

He didn't say anything. He just stared at her, his eyes as dark brown as the Stetson he carried in his hand.

Mandy frowned. "Not...not quitting for good?"

He nodded, twirling his hat in his hands. "Yeah. I'm getting too damned old to be running around the country." He gave a short bark of a laugh and his brows rose. "I bet you never thought to hear your old man say that, huh?"

Mandy sank down in a seat beside him, her thoughts clouded with bewilderment. "No, I can't say I'd ever thought to hear that. Rodeo's always been your life. For as long as I can remember, you've followed the rodeo." She knew it was more than his life, it had consumed him, leaving room for nothing else, not even his family.

"I'm fifty-five years old, Mandy. I've had more broken bones than I can count, and I guess what I'm saying is I've had enough. These last few months, especially since you got hurt, I've done some real hard thinking. Your mama and I even did some serious talking. I been feeling real guilty for years over the way I've raised you and Ben. I know your mama did most of the raising, but I've got this idea I put foolish thoughts into your head." He let out a deep sigh, increasing Mandy's bewilderment. She felt like she was in unfamiliar territory. Her father wasn't acting like he was supposed to. He'd always been a rough-and-ready cowboy. You don't cry over spilled milk, don't complain about what's already done.

"What are you saying, Daddy?"

"You're just like me, Mandy. All you want is the next buckle, the next trophy. You should have a family and kids around you before it's too late."

"I didn't want that." At least, she amended silently, not after she and Jake parted.

"Maybe you would have, if I hadn't put other thoughts in your head. I'm taking full blame. Darn it, girl, I don't want you to turn out like your old man."

"I make my own decisions, Daddy. There's no blame to be laid anywhere."

"You're headstrong," he said, as if she hadn't spoken,

giving her a somewhat sad smile. "I have to tell you now, Mandy, because I know I've never said it before, but you've always made me proud. No matter what you've decided to do with your life, I've always been proud of you."

Mandy turned away, confused by the way her father was talking. It didn't sound like him, but here he sat as bold as day, saying words she had never thought to hear from this man. As far back as she could recall they had never spoken of what was inside their hearts, never touched on the deep feelings. She suddenly felt his vulnerability, and her own emotions seemed to be just as naked.

"Daddy, I thought I disappointed you all these years," she admitted in a low voice. "I couldn't make the grade. No matter how close I got I never reached the finals."

"You could never disappoint me. You're my wild child."

"There you go, calling me that!" she said in exasperation, tossing her head. "I've always known how much you wanted me to succeed at rodeo. You didn't have to say the words. The finals would have been the culmination of those dreams."

"I only wanted that because it's all you ever talked about from the time you were little. You had the guts and determination to ride anything."

Because that's what you put in my head when I was a kid. Children were impressionable, and maybe Daddy was right about it being partly his fault, but she was an adult now with a mind of her own. Mandy stared at him, trying to grapple with what he was saying.

"Mandy, I'm no good at words, you know that. I've always lived by the seat of my pants. I'm apologizing now for all the mistakes I've made. I know I haven't done a good job as a parent for you and Ben." He dropped his chin and shook his head. "I haven't seen Ben since that time in the hospital, after you got hurt. I still remember the anger on his face. I knew then he blamed me for what happened to you." He twisted his hat in his work-worn hands.

"He had no right to do that!" Mandy exclaimed.

"I'm thinking maybe he did, but it's something I have to work out with your brother. I'm going to try, if he'll listen."

Mandy let out a deep whoosh of air, feeling as if a weight had been lifted from her shoulders. It was suddenly glaringly obvious to her that all these years she had been trying to make him proud, and felt like she had never succeeded. Why had it taken her this long to realize she had to live for herself, not for someone else's dreams? She had thought she was doing it for herself....

"I'll be happy for you, Mandy, no matter what. If you decide to make a go of it with Jake, fill this house with babies, I'll be glad."

Mandy felt overcome with emotion, a constriction gripping her insides. She leaned close and hugged him, because he was her daddy and she loved him dearly and he loved her.

Lanny awkwardly patted her shoulder and cleared his throat. "Yeah...well, that's what I wanted to tell you, and I've said my piece so now I'll be heading out."

Mandy stood when he did. She stepped back and took a good look at his handsome, familiar face. Despite what had been said, she still had an unsatisfied feeling that something wasn't right. Wetting her lips, she said, "Now, Daddy, tell me the real reason you're giving up rodeo."

Lanny hit his hat against his pant leg. "I'm getting tired, Mandy, we just went over all that—"

"The real reason," she repeated, fear curling within her. That feeling of something being amiss had intensified.

Her daddy's face went still, and Mandy watched his fingers clench his hat brim until it twisted. She waited, a deep, deep anxiety taking hold of her insides.

A rueful grin curved Daddy's mouth, yet she noticed the

vague relief in his eyes. "I've got cancer," he said. "They're giving me six months."

As Jake left the barn, he saw the taillights of Lanny Thomson's banged up, rusted pickup truck heading down his driveway. It was almost dusk. The brake lights blinked a few times, then the truck turned onto the main road and disappeared into the night.

Jake strode quickly to the house. He and Lanny had talked before Mandy arrived home. Surprisingly, Lanny had told him he was leaving rodeo. He'd wanted to know if it was true that his daughter was practically living with Jake. Jake didn't know where Lanny had come by his information, but the man seemed to have a pretty good idea of what Mandy had been up to since moving to the ranch.

Jake had kept his replies guarded, until Lanny had confessed he needed to go to his grave knowing his only daughter was happy. It was then Lanny told him he had been diagnosed with cancer.

Jake entered the house, switching lights on as he went. When he flipped the kitchen switch, he saw Mandy. She sat on the couch, her feet on the floor, elbows on her knees, with her head in her hands. The sight wrenched Jake, twisting at his insides. She looked miserable.

Jake moved toward her, wanting to hold her and take care of her. He stopped a good two feet from the couch. The years they'd been apart had made her into a strong, independent woman, but it was that independence that rose up now, making him feel as if a chasm separated them. "Mandy—are you okay?"

She speared her fingers through her hair and lifted her head to stare at him. "You know?" she asked dully. Her voice sounded thick, as if she had been crying. Jake hadn't seen her cry since the accident. Seeing her puffy eyes now made it all the worse. She cried for her father, but he had never seen her cry for herself.

He swallowed hard and nodded. "He was worried about you, Mandy. He wanted to see for himself that you were okay."

"He wanted to know if I was okay?" she asked incredulously, almost choking.

Damning the consequences, Jake dropped down beside her and pulled her close. Whether she admitted it or not, right now she needed him. He felt the shaking of her body, the quiver of her breath. She tried to hold back the emotions, but he wished she would let them go. Mandy held too much inside.

She curled into him, twisting around until she'd burrowed into his chest. Jake put both arms around her, trying to give her the comfort she sought.

"It's okay if you want to cry," he said gruffly.

"I don't cry," she muttered against his throat. "I just need you to hold me. I still can't believe it. After all these years, Daddy's giving up rodeo. Why now?" she demanded angrily. She raised her head, her cheeks tearstained and red. "Why did he wait so long? He's going to die and he finally decides enough is enough."

"Maybe he realized all he's missed. He told me that what he regretted most was not being close to you and Ben."

Mandy tipped her head back, a grimace of pain flashing across her face. "That's an understatement. I don't think I could ever claim to feel close to Daddy except when we were rodeoing. That seemed to be the only connection I had with him. Poor Ben didn't even have that. Maybe that's why I'm such a rodeo diehard." She shook her head, and Jake rubbed a palm over her shoulder blades, feeling the delicate bones beneath the skin.

"Your father loves you, Mandy, and he loves Ben, too."

"Do you think I don't know?" she demanded fiercely.

"He loved us, when he was around. As I got older I got mad for Mama's sake. It was confusing. I loved Daddy, but Mama's the one on that ranch day after day, breeding those bulls, trying to make ends meet. She did a man's job, put in a man's hours, and she tended to us, a couple of wild hellions. Daddy wasn't around. He hurt her bad. He hurt all of us. And you know what, Jake? I feel guilty about the anger inside me. I've carried it around for so long, half the time I didn't know it was there. Even after all this time I couldn't hurt him by letting him see it. I wanted to tell him how mad I was at him for what he took away from us, but I couldn't."

"People make choices that hurt others, Mandy. Maybe that realization has finally come to your father. I think you're right not to hurt him now."

"Now he's trying to make up for the past, and it's too late."

"It's never too late."

"He doesn't want me to tell Mama," she whispered brokenly. "How am I not going to tell her?" Mandy looked up, the sheen of tears evident in her eyes. "Why did he have to tell me? He didn't tell Ben, he hasn't told Mama. Why me?"

"Would you rather he kept it a secret?" he asked her, gently pushing the hair away from her tear-drenched eyes.

Immediately, Mandy shook her head. "No, I wouldn't want that, either." She let out a ragged sigh.

Jake wanted to take her pain and carry it himself.

"I don't know what I want. Part of me wishes I didn't know, the other part feels guilty about the old anger I've kept inside. I feel so mean and terrible now, knowing he's going to die."

"Your father knows you love him. All you can do now is support him and let him see your love."

"You're right, Jake." For a moment longer she held on to him tightly. "I—I need to go lie down. I have to think."

"Lie down in my room," he told her. "Come on."

Jake walked with her to the bedroom, and once there, she lay down on his queen-size bed. He pulled a quilt up over her, pushing back the light fall of hair, seeing her eyes staring at nothing, a certain hopelessness in her face. His gut tightened. Talking to Lanny today had brought back memories of his own father's last few months. Jake remembered how helpless he had felt, knowing the inevitable outcome. He had wanted to do something to slow the time, but in the end, time had run out. He knew how Mandy felt.

"I'll let you rest, then I'll go pick something up for dinner," he said, taking a step away from the bed.

Mandy reached out her hand. Jake stared at it, aware of the importance of the gesture, the measure of trust it represented. He let his fingers close around hers. He could feel the slight tremble in her fingers.

"You've always been so good to me, Jake. Sometimes I don't think I deserve your consideration. All those years ago... I can only imagine what you must have gone through with your dad. Your mother and sisters depended on you entirely. Who did you have to lean on?"

Jake stared at her in surprise. "My family was around, Mandy."

She shook her head. "No, Jake. You're the one who's always been around for everyone else. They all expected it of you, and you didn't fail any of them. Everyone has always leaned on your strength."

"Move over."

Mandy moved over on the bed, and Jake sat down beside her.

"I've got pretty wide shoulders, Mandy. I handled it."

She looked away from him. "I've been thinking about it

a lot, that night ten years ago. I get a sick feeling when I think back to that time.''

"It's over with. Let's leave it in the past where it belongs.'' Jake felt now wasn't the time to talk about the past. He moved to get up, but Mandy gripped his hand.

"Please stay,'' she whispered. "Please hold me. Can you just hold me, Jake?''

Without a word he pulled off his boots and slid onto the bed beside her. Mandy turned her back and fitted herself to him. Gradually, her body began to relax.

"How did your doctor's appointment go?'' he asked.

"Fine,'' she murmured. "I'm fine.''

"Do you want to tell me your news?'' Jake asked her, hoping to turn her thinking to other channels. She had been so full of excitement when she had arrived home. As the days went by Jake had gotten to see more and more of the exuberant, full-of-life Mandy, a vast difference from the night she had first arrived at his ranch. So very different, so very much like the younger Mandy he remembered.

"My news?'' Her voice sounded vague, then she stirred and turned toward him. Jake dropped his arm to her waist and cradled her hip with his hand. "I went to a riding clinic today.'' She took a deep, shaky breath. "It's for disabled kids…a great program, but the funding for it has virtually disappeared. Samantha—that's the woman who runs it— said she could use any extra help. I'm going to give lessons two days a week and see how it goes.''

"I think that's great, Mandy. That must be Sam Evans?''

"Yes, she said she knew you. I was really excited about it, but now, after talking to my father…'' She shrugged her shoulders. "It kind of kills the moment.''

Jake understood her mixed emotions. Her earlier excitement had been doused by the news of her father's condition. Jake wished there was something he could do to ease her mind.

"Why don't you tell me more about this riding program," he suggested. "When are you going to start?"

Mandy pulled herself upright and leaned against the headboard. She pushed the hair away from her face and drew a deep breath. "I was planning on driving over tomorrow morning, but I wonder if I should go to town and spend time with my dad."

Jake could see the confusion and worry in her eyes, feel the renewed tension in her body. Carefully, he suggested, "Your father told me he was going to see Ben early tomorrow. You could still go to the riding clinic, then make arrangements to see your father later in the day." Jake had a feeling Mandy needed this riding program. She had come a long way since arriving at his ranch. He didn't want her tossing this opportunity aside if it would help her, if she found out it was something she wanted.

"You're right, you know." Mandy's gaze met his. "It's just that I feel so heavyhearted inside. I want to go out and ride some bulls right now just to make Daddy happy before it's too late."

Jake locked his jaw tight. Bull riding. Why would she think about bull riding at a time like this? He couldn't imagine her getting on another bull.

"How can you think of riding the bulls again?" Jake said fiercely. "How can you forget what happened?" She couldn't go back to bull riding. He wouldn't allow it.

Jake pulled himself up short. Grimly, he reminded himself he didn't have a say in the matter. Mandy could do anything she pleased, and she would.

Mandy looked at him briefly. She tucked a strand of hair behind her ears and admitted slowly, "I'll never forget what happened, but I'm not going to live my life in fear. It all comes down to what I've made of my life, Jake. Quite simply, I've failed. All those years, when I'd get close to winning big time, something always happened to screw it up. Maybe I did it subconsciously."

Jake's insides twisted tighter. He dropped his arm around her shoulders. "You've never failed, Mandy," he said quickly. "You've got the buckles to prove it. You've had a grand and memorable career, and I know you're destined to go on and continue to make your mark in the world. Remember, you're the one who told me you never give up. It's when you don't try new experiences that you've failed. Whether you want to hear it or not, there are other things besides rodeo."

Mandy suddenly smiled at him. Sliding down on the bed, she threw her arms around his shoulders, pulling him down to her. Jake buried his face in her neck, loving the fragrance that was Mandy. She never ceased to surprise him with her lightning-fast changes of mood.

"You're right, Jake. It's times like this, when you remind me of what I've accomplished, that I feel I can do anything." She planted a kiss on his cheek, then rained another half dozen along his jaw and lips. Jake's body responded immediately. He tightened his arms around her.

"You're good for my ego. I think I'll keep you around."

Playfully, she leaned her full weight against him, then propped her chin in her hands, her elbows resting on his chest. "I'd like to seduce you," she said boldly. "Are you going to cooperate?" She trailed a finger down the side of his neck and, snap by snap, slowly undid his shirt.

Each popping sound brought Jake closer to the burning need he always felt for Mandy. His gaze met hers and held. She wanted him; he could see it on her face. He knew her well enough by now to know she didn't want gentleness. She wanted—needed—to forget, if only for a moment, the news she'd heard from her father.

Jake let himself respond in a frenzy of need and want. They made love quickly, explosively. He felt as if he were being consumed by the fire in Mandy, then he consumed her in turn. He wanted to protect and devour her at the same time, but he settled for reaching out and touching the stars instead. With Mandy, he felt like he could do anything, be anyone. Sometimes he even forgot the past.

He wondered how long this relationship could last. Sexual desire would continue for only so long, then would die a natural death. What if she wanted to break things off before he was ready to end it? Would he be worse off than he'd been before they began a relationship?

Jake cared about her, but he was determined it would go no further than the desire he felt now. They were too different. He had buried the pain of Mandy's leaving with family issues and work for ten years. He felt a clenching in his gut. When they felt the time was right, they would call it quits and would both walk away and get on with their lives. That had been his plan all along. Closure. It's what Mandy wanted, too. She would return to bull riding, maybe thinking of her time here as just a pleasant interlude. Jake didn't want it to be like that, but he had to let her go. It hurt too damned much otherwise.

There was no way he could watch her return to bull riding. Obviously she was still bent on doing so. Her resolve had not changed. She had never pretended otherwise. Mandy had always been up front with him about that.

Bull riding. A chill raced through Jake, one he felt clear to his toes. To ward off the confusion in his head, he tightened his arm around Mandy, feeling her snuggle against him, the skin of her shoulder warm against his ribs.

"I like our little…ahem…conversations," Mandy said in a husky murmur.

Jake bent his head, aware of her feathery hair against his cheekbone. He speared his fingers through the silky blond mass, cupping the base of her skull to tilt her head up.

He looked straight into Mandy's eyes. "You're one hell

of a lady, Mandy Thomson,'' he said deliberately. ''I'm proud to know you.''

Her smile slipped just a bit. ''Thanks, Jake. Too bad we couldn't...'' She let her voice trail off.

''What?''

''Nothing. There's no use going over the past.''

Jake felt his insides tighten. Was this goodbye? He'd said all along he wanted to get her out of his system, but he couldn't forget the last week of camaraderie they'd shared. ''What rule says we can't try to live with it? I'm willing to forgive and forget.''

Mandy jerked back from him. ''How can you say that?'' she asked, her tone bordering on anger.

She pulled up the sheet and wrapped it around her body, almost as if she had to shield herself against him, Jake thought.

''Forgive and forget—you make it sound like it was all my fault! We were both too young. Afterward, you did a good job of cutting me out of your life.''

Jake felt his own temper rise, but he knew they'd accomplish nothing by yelling at each other. ''You did the walking, Mandy.'' He clenched his jaw tightly. He wouldn't soften the words. He recalled the sting of her walking away. ''You told me you loved me and you walked away. Rodeo was more important.''

''What else could I do? I didn't know anything except rodeo.'' Mandy got up quickly from the bed. ''At first it was romantic to talk about getting married, then it became more real. I got scared. You were talking about babies, a mortgage. Then the weight of the world was suddenly dumped on your shoulders. I was one more burden on the pile.''

''It wouldn't have been like that. We'd have been stronger, the two of us together.''

Mandy shook her head, clutching the sheet as she quickly

gathered her clothing. "You didn't have time for me, Jake. I didn't blame you. I understood. Your father was hovering by death's door. Your mother, your little sisters, needed you."

"You never gave us a chance," Jake stated, no longer trying to contain the anger. "One week we had all these plans and then wham! You tell me it's better if we split."

Mandy looked around the room almost desperately. Jake took a deep breath, standing quickly and pulling on his jeans. "Mandy, we've got to talk about this calmly and rationally."

She looked at him over her shoulder, the slender curve of her back to him. "No, no, we can't. All we'll do is fight. We can't see each other's point of view. Maybe we're both too stubborn. Maybe…" she caught her breath, and Jake put out a hand to her when he heard the half sob that escaped her, "…maybe it's happening again, the inevitable tearing apart. We're having an affair, that's all. We don't care about each other enough. It's like it's unfinished business between us, Jake. Unfinished business you're intent on finishing. I've got to go."

She whirled from the room, still clutching the sheet and her clothes. Jake dropped into a chair, feeling as empty as the doorway. He put his head in his hands, pressing his forehead with his palms. He needed to examine what was going on here. He had an uneasy suspicion he was missing something. Had Mandy changed? Did she want more than what she said? Did either one of them want to go back and start again?

Telling her he forgave her had been the worst thing he could have said. Why had he added fuel? Had he really wanted to start a fire?

Chapter Fifteen

Mandy had gotten into the habit of arriving at the River-dale barn early in anticipation of her riding lessons at the clinic. Today, it looked like she was the first one to appear.

She had lined up a few apartments in town, but she hadn't had time to go look at all of them yet. She knew she couldn't stay with Jake much longer, not after what had happened. Her pride wouldn't allow her to stay with a man she loved, but who might still harbor resentment over a decade-old mistake. Despite everything, the idea of forever with Jake was something she wanted. But she wouldn't go begging to Jake. She had never begged for anything in her life.

Mandy looked at the barn. She had been giving lessons for almost two weeks and found she really looked forward to working with the kids, who ranged in age from five years up into their teens. They were all so eager to learn, but what really made it worthwhile was they weren't easily discouraged. They tried time and again, and their efforts paid off. Riding gave them the mobility they lacked on the ground.

Mandy was working there four days instead of the originally agreed upon two. By the end of her first week she and Sam had already become friends. Mandy admired Sam for her dedication to the program, despite the odds against her. The equipment was badly in need of replacing, as she had said, and some of the horses were ready for retirement. Mandy wondered what would happen to the children if the program was dropped.

Just then Sam drove up and exited her vehicle. "Mandy!" she called. With a wave, she headed toward the other barn. "Come over to the tack room! I have someone I want you to meet."

When Mandy entered, she found Sam with a tall, blond man who had a camera slung over his shoulder. Curiously, Mandy approached them. The man was casually dressed, in dark jeans and a sweatshirt, while Sam wore her customary breeches and leather boots. "Morning, Mandy," she said with a smile. "I'd like to introduce you to a friend of mine, Dan Anderson."

Dan lifted a brow, a somewhat speculative grin on his handsome face as he looked at Mandy. He thrust his hand out to her. "Mandy Thomson, it's great to meet you. Sam told me you were helping her out. I thought she was pulling my leg."

"I guess we're helping each other out."

"Ever since Sam told me you'd showed up, I've had an idea in my head. I wouldn't be adverse to interviewing you. We could let your fans know what you've been up to in the last several months."

"Uh, one thing I should mention, Mandy," Sam said quickly, "Dan's a reporter."

"Oh." That information made Mandy a bit edgy.

"Now don't go running off," Dan said, his eyes sharp,

as if he could read her thoughts of escape. "I'm really a nice guy." He placed his hand over his heart, then held up two fingers. "Scout's honor."

Mandy couldn't suppress her grin. "Since you're hooked up with Sam, who's a really nice person, I'm going to believe that."

"However," he added smoothly, "I do think you should let me interview you, Mandy. You name the time and place."

She immediately shook her head. "Thanks, but no thanks."

"It would be a great story...nonintrusive, I promise. We'll let everyone know what's going on in your life. You really dropped out of sight."

"I don't do interviews anymore," Mandy said firmly, smiling to soften the words.

"Okay, but I think it would be a great human interest story." Reaching into his jeans pocket, Dan pulled out a slim gray wallet and extracted a business card. He held it out to her, his face now serious. "If you change your mind, I'd be glad to talk to you. Really...call me anytime." He pocketed his wallet and slung the camera back over his shoulder as he turned to Sam. "I've got to go, Sam. I'll call you tonight." He dropped a kiss on her mouth, then turned back to Mandy. "I'll be seeing you, Mandy. Nice meeting you."

"Nice to meet you, too, Dan."

Mandy looked at Sam as Dan walked around the back of the barn. She heard a car start and through the open barn door she saw a car drive by. She leaned against a stall door, crossing her feet at the ankles. "I hope he isn't offended, but I really don't want to do an interview."

"Believe me, Dan isn't easily offended, but I do think he's right," Sam added quietly. "And it's not because he's my boyfriend, either. You could do this program a world of good if you got back out in the public eye and stirred things up, let people know what's going on."

"I don't know how an interview from me could help, Sam. It's been almost five months since my last rodeo. People forget. There's always a new face out there." In truth, the idea of going before the cameras again gave Mandy an edgy, uncomfortable feeling. During her rodeo years she had been interviewed countless times, but now she didn't want to entertain the thought. She felt she had been out of the public eye too long. Why would anyone care what she was up to now?

Sam snorted disbelievingly. "Come on, Mandy, you can't be that naive. You've been a name in the sport far too long for people to forget you overnight." She shrugged. "It's just a thought. At least promise me you'll think about it."

"All right, I promise. If I decide to do an interview, Dan will be the first to know." Mandy said the words, but in her mind she knew she'd never call him.

"On to other business. I talked to the program director. A few days from now they're having a budget meeting on the riding program's renewal. He didn't sound real optimistic."

Mandy felt a great wave of disappointment. "Oh, dear. I know you told me that from the beginning, but now that I've seen what the program does for the kids, it's even more of a letdown." Mandy drew a deep breath. "There must be something we can do."

"Give me an idea to work with," the other woman said.

"You'll be the first to know if I come up with something," Mandy promised, her mind searching out possible avenues. "But since it isn't going to help if we worry about that meeting, I think we'd better check out the palomino mare before the kids arrive. Yesterday she seemed to be limping a bit."

* * *

As Mandy ran a brush over Arnie, one of the riding pro-gram's horses, she kept going over in her mind the angry words she and Jake had exchanged. He'd said he would forgive and forget. Those words stirred her anger and a deep anguish. Had she really done something so terrible all those years ago? At the time she had made the best decision a seventeen-year-old could make. Why couldn't Jake see that? She had never wanted to hurt him. She had thought it out so carefully.

Trying not to think of the mess things were in, Mandy brushed harder. She suddenly stopped and leaned her arm over the horse's back and redirected her thoughts to her family.

It had become Mandy's routine to visit several times a week with Daddy at Mama's ranch. Mandy wasn't sure of the details, but Mama had invited Daddy to stay in the small, unoccupied cottage on the ranch property. All Mandy knew for sure was that the invitation had occurred the same day Daddy had broken the news about his health to Mandy. Mama might have told her the circumstances if she had asked, but Mandy felt it was between her parents, so she kept silent.

Daddy had made mistakes but because of his health crisis she truly believed that somehow they would forgive and go on. The time had finally come to pull together as a family.

Mandy gave the horse one last swipe with the brush, then led the mare into her stall and pulled the door closed. She had plans of her own to think about. She loved Jake, but was afraid they'd only keep hurting each other if she didn't leave. They seemed to want different things out of their relationship. Because of their disagreement, the atmosphere at the ranch was strained. Mandy knew things couldn't go on as they were. Everything progressed, changed; that was the excitement in living. Nothing remained the same. Sadly, she accepted that Jake no longer loved her. If he had, surely he would have said something, given some indication. Then again, she hadn't told him she loved him, either. She was a coward, plain and simple. She was too afraid of him not wanting her love. Of him rejecting it as she had rejected his years ago.

Even if Jake wanted her to stay, Mandy didn't know how that would sit with her. A relationship meant permanence, remaining in one place. She didn't know how to deal with permanence.

She had been halfheartedly looking through the papers the last few days for an apartment. She knew she had to find something. It wasn't fair to Jake or herself to prolong matters. Mandy wondered how she'd ever thought they could go back. How could two people who cared so much keep hurting each other? Why had it turned out so wrong?

The only bright spot in her life right now was that she might have come up with a way to save the riding program. She had run her ideas by Denny and Lynn, and their enthusiastic approval had convinced Mandy her plan was worth a shot. She hadn't told Sam yet; she had needed to do more research before spilling the beans. Mandy wanted the other woman to be as excited as she was. For once in her life, she was looking outward, and it felt good. If she could pull this off...

"Time to call it a day," Sam said from behind her. Mandy swung around with a startled yelp.

"I didn't know you were here! I thought you had left." Mandy studied Sam's grim face. "What's the matter?"

"I was planning on leaving but I got a call from the director. The remainder of the funding has been moved to another program." She put both hands behind her neck and let her head fall back. "It's official. The riding program is finished."

Mandy was hardly aware when the halter and lead rope in her hand slipped to the stable floor. "No. Just like that?"

"I'm afraid so. They've given me two weeks to tie things up, but we're officially done."

Mandy walked in a tight circle, frowning, then looked back at Sam. "I talked to some friends and I may have an idea to save the program. But we'd need a little time to pull it together."

"I would love to halt this, but it's not a matter of holding things up. Shoot!" Sam's voice sounded tired. "I've waived my pay for a month to keep it going for the kids. They're shutting us down."

"Those are details we can work out," Mandy insisted, refusing to be daunted.

Sam shrugged resignedly. "I warned you up front what could happen. Now it has," she finished flatly.

Mandy stared at Sam. "I'm not giving up, and you can't, either. I need your help, Sam. You've got the training. You're the one who keeps this program together. What if I can get the money, secure backers—would you want to continue the program?"

Sam began to smile and the tiredness lifted from her face. "Are you kidding? Of course I would."

Mandy's thoughts ran in ten different directions. "I'm not going to let this get away. I think I have a solution—I want to raise money by having a rodeo."

"Mandy!" Sam exclaimed. "That's a perfect solution. You know people. Your name alone will draw crowds! You could probably get some of your famous rodeo friends to come."

Mandy started laughing. Sam's enthusiasm was infectious. "Hang on, we have to put it all together first."

"We can get Dan in on this. He's got a lot of contacts. Right now he's doing some reporting for a local television station. Maybe he can arrange some preliminary interviews to get the word out." Sam clasped her hands together.

"Mandy, I have a good feeling about this. I really think we can do it."

"Let's just hope you're right about my name being a draw," Mandy cautioned her. She didn't want to build false hope, but she felt her own excitement escalating. Could she do this? Could she pull it off?

From his vantage point on the back deck, Jake saw Mandy's vehicle arrive at the house. She was doing so well. She had adjusted to her prosthesis and walked with a hardly discernible limp. Jake's chest expanded in a deep breath. She seemed happy and content. Mandy was a strong woman whom circumstances could not keep down. He knew she saw her father on a regular basis, and he thought that was her way of dealing with his terminal illness. Since their argument several days ago Jake himself hadn't seen much of her. He'd had time to do some soul-searching, but he hadn't come up with any ready conclusions.

He knew they couldn't go on like this, saying polite hellos. He stared out across the flat expanse of his land, wondering if Mandy would ever settle someplace permanently.

Restlessly, Jake hopped off the rail and strode across the deck. No matter the outcome, he had to break the stalemate between them.

He stopped just short of the house. Mandy stood in the doorway. She let go of the door, and it closed with a soft thud behind her.

"Hello, Jake."

"Mandy." He swallowed hard, gazing at her, his insides tightening as he watched her. She stood still for a moment, her jeans hugging her slim hips, her T-shirt lovingly following the curves of her breasts. She appeared dusty and tired, but looked so good to him, a tentative smile curving her lips. Jake's entire body felt as tense as a bow. He knew what had to be said.

"We need to talk."

"Yes, we do, Jake."

He retraced his steps and took up a position against the deck railing. Mandy pulled a chair close by and sat down.

"How are things at the riding clinic?" Jake figured he might as well jump in.

Mandy grimaced and shook her head. "They've dropped the program. I was warned, but it's hard to believe."

"I'm sorry to hear that. I know how much you've enjoyed working there these last few weeks."

"It might not be all bad news."

Jack sensed Mandy's excitement. Her eyes sparkled and she moved her hands expressively, as if she couldn't keep still. "I've got an idea to start up a new program. I've been talking with Lynn and Denny about planning a rodeo."

"You're going to plan a rodeo?" Dread began to pool in Jake. He'd known the day would arrive, but hadn't thought it would be so soon that Mandy would leave.

"I want to plan and sponsor a rodeo."

"Why?" Jake asked flatly.

"Denny knows some people willing to donate good, sound horses if we get the riding program underway. I was thinking that if the competitors know this is a good cause, maybe they'll donate their winnings to a riding foundation for the kids. It will start the program off right. We could even, conceivably, have a yearly rodeo to fuel the funding."

Jake could see the logic in the plan. "You've apparently thought this out. I'm impressed. When did you come up with the idea?"

"I've been kicking it around for a few days. Yesterday I realized I have to do more than think about taking action. Do you remember Emily, the young girl I met at the doctor's office? Her mom came to see me. She wanted to enroll Emily for riding lessons when the doctor gave her the go-ahead."

The sheen of tears in Mandy's eyes reinforced to Jake how much she loved working with the kids.

"You were meant for this, Mandy. I've never seen you happier."

"I do enjoy it," she said softly. "It surprises me, I guess, how much." She shook her hair back and took a deep breath. "I've got something else to tell you, Jake." Her smile slipped a little. "It looks like I've found another place. Now you can get on with your renovation plans."

"I don't give a damn about the renovations," Jake said harshly, clenching his fists against his thighs. "Don't leave."

"I have to," she said softly. "We both know it."

"You're running away again, Mandy." Jake glared at her.

"I don't see it that way." Mandy reached out her hand and touched his arm. Jake felt the heat of her fingers clean to his toes. "It's no good for either of us, Jake. I really appreciate you letting me use the apartment. It made things easier for me, but now it's time to move on."

"We agreed to take this relationship where it would go." He turned his hand and gripped her fingers. "We care about each other. Life hasn't been the same since you arrived, and I'm glad. Amy told me I was in a rut and she was right. When I came across your picture the week of the accident, the years rolled back. I had this notion I needed to see you one last time, then I could get on with my life. But things changed the moment—"

Mandy stared at him, her worst suspicions finally confirmed. "You came that night to say goodbye?" she interrupted. "Then you were going to get on with your life, heart whole and fancy-free?"

Jake's mouth felt dry. He didn't deny it.

Mandy stood up and moved away from him. "But it

didn't turn out that way, did it, Jake? You got sucked into the mess of my life.''

"I saw you and I couldn't leave," he told her quietly. "I had to stay. I don't know what would have happened if you hadn't gotten hurt.''

Mandy looked away from him. A slight breeze blew around them, lifting her hair away from her face. His blood stirred. Mandy had that instantaneous effect on him. He wanted to cherish her and rip their clothes off at the same time.

"You came to the rodeo to see me. You made me want you in my life again. It wasn't fair.'' Mandy's voice came to him low and pained. "It's still not fair. Despite all we've come to mean to each other, we still want different things. I know you don't want me to return to rodeo, but I have to.'' She added fiercely, "It's who I am.''

Jake felt his ire rise. "I remember the night you got hurt in minute detail, Mandy. I saw what happened. I watched them extricate you from under that bull, your face as white as death, lips blue, with a trickle of blood. It's a night I'll never forget. How can *you* forget what happened?''

"This isn't all about rodeo, Jake. It's about you getting what you want. I moved in here. I trusted you.'' Her words came in a rush. "I stayed when I wanted to leave, that first night. You pushed all the right buttons.''

Jake wanted to reach out to her, to ease the pain he heard in her voice. Instead, he kept his hands by his sides. "I haven't done anything to violate your trust. I guess nothing has changed in all these years. You're right, we still want different things.''

"Then maybe it's time we stopped hurting each other. You knew all along I intended to return to rodeo. I have to wonder if you've been hoping all along I would change my mind.''

"I knew you'd leave," Jake snapped. But she was correct—he *had* hoped she would change her mind.

"I feel as if I've been manipulated. You provided a place for me to live, convinced my brother to bring my horse here. I even met your friends and got reacquainted with your family. You made it very comfortable and convenient."

"You could have left anytime."

"I guess I'm too weak," Mandy said bitterly. "I cared too much about you. I've never stopped caring."

Jake felt tired. "The night you got hurt I felt drawn to you all over again. All these years I've locked you out, but a part of me kept your memory close. You're not an easy person to get over, Mandy." He paused. "I felt cheated when you left. I loved you back then—we both know that. I'm not pretending otherwise to make it easier on either of us." Jake felt a hard lump in his throat. He had to push the rest of the words out. "I don't think I ever stopped being angry at you. I buried it for a long time.

"I'm not like the rodeo cowboys you hang out with. I know there're probably any number of them lined up. I'm an ordinary guy, the same man I've always been. No frills, no fireworks. You might consider my life to be as boring as the boxes I manufacture. But guess what, Mandy? I like my life and who I've become. I wouldn't change it."

"Jake…"

"Ten years ago we *were* young, but we both know you've got a background that makes you shy away from commitment. That was your out then. I got too close and that scared the hell out of you. You admitted it yourself. It didn't matter that I adored you, that I wanted to marry you." Jake laughed, and the sound grated in his ears.

"Why can't things go on as they were? We were doing okay," she murmured.

"Relationships progress and change. You want it to stay

the same. Easy in, easy out. You're so busy covering any emotional tracks, you won't let me in.''

Mandy's voice was low and full of pain. ''All those years ago we both made mistakes. We learned that love doesn't always mean forever, and it doesn't conquer all problems. When I think of that night I left you I feel the hurt again, but I still think it was the best thing to do.''

Jake wanted to smash something.

''I've always been responsible for myself, Jake. If I screwed up, I was the only one who got hurt by the mistakes. Marriage is so much more. Others get hurt. I've seen it too many times with my parents. I was too frightened to take that risk.''

''Life is a risk, Mandy, not just marriage and relationships.''

She turned away, but not before Jake had seen the closed expression on her face. ''There's too much garbage in my past. I—I guess I'm too afraid to step beyond it.''

Mandy moved away from him, her movements jerky. She started down the deck stairs to the back field.

Jake went after her and grabbed her arms, swinging her around. ''So you're just going to throw it away again?''

''I have to!'' she said fiercely. ''I can't bear to go forward, clinging to the hope we won't tear each other apart again.'' Tears spilled down her cheeks. ''I can't do it, Jake. Don't ask it of me.''

Jake watched his dream crumble with each step Mandy took away from him. He wanted to call her back, demand that she stay. But he kept his mouth shut. Anger boiled inside, but at the root of it was bone-deep despair.

Mandy didn't realize she was running until she reached the barn door and stopped, feeling the wetness on her face. Silence surrounded her, broken only by the rasp of her own breathing. She had done it—hurt Jake for the last time.

Mandy swung open the barn door and wandered aimlessly inside. How could she and Jake have a normal relationship when her childhood memories reflected anything but normalcy and caring?

She wanted to hide, but she knew the pain wouldn't lessen. She opened the door to Jake's office and stumbled inside, her foot hitting something. She heard a small crash. Flicking on the light switch, Mandy saw she'd kicked over a box. More evidence of the disruption she had caused in Jake's life. His possessions were in boxes stored in the barn. Papers now lay strewn across the concrete floor.

Mandy bent down to pick them up and noticed her name in bold black print. Curiously, she picked up a bundle of newspaper clippings held by a rubber band. Each article detailed one of her rodeo wins—date, time, place. Some of the clippings were glossy and looked as if they'd been cut from magazines—articles about her after-rodeo hours, the honky-tonks and dance bars she and her friends had frequented. The wild time in her life she had put behind her.

Mandy rifled through the papers. The oldest date was about a year after she and Jake had split. He had been tracking her all this time....

She sat down with a thump on the floor, the box cradled in her arms. Jake had shown her nothing but support from the beginning. He had managed to keep her here that first night when she'd wanted to run. Mandy knew she loved him, and although he hadn't uttered the words she yearned to hear, she sensed that deep in his heart he still loved her, too. But she didn't feel worthy of his love or the trust it implied.

Mandy put the sheaf of papers down and pushed aside the newspaper clippings. Beneath the pile was a large four-by-five-inch newspaper photo. It was a version of the same picture she had seen before. Jake knelt beside a fallen bull. There was no doubt in her mind the bull was old Hit Man, and she lay under the dead animal. The memories of that day flashed like wildfire through her brain.

Mandy felt the sobs that racked her, but she couldn't stop them. They filled the barn—harsh, deep sobs that seemed to come from her very soul. What was she doing? Throwing Jake's love away again, tossing it back at him as if this were a tennis game?

Mandy began to calm down. She rubbed her forehead, wiped the wetness from her face with her arm. A terrible emptiness shifted through her.

That night of the accident Jake had been there the entire time she was under that bull. He couldn't put himself through that again. No wonder he didn't want her to return to the rodeo. But she had to.

Mandy knew she was fooling herself if she thought they had a future. Real life wasn't that easy. She recognized that, why didn't he? Still, the thought of leaving Jake again was almost more than she could bear. Even once in a lifetime was devastating.

She needed to think. She needed to straighten out the confusion in her mind. Mandy put the box back on the pile and walked outside, closing the door behind her.

She went to stand by the pasture gate, then knew with sudden clarity she needed to go home, to the place where she'd grown up. Start at the beginning and work from there. She whistled, a pathetic attempt at best, but Pongo came trotting over to her. She saw him through a blur.

"Come on, Pongo, we're going home."

Grabbing his halter and lead line, Mandy slipped it on his head and jumped on his bare back. She rode across the pasture, not letting herself look back.

Chapter Sixteen

Jake was beyond worried. Mandy hadn't returned and it was almost dusk. He had seen her ride out across the flats on Pongo hours before. If she had gotten hurt, chances were the horse would return to the barn. Jake doubted she had fallen, but worry made the thoughts race through his head.

Trying to remain calm, he paced the floor of his living room. Should he go out looking for her again? He had ridden out about an hour after she'd left. Jake had taken the same direction he'd seen Mandy go, and he had found Pongo's tracks. He knew they were Pongo's because the horse had a peculiar shoe on his right front hoof, a long trailer to keep the hoof positioned correctly.

After a while Jake had turned toward home. He thought Mandy would return after she cooled off, but inside he had a feeling she wouldn't. She must have kept riding. Her vehicle was parked out front, but her apartment remained dark. Jake turned the lights on in her place but he knew she wasn't coming back. Deep down inside his gut told him it was the end. She hadn't trusted him, and she had cut him out of her heart just like that. It was worse than ten years ago. Jake wondered how that could be so. Back then he had loved her. He refused to subject himself to loving her anymore.

Abruptly, he heard the sound of a car out front. He half ran to the front window. He'd give her what for, for scaring him like that. Jake was surprised and disappointed to see Ben coming up the walk. Jake threw open the front door. "Do you know where Mandy is?" he asked without pre-amble.

Ben walked into the house and dropped into a kitchen chair. "My sister rode over to Mom's ranch."

"She rode all the way to your mother's? That's twenty miles away."

Ben grimaced. "Less across the flats, the way she came. Something's going on with her, but Mom couldn't get anything out of her, so she called me." Ben looked expectantly at Jake.

"We had an argument," he said shortly. "I've been worried out of my mind. It's almost dark."

"Mandy asked me to get her vehicle. Mom dropped me off. Mandy's kind of grim, not saying much of anything."

"Damn!" Jake put a hand up to his neck and rubbed at the ache there. He could feel a headache coming on. His muscles were as tense as could be. He dropped down onto a big chair, throwing his head back and staring up at the ceiling.

"Want to talk about it?" Ben murmured.

"Mandy and I are finished. This time for good."

"But she seemed so happy here, almost settled. I thought maybe you two, you know, could make things work out...." Ben's words trailed off.

"Me, too," Jake said grimly. "Mandy warned me, but I guess I was kidding myself. I thought we had a good thing, starting over, getting along fine. At the first hint of doubt, she bolts before we can get it straightened out.''

Making a steeple out of his fingers, Jake looked at Ben. ''When I went to the rodeo that night Mandy got hurt, I thought I could put her out of my life once and for all.''

Ben groaned. ''That's why you showed up there? Did you tell her that?''

Jake nodded grimly.

''Then the accident happened,'' Ben said slowly. ''You were there. The rest is history.'' He put his head in his hands. ''I'm really sorry. Part of this is my fault for asking you to let her use the apartment. This must have been hell for you.''

''It was in the beginning, but how could I turn her away when she needed help? Your sister is some lady, Ben.''

''What happened?''

''Mandy is a hard act to follow. I found myself drawn to her again,'' Jake admitted in a low voice. ''I guess I've buried my feelings all these years, even though I've made a new life for myself. I know it all sounds crazy.'' The pain inside wouldn't go away.

''I think Mandy's pretty confused right now, Jake. She's just coming out of an emotional and physical trauma, and unfortunately, we're both carrying a lot of baggage. Now, with my dad's condition...''

''I didn't know you knew.''

''I had it out with my old man. I guess the resentment just built up to a firing point and exploded. I didn't know he was dying until he told me, and he thought Mandy had spilled it. Anyway, Mandy's always taken to the rodeo like my father. After you two split up, it's like she was driven. I sure as hell know she wasn't happy.''

Jake closed his eyes, wishing he'd had more wisdom at age nineteen. Maybe they hadn't been ready for a commitment, but he should have gone after her. Jake felt guilt creep in. *He should have gone after her.*

"It's the way we grew up, Jake. Mom and I have been worried about her for a while. A few years back it seemed like she was on a self-destructive course. This last year she's really straightened up, maybe she grew up. Then the accident..." Ben looked at Jake. "I have to tell you, I was afraid she'd slip back into her old ways when she lost her leg. I knew, somewhere in the back of my mind, that if anyone could help Mandy, it would be you."

"Your sister's one courageous woman. She's come back full force."

"She told me about her work with the riding program. She really likes working with the kids. It's too bad it had to end."

Jake rubbed a hand across his face. "Well, she's planning on putting together a rodeo to raise money for a new program. I think it's a great idea, but the idea of her bull riding again scares the hell out of me. I can't be around for that."

"And Mandy is still hell-bent on doing it," Ben said slowly. "My sister is a rolling stone, just like Dad."

"I don't really believe that, Ben. I think Mandy wants to settle, but she's afraid."

"That's a different take on things," Ben said rather doubtfully.

"I have to believe it," Jake murmured in a low voice.

"Then why the devil are you sitting here talking to me? Go get her."

Jake wanted nothing more than to do just that, but he shook his head. "I can't. Dammit, Ben, Mandy's got to come to the realization herself. It's got to be her call."

"I guess I can see your point, old buddy. I wish I could help."

"This is between Mandy and me, or rather, Mandy and herself."

* * *

Jake shifted in the desk chair, leaning back farther and resting his booted feet on the desktop. He propped the partially empty whiskey bottle against his thigh, ignoring the phone as it rang for the third time. Mandy had left three weeks ago, and he hadn't heard a word in all that time. She'd left him good and proper, just as he knew she would. But not like he wanted.

He knew that now. He had tried to be up front with her from the beginning, but he'd been lying to himself. His motives had been legitimate, perhaps, but he had lied also, this time to himself. He cared about Mandy more than he'd admitted. Maybe he even loved her. He had thought having her around would get her out of his system once and for all, but he was more deeply entrenched now than he'd ever been.

Jake frowned, staring at the stucco ceiling with sleep-deprived eyes. Surely it would get better, this empty ache he felt?

The phone stopped ringing. Jake's head felt better when it was quiet. He had a pretty good grip on things. He hadn't started drinking until this afternoon.

This week he had been notified that he would have his own exhibit at the gallery. It had been the culmination of eight years of work on his part. His carvings would hold a permanent place in the town's history. It was a great coup, but at the back of his mind Jake knew he wanted to share this success with Mandy. He had had one drink to celebrate, and that had led to another.

Maybe he wasn't handling this whole thing all that well, but at the moment he damned well didn't care. He was trying to decide how he had screwed things up so badly.

The last few weeks, since she'd left, had seemed like

forever. What would another ten years feel like? Jake wondered grimly.

The phone began to ring again. With a disgusted mutter, Jake dropped his feet to the floor and picked up the phone. "What?"

"Hello, Jake," a female voice said, apparently unperturbed by his growl. "This is Lynn, Mandy's friend."

Jake pressed a fist against his throbbing temple. "Mandy's not here."

"I know that. Listen, I want to make sure you know what's going on. I have a feeling Mandy hasn't contacted you."

"Why the hell would you think that?" he asked sarcastically. He carefully put the bottle on the desk, rubbing a hand across his eyes and shoving the hair off his forehead.

"Now, Jake, I'm calling you to help out."

"Lynn, I don't think you should be going behind Mandy's back—"

"I'm not. I've told her what I think and now I'm telling you. Mandy's been really happy since she's been out there with you. She's almost like a new person, and the gang really wants to see you guys make a go of it. Mandy deserves it. If you're the guy to make her happy, then I'm all for it."

"Well, Mandy and I are through. She walked out on her own."

"She'll come around," Lynn said confidently.

Jake felt a spark flare briefly and he sat upright. "What are you saying?"

"Mandy has to think things through. I've known her my whole life. She can be hardheaded, but she's not dumb. In fact," Lynn drawled, "I want to issue you an invitation to a rodeo."

"I heard about it on the news. Not interested." No way would he watch her climb on a bull.

"Mandy has worked herself crazy to pull this together in

this short a time. I think it would mean a lot if you showed up."

News of the rodeo seemed to be everywhere he turned. Even his mother in Florida had called when she'd gotten wind of it, no doubt spurred by his sisters' curiosity.

"We're all proud of her, and quite frankly, Jake, kind of amazed. She got some really big names to commit. And get this…all the concessions, the big-name sponsors—most of the money that comes in is going toward the new riding program. When Mandy sets her mind to something, that girl gets results."

So why couldn't she settle her sights on him?

"So why are you calling, Lynn?" Jake asked, impatient with this chitchat.

"To invite you to come. Jake! Aren't you listening? I know Mandy. She'd never have let you in her heart in the first place if she didn't care about you. A lot."

Jake swallowed hard.

"I know I'm butting in here, but we're all wondering why you let her go. That night of the accident, everyone could see how much you cared about her. You wouldn't let anyone else near her, except for the paramedics."

Jake didn't recall that part; all he remembered was his awful, choking fear that Mandy wouldn't make it.

"So, can we count on your being there?"

He took a deep breath. The decision had already been made; the place didn't really matter. He had to see her again, even if it wrenched his gut and turned him inside out.

"I'll be there."

"Good. Just make Mandy happy."

Jake hung up the phone and then began to pace the room. Could he put his heart on the line one more time? Would it make a difference if he told her he loved her? Jake cuffed himself on the side of his head.

"Wake up, Miller. You love her. Admit it, dammit. You

love her! How dumb can you be? Tell her you love her and she'll kick you in the butt like you deserve.''

She'd never have let you in her heart in the first place if she didn't care about you. A lot.

Jake couldn't let Mandy go without a fight. He'd made that mistake ten years ago. Not this time.

Mandy looked around the crowded equine center, emotion clogging her throat. Her friends, colleagues, everyone she had ever met in rodeo and called regarding the new riding clinic had come through. The spectator seats were full, the day was clear and warm, everything was perfect for the rodeo about to begin. Mandy scanned the yard. Almost everything.

She shoved away thoughts of Jake. In time, the pain would ease. She had pushed herself the last few weeks, trying to pull everything together. She hadn't let herself dwell on the pain of parting from him. Right now, she had to take care of the business at hand.

Mandy walked through the pens, making last-minute checks. Her leg began to bother her a bit—she had been on her feet for almost four hours and it was barely 10:00 a.m.—so she climbed up on a bull pen and sat on the top rail, letting her leg dangle and relax.

''Mandy. Mandy Thomson.'' She heard her name being called, and felt a strange sense of déjà vu as she slowly turned her head and looked across the rodeo yard.

Her gaze connected with light blue eyes in a handsome face. The face of the man she loved. Jake. This time he wore jeans and a western-cut, dark green shirt instead of a suit. His head was bare and he just stood there and stared at her. He wore an assured, assessing look on his face, like that night almost six months ago. Had it been only six months?

Mandy felt some of the tension and worry inside her ease

and uncoil. Jake was here. He had come, if only to say goodbye one last time.

"Mandy...Mandy, snap out of it."

She looked down. Denny was waving her hand at her and snapping her fingers.

"We need you over by the announcer's booth. The opening ceremonies will begin soon."

"Okay." Mandy smiled and began to climb down. When she dropped her feet to the dusty earth, she threw one last glance Jake's way. The space where he had stood was empty. Mandy looked around, but she didn't see him in the crowded yard. Had she imagined him standing there?

"Come on, Mandy, we're right on schedule. You need to do the opening speech." Denny squinted at her. "Are you okay? You look a little pale."

Mandy nodded, frowning as she followed Denny. She was sure she had seen Jake. It hadn't been wishful thinking, had it? She smothered a sigh. She had indulged in a lot of wishful thinking lately, all of it to no avail.

Mandy stood in the middle of the rodeo arena, a microphone clutched in her hand, feeling strange and unfamiliar as the applause started. Her opening words to the crowd had been simple, hopefully significant. She'd tried to make them understand the importance of the riding program for the children involved or yet to be involved.

Mandy heard pounding hooves and turned as Denny on her black mare cantered toward her, leading Pongo. Denny drew her horse to a sliding halt, stirring up dust with a rodeo performer's flair.

Mandy took Pongo's reins and felt the sudden hush of the crowd. Her heart pounded in her chest. With a practiced hop, she found the stirrup with her left foot, swung her right leg over Pongo's hindquarters, then reached down to pick up the other stirrup.

Sitting straight in the saddle, Mandy waved to her friends, family and fans. She urged Pongo into a canter. She had participated in more rodeos than she could count in this very arena, but never had she heard such an outbreak of cheering and shouting as she did now as she circled the ring.

Mandy rode through the gate, ducking her head to wipe her arm across her eyes, thankful for the support and generosity of everyone who had believed in her and shown up today. It would have been perfect, if only she knew for sure that Jake was here.

The arena was empty, the crowds long dispersed, with dusk well on its way. Only a few cowboys hung out by the bull pens, waiting to corral the last animal back into the holding area.

Mandy stared at the bull, a dirty white Brahma with flecks of gray across his hide, and horns that curved wickedly over a broad, flat head.

"Mandy, are you sure this is what you want?" Mama asked as she came to stand beside the stock pen that held the bull.

From her perch on the rail, Mandy pulled on her leather gloves, then pulled them off again, fiddling with the fingers. She stared out over the empty arena, her mouth set in a straight line.

"I have to. If I never get on a bull again after today, that's okay, but I have to do this. Tall Chief here is new to the rodeo circuit. What better bull to use?"

Her mama sighed. "I recognize that determined tilt of your head, Mandy. I know you want to prove something to yourself, and I can't fault you for that, but this bull has a mean streak a mile wide."

"It's only a six-second ride, Mama," Mandy said confidently. The words echoed inside her head. How many times had she said the same thing to her mother over the years?

Mandy shook her head to clear it. She wondered if Mama recognized her fidgeting for what it was. Despite her brave words, Mandy recalled all too clearly the nightmare of her last six-second ride. She still didn't know if she could go through with this.

"I know better than to argue with you, Mandy. Since you've been little, once you make up your mind there's no swaying you."

"It's a sorry fact, but it is a fact, Mama." Still, Mandy made no move to climb over the chute, where the bull moved restlessly. He hadn't been still since some of the boys had herded him in there.

Mandy felt full of doubt, but one thing was clear—she had to try and ride. She also knew she had a decision to make concerning Jake. The way she had left was wrong, but the panic that had ripped through her had been real and inflammatory. She wasn't that mixed-up seventeen-year-old anymore. She was a woman, and she had to face up to her life, not run from it. When had she begun living her life in fear? She was no coward.

Since the day she had ridden away from Jake's ranch, she carried a constant ache inside, a deep hurt that wouldn't turn her loose. She missed Jake…missed their times together. A part of her felt incomplete.

"Do you regret leaving?" Mama asked, as if she had read her thoughts.

Mandy narrowed her eyes and twisted around to stare at her mother's placid face. "Regret it?"

Mama straightened her lips and put her hands on her hips. "If loving that man puts that look of misery on your face, then you're better off without him—"

"Jake is a good man," Mandy told her quickly.

"—especially if he's mistreated you."

Mandy ducked her head, staring at the reddish-brown dirt below her. "Jake wouldn't harm me. If anything, he cares about me too much. Maybe more than he knows," she added.

"I've never heard of a man loving a woman too much."

Mandy hunched her shoulders. "I've never felt like this. I've always loved Jake, but it seems so much worse now. I've lived with the loss for ten years. With time the ache got bearable. But now…" Mandy shook her head. "It's like I'm incomplete without him in my life. It's worse than after the accident, when everything felt like it was over. All I could see was a long, dark tunnel with no light in front of me."

"Maybe Jake's more vital to you than anything you've ever experienced."

"I walked away from him a second time, Mama. Jake thought I took off all those years ago because I didn't love him. He didn't understand it was the only thing I could do."

"Sometimes you have to give yourself leeway to change your mind, Mandy. Life isn't black-and-white, right or wrong. If Jake's half the man I think he is, he'll want you back, and he'll understand."

"I guess I keep hoping that, Mama. It's all I've thought about since I've been home. I miss Jake, the times we had, his consideration. He's a good man," she finished quietly. Saying the words made her realize how very true they were. Her love for Jake filled her totally, soothing that emptiness gnawing at her.

"Well, it's your life, Mandy. You know I'd never interfere," Mama said placidly.

Mandy gave her mother a slow grin, the first real one in days. "At least, not so I'd know it."

"I've never meddled in your life or your brother's." Without missing a beat, her mama tossed back her hair and added, "Now are you sure you have to ride this devil?"

"Yes."

"No one will think less of you if you don't."

"I'll know."

"If you're determined, then do it while I'm here. Your father's watching from the stock pen over there. I wasn't with you the last time. The least I can do is be here now."

Mandy looked warily at her mama, seeing the worry in her dark blue eyes. She climbed down from the fence and stood beside her mother.

"I need to do this, Mama. It's as simple as that."

Mama put her arm around Mandy and squeezed her shoulders. "Then you do what you have to do."

Mandy exhaled slowly. "I love you, Mama."

"I know, sweetheart."

"I haven't always made the right decisions. I have a knack for making a mess of things—"

"You've grown up, Mandy. You're learning from your mistakes, that's what's important. You're smart. I raised you smart. You'll make the right choice."

Mandy felt moisture on her lids, and quickly swiped a hand across her eyes.

"Jake's a good man. A blind man could see he loves you."

"He wants to take care of me," Mandy blurted, snapping her gloves against a jeans-clad leg. "I don't need anyone doing that."

"A man looking out for you." Mama shook her head. "I know what you mean, Mandy. I'd leave, too, if I had someone caring about me."

Mandy let out an exasperated breath. "He's followed my rodeoing for years! The man's got more articles than I do."

"He's spent a lot of time thinking about you. He's been devoting time to you. He's used to taking care of the females in his life. He seems very straightforward and that's a good trait, but then, I don't know Jake very well."

"Mama!" Mandy said in exasperation. "You sound like you're endorsing him."

Her mother laughed. "And you sound like you're trying to hang a man whose only crime that I can see is loving you. Is that the part that scares you, Mandy? A man that really cares about you? A man you can grow some roots with?"

Mandy scuffed the toe of her boot on the dusty ground. "I haven't been asked yet, but, yeah, it scares me," she whispered, daring to admit it out loud. She felt a sniffle coming over her and she cleared her throat instead.

"Love can be wonderful," Mama said very gently. "Didn't I ever teach you that?"

Mandy threw her head up in disbelief. "How can you say that? You loved Daddy, and he hurt you."

"We had lots of good times, too. Jake isn't like your daddy, Mandy."

"Jake would never hurt me the way Daddy hurt you." In the following silence Mandy heard the restless movement of the bull in the chute, and concentrated hard on those sounds. Feet stomping dry dirt, tail swishing at flies, the brush of hide against the metal bars...

She stuffed her hands in the front pockets of her jeans.

"Your father is a good man, but he has his weaknesses. There were women, I won't deny it. I ran him off and he went back to rodeoing full-time."

"If he loved you—and Ben and me—he would have stayed."

"Mandy, don't ever think your daddy didn't love us. He had a big heart." Her mother sighed reminiscently, but it wasn't a sad sound. "I made my own share of mistakes. It's not good when you let anger speak for you."

Mandy clenched her fists. "Sometimes I hate him—"

"No, you don't, Mandy," Mama said softly, laying a hand on her arm. "You love your daddy, and that's the way it should be. We all have to make peace with the past. I've watched you rush down some frightening roads, and I've ached for you. I'd hoped you'd pick up a normal life, a life you could be happy with.''

''One that doesn't include rodeo.''

''There's nothing wrong with rodeo, but you need something more.''

''In the hospital after the amputation—I'll never forgive myself for what I said to you when you told me they couldn't save the crushed leg,'' she whispered. Mandy stepped in close to her mama and put her arms around her again. ''How could I have blamed the loss of my leg on you, accusing you of never wanting me to ride the bull?''

''Even the strongest know fear, Mandy, and that was a most fearful time. You're my daughter. I'll always love you, no matter what.'' Her mama hugged her back, and Mandy closed her eyes, realizing how good it felt to wind her arms about her mother's slim frame. She felt as if she'd missed this, all these months. It was her own fault for staying away, her own self-imposed punishment.

Mama stepped back and laughed, the sound a bit shaky. ''Well, now, are you going to ride this bull or should I tell these boys to turn him loose?''

Mandy let her gaze meet her mama's. ''I'm going to ride him, and then I'm going to get on with my life. Maybe I've finally got my priorities straight.'' She drew a deep breath, then gave her mother a smile as big as the outdoors. ''I'm going to find Jake—see if he'll take me back.''

Her mama nodded and stepped back. If she was afraid, she hid it well. ''Give him hell, Mandy,'' she said softly.

Mandy climbed up onto the gate holding the bull. She climbed using her good leg. She swung her prosthesis over the top bar, then her other leg. She stood looking down at the bull, her hands gripping the rail tightly.

Mandy felt as if she were moving in slow motion. She could feel the beat of her heart, hard and heavy in her chest, could hear the breath as it left her lungs. It felt like so many times before, the thoughts wild and crazy in her head. This time, though, her hands were clammy, or had they always been clammy before a ride?

She pulled on her gloves, awkwardly climbed down on the bull, felt him shift under her, move uneasily. Quickly, she put rosin on her glove, wound the rope and gave the signal to open the gate. Someone responded, because the gate swung out and her breath left her dry mouth. The bull leaped forward, the motion jerking and yet familiar.

Mandy rode him, spurred him, and they twisted and turned. She heard the distant shouting of the cowboys, who had appeared from nowhere, then the clamor of an old steel bell. The sound didn't make sense, until she realized the ride was over.

Mandy threw her leg over the bull's side and let go of the rope. She jumped to the ground and landed on her feet. Both feet. She stood still and breathed, all in one piece, her chest heaving, her heart easing down past her throat now that it was over. She had done it. The bull kicked up his heels and was herded out another gate.

Time righted itself as Mandy stood in the dirt on two legs. She felt dazed, relieved, scared and satisfied. She pivoted on her heel. Only then did she see Jake standing there beside her mama and daddy.

Jake looked like hell. He looked like he had been rode hard and put away wet...and he looked wonderful to Mandy. In his hands he clutched a spray of white carnations. The flowers looked as worn as Jake, the stems bent and limp.

"You did it, Mandy girl," Daddy said, nodding his head solemnly. "I'm proud of you. You've got guts."

Mandy heard her father's comments, but she kept her eyes on Jake, hardly aware of the others moving away.

"I did it," Mandy said softly, walking toward Jake, her eyes only on him. "I did it, Jake."

Stunned, she watched him turn on his heel and walk away.

"Jake!" she called. "Jake!" He kept walking. The flowers he had carried lay in the dirt where he'd dropped them. Panic gripped Mandy. Had Jake finally given up on her? *No, Jake, no!* But the words didn't come.

Mandy floored the gas pedal. She'd probably get a ticket. She ducked her head as her vehicle hit a pothole. Quickly, she yanked her seat belt out and hooked it. Why had Jake left like that without a word? Mandy tried to still the real fear burgeoning in her chest. Maybe she had blown it so bad this time she'd never get him back. He had to know he loved her! He had to. How could she live if they parted again? The last few weeks had been a terrible hell. Surely he knew they needed each other? She had never stopped loving him. Mandy bit her lips and drove too fast around a corner. She pulled the wheel around quickly, almost losing control.

"Calm down. You'll kill yourself before you can tell him you love him." What if she'd misread his feelings and he didn't love her, after all? What then? Mandy tossed her head and peered through the dusty windshield. She'd tell him anyway that she loved him. If he trampled her pride, so be it. But she bit her lips again and prayed it wasn't too late.

Mandy pulled into the driveway of Jake's ranch and roared toward the house. She jerked the vehicle to a halt and jumped out, not even bothering to close her door. She didn't see Jake's truck. Mandy ran around the house, ignoring the dart of pain in her right leg.

"Jake?"

The house remained quiet and still. Mandy heard her rasping breath in the softly falling dusk. Where was Jake?

She ran down the hall to his office and found it empty. Mandy turned and walked back to the living room. She exited the house by the kitchen door and stood indecisively. Where was he?

"Why aren't you out celebrating?" His voice came from around the house. Mandy yelped, startled, as Jake walked toward her, his thumbs hooked in his belt loops. She took an eager step toward him, relief making her want to grab him and kiss him.

"Jake, you're here! I didn't see your truck and I couldn't imagine where you were. I left right after you did. Why did you leave like that? I really need to talk to you. I've been so selfish, so caught up in my own wants I've…"

Jake stood there not saying a word, one brow raised, a bored look on his face.

Mandy swallowed hard. "Jake?" Her voice sounded thin and scared, exactly the way she felt. "I—I did it, Jake. I beat my fear."

Jake wondered why she'd come to rub it in. He was already hurting like hell and didn't want to see her again. It had been a stupid move on his part to go to the rodeo, anyway.

"You did it," Jake repeated, his voice hoarse. Desperately, he cleared his throat. He still hadn't recovered after arriving in time to see Mandy on the back of that two-thousand-pound stomping, twisting animal. It had brought back memories of the night she got hurt, and it had sunk him into a misery so deep he couldn't act normally.

Jake made an effort to pull himself together. "Mandy, I came to the rodeo today to say that if you want to go back to rodeoing, I'll support your decision. Dammit, Mandy, if you just want to live together, then we'll damned well do that, too, and forget about any of the rest of it." Jake closed his eyes a moment, feeling the cost to himself, knowing what he had to say next.

He opened them to find Mandy close to him. "I came

prepared to agree to almost any terms to keep you," he confessed. "I love you so much it hurts."

A look of wonder filled Mandy's eyes, but Jake shook his head and touched her cheek briefly. He could feel the anger and despair eating at him, burning into his gut.

"But I can't, Mandy. I turned coward, if that's what you want to call it, when I saw you on that bull. I can't watch you riding bulls. Those six seconds just about tore my insides out." Jake had thought he was going to embarrass himself and puke in the dirt. Lanny Thomson had come to stand beside him, and luckily, Jake hadn't, but it had been real close.

"It's over," he said harshly. "I'm not going to try and hold you down. I love you, Mandy, but I don't want you." Emotion, hot and tight, gripped his throat.

The exhilaration on her face almost undid him. She looked so alive, so ready to take on life's challenges. How could he bear to let her go? But he wasn't letting her go. He was pushing her away. It was a matter of survival, for both of them.

The leaving would be worse than ten years ago. They'd been kids back then, and he'd loved her, but now there was a different depth to his passion. A deep caring and need to keep her with him, see her through life's hardships, at any cost. Except this one. He would slowly die; Jake knew it for sure.

"I love you, Jake." Her arms wound around him, and Jake stood stock-still, his own arms stiff at his sides as he tried to take in what she had said. He didn't feel as if he could respond properly. She squeezed him. "Do you hear me? I love you. You're the first to know I just rode my last bull. I'm begging you, Jake, to give me another chance. Take me back. Please."

Jake jerked Mandy away from his chest and stared at her. "What?" he demanded. Elation gripped him, but he didn't trust it. He pulled her back to him before she could answer. "Don't say anything else."

Mandy's voice came to him muffled, but the words were sweet. "I've loved you for what seems like forever, but it was scary, a totally new phase of my life. Until today I never realized how much bull riding weighed on me. Even knowing that, I had to ride one last time. Now I feel like I've closed that part of my life. I want to move on." Mandy looked up at him uncertainly. "That is, if you still want me. Do you want me, Jake? Can we make this work?"

He felt as if a light had begun to shine once more. "I won't lie. I thought I could handle it if you went back to bull riding, but when I watched you, I realized I couldn't. All I could remember was the night of the accident. I'll never forget what you went through."

"I remembered it, too," she admitted. "The bull riding is over, though I'll still rodeo part-time. I've been offered an opportunity to write articles promoting women in rodeo." She stepped back from him and Jake looked around. Darkness had fallen. They stood alone in the night air, a warm breeze caressing them, rustling the trees.

"I'm sorry, Jake, about what happened between us three weeks ago. I was selfish and unfair." Mandy looked down at her feet and rocked on her heels. He couldn't see her face, which was hidden by a curtain of hair. "But I was so scared."

When she looked up at him Jake was jolted by the tears running in a steady stream down her cheeks, the wetness making tracks through the dust clinging to her creamy skin. Feeling a sense of wonder, he touched a fingertip to the tears. Her vulnerability was there for him to see.

"I used my father's mistakes, and my own, to try and deny what was between us. I was running again."

"I can understand fears, Mandy, I've confronted my own. I've been lying to myself. I never stopped loving you. When you left, all those years ago, I was angry, but I know in my heart it was too soon for us. I guess it was easier to blame you, but I couldn't stop caring. That's why I let you come and stay at my place, even though I thought I was looking for some kind of closure. Ten years ago I should have come after you. Maybe that's why I was so entrenched in anger. I felt guilt over letting you go so easily.''

"We both had some growing up to do."

Mandy linked her hand with his. It had been a long day. Jake could see the hope on her face. It was the same emotion squeezing his heart.

"I want you, Mandy, but I won't settle for anything less than marriage."

Mandy's smile was blinding, her eyes sparkling. She threw her arms around his neck once again. "Oh, Jake, I'll marry you. I will! I need you in my life. You make me whole."

Jake dipped his head, tasted the sweetness that was Mandy. Tough and tender Mandy. His Mandy.

She gave a gurgle of laughter, then put her arms out and stretched them upward to the sky. She twirled away, and then back. "I feel so full of renewed energy, I could dance all night."

One moment she was smiling at him, the next, without warning, her leg gave out. Mandy slid to the ground as easily as you please.

"Mandy." Jake reached his hand out to her.

She looked at it, at the wide palm, then let her eyes travel up to his face. From her perch on the ground, in the dirt, she started laughing.

"I was warned this could happen from time to time. Are you prepared to pick me up when my leg kicks out, Miller?" Mandy asked him sassily, confident of his answer.

"Every time," Jake assured her solemnly, his fingers already closed on hers.

He pulled her up against him. She let her head rest against his chest for a moment, then she stepped back and dusted off her jeans. With both hands she reached up and gripped Jake's shoulders, cocked her head sideways, then planted a slow kiss on his mouth. Leaning back, arms again encircling his neck, she gave Jake a dazzling smile.

"I'm going to count on you, cowboy, as long as you know you can count on me."

Epilogue

Mandy gently traced a fingertip along the feathered wing of an eagle, a recent addition to one of Jake's carvings. The guests had finally left the gallery, the lights were dimmed and it was time to go home. Home with Jake, her husband.

Mandy threw back her hair, excitement making her heart beat rapidly. She would burst if she didn't share her news with Jake. She didn't know how she had managed to keep the secret for an entire day. And what a day! Full of preparations for Jake's show, the crowning glory of which had been this centerpiece. Mandy stared at the carving Jake had surprised her with—a head-and-shoulders likeness of herself in beautiful honey-hued wood. She was forever captured, reaching one hand upward, fingertips touching the stars. Jake had depicted her life—reaching for stars that seemed out of reach and coming full circle to completion.

When she heard approaching footsteps, she placed the long-neck bottle she held in her hand on the table behind her. Quickly, she faced Jake.

When he caught sight of her his mouth curved in a smile she knew well. A warm, sensual smile that promised great delights later. Mandy felt as if his arms had just wrapped around her.

Jake was devastating in black, right down to the boots on his feet. The only splash of color was his turquoise necktie. He reached out an arm and pulled her close. Mandy's pulse raced in anticipation. "Why do you suppose it's taken me all day to get you this close to me?" she murmured.

Jake ran his gaze over her, then gave her a rueful smile. "Mandy, do you have any idea what that tight-fitting little dress and those spike heels have been doing to me all night? Do you know what I've been thinking while this place was packed with people?"

"I can guess." Provocatively, she pressed close and laced her fingers behind his neck. No need to tell him she had picked the dress deliberately for that effect. "Why do you think I learned how to walk on these darned heels? It's all for your benefit."

"We have the place to ourselves...." he said suggestively, one brow arched. "There's a workroom down the hall...."

Mandy laughed, unable to contain the excitement a moment longer. Reaching behind her, she pulled out the bottle of sparkling cider with a flourish. "First things first. This occasion calls for a little something special to celebrate." Mandy uncorked the bottle with a soft pop. Grabbing the paper cups she had found, she poured a liberal amount of the clear, bubbling liquid into each.

"Here is yours." She handed him a cup.

Mandy swirled the liquid in her own cup, then lifted her gaze to her husband. She gave him a deliberately wicked smile. Lazily, she let her fingertips trail down his neck and along his shoulders. Mandy placed her palm flat against his chest, feeling the flex of muscle beneath, all too aware of the glint in his eyes.

"First, I'd like to make a toast to one glorious year of marriage," she said huskily. When Jake would have spoken, she pressed a finger to his mouth and shook her head. She raised her glass again. "Here's to many more successful showings. And..." Mischievously, she indicated he should take a drink. "Let's toast the newest addition to our lives." Mandy moved his hand from her hip to her flat stomach. "Daddy."

Jake choked and put the cup down. He cleared his throat. "You're—" His voice rasped and didn't cooperate.

Mandy patted him on the back, laughing, crying, surprised by the wetness on her cheeks.

Jake's arms wrapped around her fiercely. "Mandy," he finally managed to gasp. "Sweetheart."

"I'm pregnant, Jake." Mandy knew the smile on her face had to be foolish, it felt so huge, but she didn't care. She leaned back so she could see his face. She didn't want to miss one moment of his reaction.

"Pregnant."

Mandy swallowed with difficulty, seeing and feeling Jake's wonder, the joy. It radiated from him.

"I'm so happy, Jake. I can't imagine my life, our life, being anything other than what it is, and now we have so much more to look forward to."

"So that's why you cut back the rodeo schedule recently," he murmured, feathering kisses up the side of her neck. "And you brought in more help for the riding program."

Mandy closed her eyes, hardly able to think with Jake's lips on her skin. "Yes. It's been a hectic time, but I found a few people...to fill in...."

"About that workroom...."

"Mmm, I feel the need to lie down. There's been too

much excitement today.'' Mandy suddenly opened her eyes wide. ''That's not to say I can't stand a bit more,'' she amended.

Jake's growl was muffled in her shoulder as he swung her off her feet. Mandy squealed and quickly wound her arms around his neck.

They almost made it to the workroom.

*   *   *   *   *

Beloved author
Sherryl Woods
is back with a brand-new miniseries

THE CALAMITY JANES

Five women. Five Dreams.
A lifetime of friendship....

On Sale May 2001—DO YOU TAKE THIS REBEL?
Silhouette Special Edition

On Sale August 2001—COURTING THE ENEMY
Silhouette Special Edition

On Sale September 2001—TO CATCH A THIEF
Silhouette Special Edition

On Sale October 2001—THE CALAMITY JANES
Silhouette Single Title

On Sale November 2001—WRANGLING THE REDHEAD
Silhouette Special Edition

"Sherryl Woods is an author who writes with
a very special warmth, wit, charm and intelligence."
—*New York Times* bestselling author
Heather Graham Pozzessere

Available at your favorite retail outlet.

Where love comes alive™

Visit Silhouette at www.eHarlequin.com   SSETCJR

CALL THE ONES YOU LOVE OVER THE HOLIDAYS!

Save $25 off future book purchases when you buy any four Harlequin® or Silhouette® books in October, November and December 2001,

PLUS

receive a phone card good for 15 minutes of long-distance calls to anyone you want in North America!

WHAT AN INCREDIBLE DEAL!

Just fill out this form and attach 4 proofs of purchase (cash register receipts) from October, November and December 2001 books, and Harlequin Books will send you a coupon booklet worth a total savings of $25 off future purchases of Harlequin® and Silhouette® books, AND a 15-minute phone card to call the ones you love, anywhere in North America.

Please send this form, along with your cash register receipts
as proofs of purchase, to:
In the USA: Harlequin Books, P.O. Box 9057, Buffalo, NY 14269-9057
In Canada: Harlequin Books, P.O. Box 622, Fort Erie, Ontario L2A 5X3
Cash register receipts must be dated no later than December 31, 2001.
Limit of 1 coupon booklet and phone card per household.
Please allow 4-6 weeks for delivery.

I accept your offer! Please send me my coupon booklet and a 15-minute phone card:

Name: _____

Address: _____ City: _____

State/Prov.: _____ Zip/Postal Code: _____

Account Number (if available): _____

---

097 KJB DAGL
PHQ4012

If you enjoyed what you just read,
then we've got an offer you can't resist!

Take 2 bestselling love stories FREE!

Plus get a FREE surprise gift!